EVERY MOVE YOU MAKE

David Malouf is the author of *Dream Stuff* ('These stories are pearls,' *Spectator*) and *Antipodes*, and of acclaimed novels including *The Great World* (winner of the Commonwealth Writers' Prize and the Prix Femina Etranger), *Remembering Babylon* (shortlisted for the Booker Prize and winner of the IMPAC Dublin Literary Award), *Johnno, An Imaginary Life* and *Conversations at Curlow Creek*, as well as his autobiographical classic, *12 Edmondstone Street*. He has also written poetry and opera libretti. Born and brought up in Brisbane, he lives in Sydney.

ALSO BY DAVID MALOUF

Novels

Johnno
An Imaginary Life
Fly Away Peter
Child's Play
Harland's Half Acre
Antipodes
The Great World
Remembering Babylon
The Conversations at Curlow Creek
Dream Stuff

Autobiography

12 Edmonstone Street

Poetry

Bicycle and Other Poems
Neighbours in a Thicket
The Year of the Foxes and Other Poems
First Things Last
Wild Lemons
Selected Poems

Libretti

Baa Baa Black Sheep
Jane Eyre

DAVID MALOUF

Every Move You Make

VINTAGE BOOKS
London

Published by Vintage 2008

2 4 6 8 10 9 7 5 3 1

Copyright © David Malouf 2006

David Malouf has asserted his right under the Copyright, Designs
and Patents Act 1988 to be identified as the author of this work

First published in Great Britain in 2007 by
Chatto & Windus
Random House, 20 Vauxhall Bridge Road,
London SW1V 2SA

www.vintage-books.co.uk

Addresses for companies within The Random House Group Limited
can be found at: www.randomhouse.co.uk/offices.htm

The Random House Group Limited Reg. No. 954009

A CIP catalogue record for this book
is available from the British Library

ISBN 9780099502586

The Random House Group Limited supports The Forest
Stewardship Council (FSC), the leading international forest
certification organisation. All our titles that are printed on
Greenpeace approved FSC certified paper carry the FSC logo.
Our paper procurement policy can be found at
www.rbooks.co.uk/environment

Mixed Sources
Product group from well-managed
forests and other controlled sources
www.fsc.org Cert no. TT-COC-2139
© 1996 Forest Stewardship Council
FSC

Printed

Contents

When I consider the brevity of my life, swallowed up as it is in the eternity that precedes and will follow it, the tiny space I occupy and what is visible to me, cast as I am into a vast infinity of spaces that I know nothing of and which know nothing of me, I take fright, I am stunned to find myself here rather than elsewhere, for there is no reason why it should be here rather than there, and now rather than then. Who set me here? By whose order and under what guiding destiny was this time, this place assigned to me?

Pascal, *Pensées*

The Valley of Lagoons

The Valley of Lagoons

—

WHEN I was in the third grade at primary school it was the magic of the name itself that drew me.

Just five hours south off a good dirt highway, it is where all the river systems in our quarter of the state have their rising: the big, rain-swollen streams that begin in a thousand thread-like runnels and falls in the rainforests of the Great Divide, then plunge and gather and flow wide-banked and muddy-watered to the coast; the leisurely watercourses that make their way inland across plains stacked with anthills, and run north-west and north to the Channel Country, where they break up and lose themselves in the mudflats and mangrove swamps of the Gulf.

I knew it was there and had been hearing stories about it for as long as I could remember. Three or four hunting parties, some of them large, went out each year at the start of August, and since August was the school holidays, a good many among them were my classmates. By the time he was sixteen, my best friend Braden, who was just my age, had been going with his father and his two older brothers, Stuart and Glen, for the past five years. But it was not marked on the wall-map in our third-grade schoolroom and I could not find it in any atlas; which gave it the status of a secret place, accessible only in the winter when the big rains eased off and the tracks that led into it were dry enough for a ute loaded down with tarpaulins, cook-pots, carbide lamps, emergency cans of petrol, and bags of flour, potatoes, onions and other provisions, to get in without sinking to the axle: a thousand square miles of virgin country known only to the few dozen families of our little township and the surrounding cane and dairy farms that made up the shire.

It was there, but only in our heads. It had a history, but only in the telling: in stories I heard from fellows in the playground at school, or from their older brothers at the barbershop or at the edge of an oval or on the bleachers at the town pool.

These stories were all of record 'bags' or of the comic mishaps and organised buffoonery of camp life – plus, of course, the occasional shocking accident – but had something more behind them, I thought, than mere facts.

Fellows who went out there were changed – that's what I saw. Kids who had been swaggering and loud were quiet when they spoke of it, as if they knew more now than they were ready to let on, or had words for or were permitted to tell. This impressed me, since it chimed with my own expectations of what I might discover, or be let into, when I too got there.

I stood in the shadows at the edge of what was being told, tuning my ear to the clamour, off in the scrub, of a wild pig being cornered while a kid no older than I was stood with an old Lee Enfield .303 jammed into the soft of his shoulder, holding his breath.

An occasion that was sacred in its way, though no one, least of all the kid who was now retelling it, would ever speak of it that way.

All that side of things you had to catch at a glance as you looked away. From the slight, almost imperceptible warping upwards of a deliberately flattened voice.

IN the first freshening days of June, and increasingly as July came on, all the talk around town, in schoolyards and changing sheds, across the counter at Kendrick's Seed and Hardware, along the veranda rails and in the dark public bars of the town's three hotels, where jurymen were put up when the district court was in session, and commercial travellers and bonded schoolteachers and bank clerks roomed, was about who, this year, would be going, and in which party and when.

In the old days, which were still within living memory, they had gone out on horseback, a four-day ride, the last of it through buffalo grass that came right to the horses' ears, so that all you had to go on was bush sense, and the smell in the horses' nostrils of an expanse of water up ahead.

Nowadays there were last year's wheel-marks. A man with a keen eye, crouched on the running-board of a ute or hanging halfway out the offside cabin window, could indicate to the driver which way to turn in the whisper of high grassheads, till the swishing abruptly fell away and you were out in the shimmering, insect-swarming midst of it: sheet after sheet of brimming water, all lit with sky and alive, like a page of Genesis, with spur-winged plover, masked plover, eastern swamphen, marshy moorhen, white-headed shelldrake, plumed tree duck, gargery teal, and clattering skyward as, like young bulls loose in pasture, the utes swerved and roared

among them, flocks of fruit pigeon, squatters, topknots, forest
bronzewings . . .

My father was not a hunting man. The town's only solicitor,
his business was with wills and inheritance, with land contracts,
boundary lines between neighbours, and the quarrels, sometimes fierce, that gave rise to marriage break-ups, divorce, custody
battles and, every two or three years, the odd case of criminal
assault or murder that will arise even in the quietest commu-
nity. He knew more of the history of the shire, including its
secret history, its unrecorded and unspoken connections and
disconnections, than any other man, and more than his clients
themselves did of how this or that parcel of their eighty- or
hundred-acre holdings had been taken up out of what, less than
a hundred years ago, had been uncharted wilderness, and how,
in covert deals with the bank or in deathbed codicils, out of
spite or through long years of plotting, this or that paddock,
or canebrake, or spinney, had passed from one neighbour or
one first or second cousin to another.

When he and my mother first came here in the late thir-
ties, he'd been invited out, when August came round, on one
of the parties – it was a courtesy, an act of neighbourliness, that
any one of a dozen locals would have extended to an acceptable newcomer, if only to see how he might fit in.

'Thanks, Gerry,' I imagine him saying in his easy way – or
Jake, or Wes. 'Not this time, I reckon. Ask me again next year,
eh?' And had said that again the following year, and the year
after, until they stopped asking.

He wasn't being stand-offish or condescending. It was simply
that hunting, and the grand rigmarole, as he saw it, of gun talk
and game talk and dog talk, was not his style. He had been a

soldier in New Guinea and had seen enough perhaps, for one lifetime, of killing. It was an oddness in him that was accepted like any other, humorously, and was perhaps not entirely unexpected in a man who had more books in his house than could be found in the shire library. He was a respected figure in the town. He was even liked. But he wore a collar and tie even on weekdays, and men who were used to consulting him in a friendly way about a dispute with a neighbour, or the adding of a clause to their will, developed a sudden interest in their boots when they ran into him away from his desk.

My mother too was an outsider. Despite heavy hints, she had not joined the fancy-workers and jam- and chutney-makers at the CWA, and in defiance of local custom sent all three of us to school in shoes. This was understandable in the case of my sisters. They were older and would grow up one day to be ladies. It was regarded as unnecessary and even, perhaps, damaging in a boy.

After more than twenty years in the district my father had never been to the Lagoons, and till I was sixteen I had not been there either, except in the dreamtime of my own imaginings and in what I had overheard from others.

I might have gone. Each year, in the first week of August, Braden's father, Wes McGowan, got up a party. I was always invited. My father, after a good deal of humming and ha-ing and using my mother as an excuse, would tell me I was too young and decline to let me go. But I knew he was uneasy about it, and all through the last weeks of July, as talk in the town grew, I waited in the hope he might relent. When the day came at last, I would get up early, pull on a sweater against the cold and, in the misty half-light just before dawn, jog down the deserted main street, past the last service station at the edge of town, to the river park where the McGowans' Bedford ute would be waiting for the rest of the party to appear, its tray piled high with tarpaulins, bedrolls, cook-pots, a gauze meat safe, and my friend Braden settled among them with the McGowan dogs at his feet, two Labrador retrievers.

Old Wes McGowan and his crony, Henry Denkler, who was also the town mayor, would be out stretching their legs, stamping their boots on the frosty ground or bending to inspect the tyres or the canvas water bag that hung from the front bumper-bar. The older McGowan boys, Stuart and Glen, would be squatting on their heels over a smoke. I would stand at the gate of the ute chatting to Braden for a bit and petting the dogs.

When the second vehicle drew up, with Matt Riley, the 'professional', and his nephew Jem, Matt too would get down and a second inspection would be made – of the tyres, of the load – while Jem, with not much more than a nod, joined the McGowan boys. Then, with all the rituals of meeting done, Henry Denkler and Wes McGowan would climb back into the cabin, Glen into the driver's seat beside them, Stuart into the back with Braden and the dogs, and I would be left standing to wave them off; and then, freezing even in my sweater, jog slowly back home.

The break came in the year after I turned sixteen. When I went for the third or fourth year running to tell my father that the McGowans had offered to take me out to the Lagoons and to ask if I could go, he surprised me by looking up over the top of his glasses and saying, 'That's up to you, son. You're old enough, I reckon, to make your own decisions.' It was to be Braden's last trip before he went south to university. Most of the shooting would be birds, but to mark the occasion as special Braden would also get a go at a pig.

'So,' my father said quietly, though he already knew the answer, 'what's it to be?'

'I'd really like to go,' I told him.

'Good,' he said, not sounding regretful. 'I want you to look out and be careful, that's all. Braden's a sensible enough young fellow. But your mother will worry her soul case out till you're home again.'

What he meant was, *he* would.

BRADEN McGowan had been my best friend since I was five years old. We started school on the same day, sharing a desk and keeping pace with one another through pot-hooks and the alphabet, times tables, cursive, and those scrolled and curlicued capitals demanded by our Queensland State School copybooks. We dawdled to and from school on our own circuitous route. Past the Vulcan Can Company, where long shiny cut-offs of raw tin were to be had, which we carted off in bundles to be turned into weapons and aids of our own devising, past the crushing-mill where we got sticks of sugar cane to chew. Narrow gauge lines ran to the mill from the many outlying farms, and you heard at all hours in the crushing season the noise of trundling, and the shrill whistle of the engine as a line of carts approached a crossing, and rumbled through or clanked to a halt.

In the afternoons after school and in the holidays, we played together in the paddocks and canebrakes of the McGowans' farm, being, as the mood took us, explorers, pirates, commandos, bushrangers, scouts on the track of outlaws or of renegade Navaho braves.

Usually we had a troop of the McGowan dogs with us, who followed out of doggy curiosity and sometimes, in the belief that they had got the scent of what the game was, moiled around us or leapt adventurously ahead. But for the most part they simply lay and watched from the shade, till we stretched out beside them and let the game take its freer form of untrammelled thinking-aloud that was also, with its range of wild and rambling surmise, the revelation – even to ourselves, though we were too young as yet to know it – of bright, conjectural futures we would have admitted to no one else.

'You two are weird,' Braden's brother Stuart told us with a disgusted look, having caught on his way to the bails some extravagant passage of our talk. '*God*, you're weird. You're *weird*!'

Stuart was four years older. He and the eldest of the three brothers, Glen, had farm work to do in the afternoons after school. Braden in those days was still little and free to play.

They were rough kids, the McGowans, and Stuart was not just rowdy, I thought, but unpredictably vicious. He scared me.

I had come late into a family of girls, two sisters who, from the beginning, had made a pet of me. Going over to the McGowans' was an escape to another world. Different laws were in operation there from the ones I was used to. Old Mr McGowan had a different notion of authority from the one my father followed. Quiet but firmer. His sons, who were so noisy and undisciplined outside, were subdued in his presence. Mrs McGowan, unlike my mother, had no interests beyond the piles of food she brought to the table and the washing – her men's overalls and shirts and singlets, and the loads of sheets and pillowcases I saw her hoist out of the copper boiler when I came to collect Braden on Monday mornings.

She too had a softening influence on the boys. They might complain when she called them in from kicking a football round the yard, or working on a bike, to fetch in an armful of wood for the stove or to carry a basket of wet sheets to the line, and they squirmed when she tried to settle an upturned collar or hug them. But they did do what she asked in the end, and even submitted, with a good show of masculine reluctance, to hugging.

I liked the roughness and ease I found at the McGowans', but even more the formality, which was of a kind my parents would have wondered at and found odd, old-fashioned.

My sisters, Katie and Meg, were exuberantly opinionated. Our mealtimes were loud with argument in which we all talked over one another, our parents included, and the food itself was forgotten.

There was no arguing at the McGowans'. Glen and Stuart, rough and barefooted as they were, showed their hands before they were allowed to table, sat up straight, kept their elbows in, and lowered their heads for grace – the McGowans said grace!

They passed things without speaking. Barely spoke at all unless their father asked a question, or in response to a story he told, or to tell their mother how good the stew was in hope of a second helping.

I loved all this. When Braden began to have his own jobs to do after school, I stayed to help. I learned to milk, to clean out the bails, to handle a gun and shoot sparrows in the yard, and rabbits in the brush, then stayed for the McGowans' early tea. I wanted to be one of them, or at least to be like them. Like Glen. Like Stuart even. I wasn't of course, but then neither was Braden.

When we were very young it did not occur to me that Braden might be odd. He was often in trouble at home for being 'dreamy', but then so was I. 'What's the matter with you,' Stuart would demand of him, genuinely exasperated, 'are you dumb or something?'

He wasn't, but he found a problem at times where the rest of us did not, and to a point of inertia that infuriated Stuart (who suspected him, I think, of doing it deliberately) was puzzled by circumstances, quite ordinary ones, that the rest of us took for granted. Other kids found him slow. Some of them called him a dill.

I understood Braden's puzzlement because I shared it at times, and since we were always together, I took it that we were puzzled in the same way. I had for so long been paired with Braden, we had shared so many discoveries and first thoughts, that I had assumed we were in every way alike; that in all the hours we had spent spinning fantasies and creating other lives for ourselves, we had been moving through the same landscape and weather, and were one. When Stuart told us, 'You two are weird. You're weird,' I was pleased to see in his savage contempt the confirmation that in Stuart's eyes at least we were indistinguishable.

I did not want to know what I had already begun in some part of me to suspect. That Braden's oddness might be quite different from anything I could lay claim to.

For as long as I could remember, we had known, each one, what the other was thinking. The same things amused or excited or scared us. Now, almost overnight, it seemed, Braden knew stuff I had never dreamed of. His mind was engaged by questions that had never occurred to me, and the answers he came up with I could not follow. It was a habit of mind, I thought, that must have been there from the start, but moving underground in him and hidden from me; a music, behind the rambling stories he told, that I had all along been deaf to.

At the same time, in the six months before he turned fifteen, he put on height, six inches, and bulked up to twelve and a half stone. He was suddenly a big fellow. Bigger than either of his brothers. Not heavy, but big.

Then one day he showed me, in a copy of *Scientific American*, what it was that he was into. Cybernetics. I had never heard the word, and when he tried to explain it to me in his usual style, all jumps and sideways leaps into a silence I had believed I could interpret, I was lost.

I understood the science well enough. Even the figures. What I could not grasp was the excited vision of what he saw in it: a realm of action he saw himself moving through as if it had come into existence precisely for him. And this was the opening of a gap between us. Not of affection – no question of that – but of where our lives might take us. Braden, who had always been so vague and out of it, was suddenly the most focused person I knew. Utterly single-minded and sure of what he wanted and what he was for.

For the first time in my life I felt lonely. But not so lonely, I think, so finally set apart as *he* felt. From his family. His brothers. Who were still puzzled by him but in a new way.

Here he was, a big boy who had outgrown them and his own strength, and ought, in springing up and filling out, to have become a fellow they could deal with at last on equal terms. Instead he seemed odder than ever. More difficult to get through to. Content to be away there in his own incommunicable universe.

Glen, who had always had a soft spot for the boy, was confused, but also I think impressed. He still teased him, but in a soft-handed affectionate way. As if Braden's difference, which had always intrigued him, had turned out to be something he might respect.

Glen, because he was so much older, had for the most part left us alone. We had always been a source of mild amusement to him, but except for the odd burst of impatience he had, in a condescending, big-brotherly way, ignored us. Stuart could not.

In the early days the mere sight of us drove him to fury. All jeers and knuckles, he was always twisting our arms and jerking them up under our shoulder blades to see how much we could take before we turned into crybabies and cissies.

He felt easier with me, I think, because I fought back. Braden disarmed him by taking whatever he could dish out with scornful defiance, never once, after our baby years, yielding to tears.

All this, I knew, belonged to a side of their life together that I had no part in, to hostilities and accommodations, spaces shared or passionately disputed, in rooms, at the table, in their mother's affection or their father's regard or interest.

But the fullness of the change in Braden, when it finally revealed itself, dismayed Stuart. He simply did not know what to do with it.

I think it scared him to have someone who was close, and who ought therefore to have been knowable, turn out to be so far from anything he could get a hold on. It suggested that the world itself might be beyond his comprehension, but also beyond his control. The only way he could deal with Braden was by avoiding him. Which made it all the more odd, I thought, that he began at the same time to latch on to me.

He had left school by now, was working in a garage and ran with a set of older fellows, all of whom were wild, as he was, and had 'reputations'. But suddenly we were always in one another's path.

He would appear out of nowhere, it seemed, on my way back from the pool, and offer me dinks on his bike. And when he exchanged his Malvern Star for a Tiger Cub he would stop, talk a bit, and offer to take me pillion.

I was wary. I had too often been on the wrong side of Stuart's roughness to be easy with him. It was flattering to be treated, in my own right, as a grown-up, but I did not trust him. He was trying to win me over. Why? Because he had seen the little gap that had opened up between Braden and me and wanted to widen it? To bring home to me that if Braden was odder than any of us had thought, then I had proved to be, like Stuart himself, more ordinary?

I resented his attention on both counts, and suspected that his unlikely interest in me was a form of mockery. It took me a while to see that mockery was not Stuart's style, and that by seeking me out, a younger boy and the brother of a girl he was sweet on (I learned this amazing fact from a bit of conversation overheard while I was sunbaking on the bleachers at the pool), he was putting himself helplessly in my power; making himself vulnerable to the worst mockery of all. That he trusted me not to take advantage of it meant that I never would of course, but I hated the familiarity with which he now greeted me as 'Angus, old son', or 'Angus, old horse', as if there was already some special relationship between us, or as if getting close to me brought him closer somehow to her. My own belief was that Stuart McGowan was just the sort of rough, loud fellow she wouldn't even look at. Then suddenly he and Katie were going out together, and he was at our house every night of the week.

Taking a break from my homework or the book I was absorbed in, and going through to the kitchen to get a glass of water or cold milk from the fridge, I would hear them whispering together on the couch in our darkened front room, and would turn the tap on hard to warn them I was about.

Or if it was late enough, and Stuart was leaving, I would run into them in the hall: Stuart looking smug but also, somehow, crestfallen, Katie hot and angry, ready I thought to snap my head off if I said more in reply to his "lo, Angus, how's it going?' than a 'Hi, Stuart,' and ducked back into my room.

The truth was, I had no wish to know what was going on between them. I did not like the look of shy complicity that Stuart cast me, as if I had caught him out in something, but in something that as another male I must naturally approve.

Two or three nights each week he ate with us. I have no idea what he thought of the noisy arguments that marked our mealtimes. Perhaps it attracted him, as I was attracted by the old-fashioned formality I found at the McGowans'.

Occasionally, to kill time while Katie was helping in the kitchen, he would drift to the sleepout on the side veranda where I would be sprawled on my bed deep in a book. I would look up, thinking, 'God, not again,' and there he would be, hanging awkwardly in the open doorway, waiting for me to acknowledge him and taking my grunt of recognition as an invitation to come in.

Oddly restrained and self-conscious, he would settle at the foot of the bed, take a book from the pile on the floor, and say, with what I thought of as a leer, 'So what's this one about?' The way he handled the book, his half-embarrassed, half-suggestive tone, the painful attempt to meet me, as I saw it, on unfamiliar ground, made me uncomfortable. 'You don't have to pretend you're interested,' I wanted to tell him, 'just because you're going out with my sister.' On the whole, I preferred the old Stuart. I thought I knew better what he was about. It did not occur to me that what I was reading, and what I found there, might be a genuine mystery to him; which disturbed his sense of himself, and had to do with how, in this strange new household he had blundered into, with its unfamiliar views and distinctions, he might learn to fit in.

He would run his eyes over a few pages of the book he had

in hand and shake his head. Thinking, I see now, of her, of Katie, and waiting for me to provide some clue – to me, I mean, to *us* – that would help him find common ground with her.

I would make a rambling attempt to explain who Raskolnikov was, and Sonia, and about the horse that had fallen down in the street. He would look puzzled, then stricken, then, trying to make the best of it, say, 'Interesting, eh?' Waiting for some sign perhaps that I recognised the effort he was making to enter my world, and what this might reveal about *him*: about some other Stuart than the one I thought I knew, and knew only as a 'bad influence'. After about ten minutes of this, I would swing my legs off the bed and say, 'Tea must be about ready, we'd better go out,' and to the relief of both of us, or so I thought, it would be over.

I had begun to dread these occasions of false intimacy between us that were intended, I thought, to be rehearsals for a time when we would be youthful brothers-in-law, close, bluff, easily affectionate. If he could get me to accept him in this role, then maybe she would.

Once, as he moved towards the door, I caught him, out of the corner of my eye, making a quick appraisal of himself in the wardrobe mirror. Starched white shirt with the sleeves rolled high to show off his biceps. Hair slicked down with Potter and Moore jelly. In the hollow of his underlip the squared-off, dandified growth of hair he had begun to affect in recent weeks, a tuft, two or three degrees darker than his hair colour but with flecks of gingery gold, that I had over-looked at first – I thought he had simply neglected to shave there. When I realised it was deliberate I was confused. It seemed so out of character.

Now, watching him take in at a casual glance the effect he

made in my wardrobe mirror, I thought again. What a bundle of contradictions he is, I told myself.

He gave me a sheepish grin, and stopped, pretending to examine his chin for a shaving nick. But what his look said was, Well, that's how it is, you can see that, eh, old son? That's what they do to us.

When Katie first began to go out with him I'd felt I should warn her. That he was wild. That he had a 'reputation'. Only I did not know how to begin. We had always been close, and had grown more so since my older sister Meg got married, but for all that, and the boldness in our household with which we were willing to air issues and deliver an opinion, there were subjects, back then, that we kept clear of, areas of experience we could not admit knowledge of.

And it seemed to me that Katie must know as well as I did, or better, what Stuart was like. She was the one who spent all those hours of fierce whispering with him in the dark of our front room.

For weeks at a time they would move together in what seemed like a single glow. Then I would feel an anger in her that needed only a word on my part, or a look, to make her blaze out, though the real object of her fury, I thought, was herself. Stuart, for a time, would no longer be there, on the back veranda or in the lounge after tea. Things were off between them. When I ran into him at the baths, or when he stopped and offered me a lift on the Triumph, he would look hangdog and miserable. 'How are you, Angus, old son?' he'd ask, hoping I would return the question.

I didn't. The last thing I wanted was to be his confidant; to listen to his complaints about Katie or have him ask what she was saying about him, what I thought she wanted. These periods would last for days, for a whole week sometimes. Then he would be back, all scrubbed and spruced up and smelling like a sweet shop. Narrow-eyed and watchful. Like a cat, I thought. But also, in a way he could not help and could not help showing, happily full of himself and of his power over her. Couldn't he see, I thought, how mad it made her, and that it was this in the long run that would bring him down?

THE crisis came a year or so after they first began.

Nothing was said — my parents were the very spirit of tact in such matters — but I guessed Katie had given him his marching orders. Again. *Again.* Because for two nights running he did not appear. Then, late on the second night, I looked out and the little Anglia he sometimes ran around in was parked under the street light opposite.

It was there at nine and was still there at half past ten. What was he doing? Just sitting there, I guessed, hunched and unhappy, chewing on his bitten-down nails.

To see if she had some other fellow calling?

More likely, I thought, just to be close to her. Or if not her, the house itself. To reassure himself that since we were all in and going about our customary routine, no serious breach had occurred. Then, remembering the old Stuart, I thought, No, it's his way of intimidating her. It's a kind of bullying. Didn't he know the first thing about her? Had he learned nothing in all those hours in the dark of the lounge room or the back veranda? Did he think that because she had sent him packing on previous occasions, all he had to do now was apply pressure and wait?

I could have told him something about those other occasions. That she was the sort of girl who did not forgive such demonstrations of her own weakness or those who caused them.

There was only a limited number of times she would allow herself to be so shamefully humiliated. I stood hidden behind the slats of my sleepout and watched him there. Was she watching too?

I was surprised. That he should just drive up like that and park under the street light where everyone could see him. Was he more inventive than I'd guessed?

It seemed out of character too. Melodramatic. The sort of thing people did in the movies. Was that where he had got it?

Next morning at breakfast I glanced across at Katie to see if she too had seen him, and got a defiant glare. Then that night, late, when I went out to the kitchen to get a drink, she confronted me.

'So what do *you* think?' she demanded.

It was a clammy night. Airless. Without a breath. She was barefoot, her hair stuck to her brow with sweat. We stood side by side for a moment at the kitchen window.

'He's been there now for three nights running,' she said. 'It's ridiculous!'

I passed behind her and opened the fridge.

'Maybe you should go down,' she said, 'and sit with him.'

'What? What would I want to do that for?'

'Well, you're mates, aren't you?'

I had turned with the cold-water bottle. She took it from me and rolled it, with its fog of moisture, across her damp forehead, then her throat and chest.

'Is that what Stuart says?'

'Not what he *says*. Stuart never says anything, you know that.'

'What then? What do you mean?'

'Oh, nothing,' she said wearily. She handed the bottle back. 'Let's drop it.'

'Braden's my friend,' I told her. 'If Stuart wasn't here every night I wouldn't even see him from one week's end to the next.'

'OK,' she said, 'let's drop it. Maybe I don't understand these things.'

'What things?'

'Oh, boys. Men. You're all so − *tight* with one another.'

'No we're not. Stuart and I aren't − tight.'

'I thought you were.'

'Well, we're not.' I finished my glass of water, rinsed it at the sink and went to pass her.

Suddenly, from behind, her arms came round me. I felt the damp of her forearms on my chest, her face nuzzling the back of my neck.

'Your hair smells nice,' she said. 'Like when you were little.'

I squirmed and pretended to wriggle free, but only pretended. 'Stop,' I said, 'you're tickling,' as she held me tighter and laughed.

'There,' she said, glancing away to the window, 'he's gone.'

Neither of us had heard the car move off. She continued to hold me. 'Stay a minute, Angus,' she said. 'Stay and talk.'

'What about?'

'Oh, not him.' She let go of me. 'That wouldn't get us far.'

I sat at the kitchen table, awkward but expectant, and she sat opposite.

In the old days we had been close. When I came out of my room at night to get a glass of water or milk from the fridge, she would join me and we would sit for a bit, joking, exchanging stories, larking about. Stuart's arrival had ended that. He was always there, and when he wasn't she avoided me. Either way, I missed her and blamed Stuart for coming between us. We liked each other. She made me happy, and I made her happy too.

'I know you're on his side,' she said now. 'But there are things you don't know about.'

'I'm not on his side,' I told her. 'Are there sides?'

She laughed. 'No, Angus, there are no sides. There never will be for you. That's what I love about you.'

I was defensive. 'What's that supposed to mean?'

'It means you're nicer than I am. Maybe than any of us. And I love you. Listen,' she said, leaning closer, 'I'm going away.'

'Where to?'

'I don't know yet. Maybe I'll go and stay with Meg and Jack for a bit. Or I'll take the plunge and just go to Brisbane.'

'What would you do down there?'

'Get an office job, work in a shop – what do other girls do? I'm doing nothing here. Reading a lot of silly novels – what's the use of that? You know what this place is like. You won't stay here either.'

'Won't I?'

It pleased me at that time when people told me things about myself. Sometimes they surprised me, sometimes they didn't. Even when they confirmed what I already knew I was filled with interest.

'I've *got* to get out,' she told me passionately, 'I've *got* to. Nothing will ever happen if I stay here. I'd end up marrying Stuart, or someone just like him, and it'd kill me. It doesn't matter that he wants me, or thinks he does, or what I think of *him*. Even if he was kind – which he wouldn't be in fact. He'd be a rotten husband. What he really loves is himself. Maybe I won't get married at all. I don't know why everyone goes on all the time about marriage, as if it was the only thing there is.'

I was bewildered. She was telling me more than I could take in.

'So when?' I asked. 'When will you go?'

'I don't know,' she said miserably. 'I've got no money.'

'I have. I've got forty pounds.'

She leaned across the table and took my hand. 'I love you, Angus. More than anyone. Did you know that?' Then, after a pause, 'But you should hang on to your money, you'll need it yourself if you're ever going to get out of this dump. I'll get it some other way. Now go to bed or you won't be able to get up in the morning. It's after eleven.'

I got up obediently, and was at the door when she said, 'I suppose you'll be inseparable now.'

'Why?' I asked her. 'Why should we be?'

'Because that's the way he is. Once he realises this is the end, really this time, he'll want you to see what a bitch I am and how miserable he is.'

'That's all right,' I said. 'I won't listen.'

'Yes you will. But don't worry—'

'Katie—'

'No, no,' she said. 'Go to bed now.'

She came and kissed me very lightly on the cheek.

'We'll talk about it some other time. I told you, I love you. And thanks, eh? For the offer of the money. You sleep well now.'

THAT was in mid-April. The weeks passed. There was no reconciliation. Stuart stopped driving up to keep a watch on the house. Katie did not go away.

But she was right about one thing. Despite my reluctance, Stuart and I did become mates of a sort. Hangdog and subdued, he was in no mood to go out on the town with his mates, the daredevil rowdies he normally ran with, who did shift work at the cane mill, or were plumber's mates, apprentice builders, counter-jumpers in drapery shops or hardware stores, or helped out in their father's accounting business. Fellows whose wildness, which involved a lot of haring around late at night, scaring old ladies and Chinamen or the occasional black, was winked at as a relatively harmless way of letting off steam; the sort of larrikin high jinks that on another occasion might take the form of dashing into a burning house to rescue a kiddie from the flames or dragging a cat from a flooded creek or, if there was another war, performing feats of quicksilver courage that would get their names on the town memorial.

What Stuart needed me for, I decided, was to be a witness to his sorrows. Which he thought I might best be able to confirm because so much of what he gave himself up to came out of books. He was literary in the odd way of a fellow who did not read and who trusted my capacity to appreciate what he was feeling because I did. Perhaps he believed that if I took him seriously, then she would; though with a fineness of feeling I had not expected, he never once, in all our times together, mentioned her. Which made me more uneasy than if he had, since at every moment she was there as an unasked question between us, and as the only reason, really, why I was there at all.

He would pick me up in the Anglia at the bottom of our street, usually around nine when I had finished my homework, and we would drive out to some hilltop and just sit there in the cool night air, with the windows down, the sweet smell of cane flowers coming in heady wafts and the night crickets shrilling.

Stuart's self-pitying tone, and his self-conscious half-jokey way of addressing me as 'Angus, old boot', or 'Angus, old son', suggested more than ever, I thought, a character out of some movie, or a book he had been impressed by, and had more to do with the way he wanted me to see him, or the way he wanted to see himself, than with anything he really was.

Then it was July at last. The McGowans asked me to go out to the Lagoons. And I was going.

JUST before sun-up the McGowans' heavy-duty Bedford ute swung uphill to where I was waiting with my duffel bag and bedroll on our front veranda. Behind me, the lights were on in our front room and my mother was there in her dressing gown, with a mug of tea to warm her hands, just inside the screen door. I was glad the others could not see her, and hoped she would not come out at the last moment to kiss me or to tuck my scarf into my windcheater. But in fact, 'Look after Braden,' was all she said as I waved to the ute, shouted 'See you' over my shoulder, and took three leaps down to the front gate.

Glen was driving, with his father and Henry Denkler in the cabin beside him. Braden, Stuart and the dogs were in the back. Stuart leapt down, took my bedroll, and swung it up into the tray where Braden, on his feet now, was barely managing the dogs. 'Hi, Angus,' Stuart said, 'all set for the boat race?' He laid his hand on my shoulder, but his glance, I saw, went to the house, in case *she* was there.

If she was, she did not make herself visible.

I climbed over the gate of the truck and Stuart followed. We staggered, the dogs around our legs, and Braden, to make room for us, settled on the pile of bedrolls at the back.

'Get down, you stupid buggers,' Stuart told the dogs, and grabbing the head of one of them under his right arm, plumped down heavily next to Braden.

I sat opposite, drawing the other dog, Tilly, between my knees. Braden banged the flat of his hand on the cabin roof and we were off.

He had said nothing as yet. Now he looked at me, grinned, and pulled his hat down firmly over his ears.

'Hi,' I said. 'Cold, eh?' was all he said in return.

Stuart laughed. 'He's always cold, aren't you, Brade? The warm blood in this family ran out with me.'

Stuart was wearing an old plaid shirt frayed at the collar and with the sleeves rolled loosely at the elbow. No jacket, no woolly.

Braden, hunched into his thick turtle-necked sweater, made a face and looked away. A draught of cold air streamed over us as we rolled down to the town bridge with its drift of bluish mist and up to where the other ute, with Matt Riley and his nephew Jem and their dogs, was parked at the petrol station before the entrance to the highway. Matt Riley, the white breath streaming from his mouth, was out of the ute, checking one of the offside tyres. Jem was driving.

I had known Matt Riley for as long as I could remember, though we had never had a proper conversation. His wife Eileen was our ironing lady. Every Monday morning he dropped her off in his ute, and he was there when I got home, silent, drinking tea at our kitchen table, waiting to take her back again. She ignored his presence, laying aside the shirt she was working on to make me a malted milk.

I was fond of Eileen. She was full of stories, told in a language, all jumps and starts, that I had got so used to at last that it seemed the only language for what she had to tell. I had never asked myself what might be peculiar about it, or where it came from. As I never asked myself why Matt Riley was so subdued and retiring in our kitchen and yet so quietly sure of himself, and so readily deferred to, when he was inspecting tyres or setting right an unbalanced load.

As for Jem, he had been one of the big boys when I started school. In the same class as Glen McGowan. A dark, sulky fellow, I thought. Although he was a big boy he could neither read properly nor write. At fourteen he had gone off to become a roo-shooter like his uncle.

He was no longer sulky. Just big and silent, almost invisible. His Uncle Matt's shadow.

AN hour later we had left the bitumen and were bouncing due west on a clay highway cut clean through the scrub. The sun was up and had burned off the early-morning chill. The dogs were alert but quiet. Braden, his knees drawn up, one of the dog leads round his wrist, was dozing, his head toppled forward under his hat. Stuart, after a bit, leaned across, unwound the lead and passed it to me. The big dog, Jigger, turned its head in my direction but did not stir. 'Good dog, Jigger,' I told him, roughening the gingery ears, 'good old boy.' He lowered his head and settled.

I was beginning to feel good. We were riding high up on the camber of the yellow-clay road, which had been washed by the rains so that it was all exposed pebbles with eroded channels on either side, then tough grass, then forest.

Stuart shook a cigarette out of the packet in the breast pocket of his shirt, dipped his head to take it between his lips. He offered me one. I shook my head. Smoke blew towards me. Sharp and sweet.

'Big day, eh, Angus?'

It was. He knew how long I had wanted this. To come out here, be one with the others, part at last of whatever it was. The sky above us was high and cloudless, as it is up here in winter. Stuart followed my gaze as if there was something up there that I had caught a glimpse of, a hawk maybe; but there was nothing. Just the huge expanse of blue that made the air so clean as it tumbled over us; as if all this – sky, forest, the warmth of the big dog between my knees – was part of the one thing, a consciousness – not simply my own – that belonged not only to the body I was in, back hard against the metal side of the truck, muscles flexed in my calves and thighs, belly empty, but also to something out there that I had melted into as one melts into sleep, and was infinite.

I did sleep, and was woken by Stuart punching me lightly in the shoulder. 'Wake up, Australia!'

We climbed down. The other ute was already parked.

We were at the little junction station where the Chillagoe line branches west into anthill country: a water tank and pump, a general store, and the two-roomed cottage-cum-stationmaster's hut. It was the established custom for parties going out to the Lagoons to stop here for breakfast, before going down to the general store to fill the emergency petrol cans.

'I'm famished,' Braden announced. It was after eight.

I agreed.

'Don't worry, son, you'll get a good feed here,' Matt Riley told me. 'Trust Miss Appin, eh, Jem?'

Like most of the older members of the party, Matt Riley had been stopping here for nearly forty years.

Suddenly in a storm of dust a dozen or so guineafowl darted out from under the house, which stood on three-foot stumps, and got between our legs and began to peck around the tyres of the trucks. There was a clatter of hooves, and a young nanny goat skittered down the stairs from Miss Appin's dining room, with three more guineafowl at her heels, and behind them Miss Appin herself flourishing a tea towel in her fist.

'Morning, Millie,' Henry Denkler called across to her, and took the hat from his stack of white hair and made a decent sweep with it. 'Mornin', Millie,' Wes McGowan echoed.

'Drat the thing,' Miss Appin shouted after the goat, which had propped in the yard ten paces off and with its wide-set, sad-looking eyes stood its ground looking offended.

'Garn,' Jem told it, and at something in his unfamiliar growl it started and fled.

'Good on you, lad,' Miss Appin told him. Then, reverting to her role as hostess, 'It's all ready, gentlemen. Eight of you – is that right?'

I knew about Miss Appin. She had been described to me a dozen times by kids at school who had been out here and known what to expect, but had still, when they came face to face with her, been startled.

Forty years before she had been a beauty. Her family ran the biggest spread in this part of the state. She was one of those girls that a young Wes McGowan or Henry Denkler might dream of but could not aspire to. The best horsewoman in the district, she had been to school in Europe, spoke French and had been 'presented' at Government House in Brisbane.

But at twenty, in a single moment, fate had exploded out of a trusted corner and turned her whole world upside down. A horse had kicked in all one side of her face, flattening the bony ridge above her right eye, shattering her cheekbone and jaw. Over the years, the damaged side of her face had aged differently it seemed from the other, so that they appeared to belong to different women, or to women who had lived very different lives. Only one of these faces smiled, but you saw then why a girl who had been so lively and pleased with herself might have chosen to live in a place where she saw no more than a few dozen people each week, and most of them the same people, over and over.

Miss Appin was responsible for changing the points on the line, and had turned her front room into the station buffet, where twice a week, while the two-carriage train waited and took on water, she served freshly baked scones and tea out of thick white Railway crockery, and in winter, breakfast to shooting parties like ours that called up beforehand and put in their order.

Two tables with chequered cloths had been laid for us. Otherwise, the small neat room was a front room like any other. There was an upright piano with brass candelabra and the walls were covered from floor to picture rail with photographs of Miss Appin's nephews and nieces, all of them known, it seemed, to Henry Denkler and Wes McGowan and even, though he was shy to admit it, to Matt Riley: family parties on lawns, the ladies with their skirts spread; young men with axes at wood-chopping shows or looking solemn in studio poses in the uniforms of the two Wars; other boys (or the same ones when younger) in eights on a sunlit river or standing at ease beside their oars; five-year-olds in communion suits with bow ties, or like baby brides in a cloud of tulle. Three or four guineafowl crept back, and flitted about under the tables. There was a smell of bacon.

'Come on now, Braden,' Miss Appin jollied, 'and you too – what's-your-name – Angus, was it? – I need a couple of willing hands.'

She ushered us into the little blackened scullery and we fetched back plates of eggs, a great platter of sizzling rashers, bread, butter, scones. We were ravenous, all of us. But when we were seated even Jem Riley, who was a rough fellow, ate in a restrained, almost dainty way, swallowing quietly, blushing at every mouthful in an effort to keep up to the standard set by Henry Denkler and Wes McGowan, which was clearly what they thought was due to Miss Appin's 'background'. As soon as he had gulped the last of his tea, Jem excused himself and bolted. He would drive their ute down to the store and fill the emergency cans.

Glen, in a high state of amusement at Jem's confusion, got to his feet, thanked Miss Appin with an old-world formality that delighted his father and which the McGowan boys could turn on quite effortlessly when occasion demanded, and went after Jem to help.

'So then, Millie,' Wes McGowan began, pushing back from the remains of his breakfast while Braden and I tucked into seconds, 'what have you got to tell us about this *pig*?'

A seven-mile drive south of Miss Appin's, the old Jeffries place where the boar had been sighted was no more now than an isolated chimney stack in a pile of rubble and a steel windmill whose spindly tower and blades could be seen in the long grass off the north–south highway.

We drove in slowly – there was no longer a track – and parked in a clump of water gums. I was directed to take charge of the McGowan dogs, Jigger and Tilly, but also of Matt Riley's dog, Archer, an Irish setter as new to all this as I was and very nervous, though Jem assured me, as the dog rubbed against him and licked his hand, that he was sweet-natured enough if you handled him right. And it was true. When I leaned down and hugged him a little, he immediately shoved his nose into my groin. I settled in the shade of the water gums, but the three dogs, excited by the sense that something was about to begin, remained standing, heads raised, lean flanks trembling, pulling hard at the leash. It was just after ten. The sun was fierce, the long grass a wave of cicada-voices rising and skirling, then lapsing, then rising again.

Matt, with Jem as usual at his side, went off to do some scouting and it was confirmed. There was a pig, a good-sized one.

Wes McGowan, whose party this was, had ceded authority for the moment to the professional. He was seated now, sweating under his hat, in the shade of the Bedford, having a quiet smoke.

Matt Riley, meanwhile, had taken Braden aside and was giving him instructions, pointing across the open grassland to where the boar was holed up and sleeping in the sun, somewhere between the windmill and the darker treeline that marked the course of a creek.

The other old-timer of the party, Henry Denkler, had set up a folding stool, and with his hat drawn down and his .303 across his arm, was dozing, for all the world as if he was having a quiet snooze in his own backyard in town.

The others, Glen, Stuart, Jem, were squatting on their heels in the shadows behind me. Not speaking. All their attention, like mine, was on the group Matt Riley and Braden made, Braden the taller by a head, which was all Matt-talk, low-voiced and slow, no more, as I strained my ears to catch it, than a few broken sibilants at moments when the cicadas cut out.

Braden was nodding. Allowing himself to be sweet-talked into a kind of high-pitched ease. Yet another area in which Matt was a professional.

I glanced back quickly at the others.

They too had been gathered in. A moment ago, Glen and

Stuart had been as tense almost as the dogs, out of concern perhaps for Braden – more family business. They were subdued now. Almost dreamy. As if Matt had worked his spell on them also, as he had done three or four years back, when they had been where Braden stood now.

I too had a place made for me, but it was up to me what I made of it. I held fast to the dogs, watching their shoulders quiver in expectation. Something of their animal sense that we were set down now in a single world of muscle and nerve, mind both present and dreamlike afloat, communicated itself to me, entered my fists, where they held fast to the twined leashes and took the strain of the dogs' forelegs and rump, ran back down my forearms to my chest and belly, set my heart steadily beating.

Matt had his hand now on Braden's shoulder and was singing to him – that's how I heard it. Slowing him down. Creating in him a steady state of being inside himself. In the eye that would sight along the barrel of the rifle. In the index finger that would gently squeeze the trigger. In the softness of his shoulder that would take the impact of the shot down through his spine, his buttocks, the muscles at the back of his calves to the balls of his feet where they were spread just wide enough to balance the six feet two of him squarely on the earth.

I wished that Matt was singing, in that low voice whose words I missed but whose tune I was straining to catch, to me, or to something *in* me. That he was discovering for me that state of detachment but deep immersion, beyond mere attention or nerve, that, once I had hit upon it, I might go back and back to – the sureness of something centred that I lacked.

I watched Braden and thought I saw it entering him. When Matt nodded and released his shoulder at last he would be fully equipped. They would go forward and the others would get up and follow, even Henry Denkler, waking abruptly from his doze as if even in sleep he too had been quietly listening. Twenty minutes from now, Braden would have it for ever. Even if he never returned to any of this, it would be his.

It was this, rather than the business of simply putting a shot into the brain of a maddened beast, that he had come out here to get hold of so that these witnesses to it – his father, his brothers, the professional, Matt Riley, Henry Denkler – would know he had it, that they had passed it on.

On some signal from Matt Riley that I failed, for all my tenseness, to register, Wes McGowan got to his feet, came to where I was sitting and leaned down. His big hand covered Tilly's skull, tickling her with his finger behind the ears. 'Angus,' he told me, 'I want you to stay back here with the dogs.'

I swallowed hard, nodded glumly. I'd known this was coming, and Mr McGowan, not to embarrass me by witnessing my youthful disappointment, turned away. I knew what he was doing. He was keeping me out of harm's way. But there was something else as well. If anything went wrong out there my inexperience might be dangerous, and not only to myself.

'Come on, boys,' I told the dogs, and I put my arms around Tilly, who turned and licked my face.

Glen and the others were on their feet now. Braden cast me a quick look and I nodded. I too got to my feet. The little party formed in three lines, Matt Riley and Jem in front to do the tracking, Braden, Glen and Stuart behind. They set off through the waist-high grass. Once again I would be on the sidelines watching, as I had been so often before when it was a matter only of the telling. I urged the dogs up into the tray of the Bedford and, scrambling up behind them, stood straining my eyes for a better view.

The shoulders and hats, which were all I could see above the sunlit grasstops, moved slowly forward. Twenty, thirty yards further and Matt Riley sheered off to the left. The rest of the party came to a stop. Waited. I could hear the silence like a hotter space at the centre of the late-morning heat. Big grasshoppers were blundering about. Flies simmered and swarmed. The dogs, on tensed hind legs, leaned into the still air, tautening the leash. 'Easy, Jigger,' I whispered to the younger dog, though he paid no attention. His mind was away up ahead, low down in the grass roots, close to the earth. 'Tilly,' I told the other, 'quiet, eh? Be quiet now.' My own mind too was out there somewhere. Beside Braden. Who would be sweating hard now, every muscle tense, preparing for the moment when he would move on out of himself. I saw Matt Riley, without looking behind, raise his arm.

'Quiet now, Tilly.'

I laid my hand on the old dog's quivering flank. The sky hung above like a giant breath suspended over the shifting light and shadow of the grass and I watched the hats, and below them the upper bodies, part the still grassheads as they waded towards the treeline. They were moving in dreamlike slow motion, Matt Riley still in front. 'What can you see now, Tilly?' I whispered.

They had stopped again. I saw Matt, still without turning, beckon to Braden.

He moved forward and Matt passed to his right. Braden was half a head taller than anyone else among them except Henry Denkler, who towered above the rest.

Matt raised an open hand, and I saw Braden lift the .303 very slowly to his shoulder.

The cicadas stopped dead in the heat. There was a sound, more like a happening in the sky I thought than a shot, and dozens of birds that had been invisible in the grass were suddenly in the air, wildly flapping.

There was a swift movement among the hats, then another shot, and the dogs were barking and straining so hard at the leash that I was almost pulled out of the truck, too busy shouting at them to shut up, and cursing and jerking at the leash, to see what was happening off in the distance, till there was another shot and I risked it, and saw the knot around what I knew must be the kill.

At that moment, a quarter of a mile to my left and well out of the vision of the others, I saw the two ancient carriages of the Chillagoe train come puffing across the horizon, pouring out smuts. It would have made its mid-morning stop at Miss Appin's, taken on water, and was now heading west into anthill country.

I could see Wattie McCorkindale, the driver, in the cabin, a tough nut of a man with tight grey curls like a woolly cap. I passed him each morning on my way to school, always in the same faded, washed-out overalls and carrying his black lunch tin. Beside him, in the cabin, was his mate, Bill Yates.

For a moment, as it swung close, I heard the hammering of the wheels on the track, then it swung back again, and it was the little gated platform at the rear that was facing me, and a woman was there, shading her eyes as she peered into the sunlight. She must have heard the shots. I was tempted to wave. I wondered what she must be making of all this. The shots, then a lone boy standing in the tray of a ute, in a grassfield in the middle of nowhere, holding hard to a mob of crazy hounds. Meanwhile, the party of pig-shooters, in a tight bunch now, was coming back.

Braden was flushed and looked innocently pleased with himself. Stuart and Glen were on either side of him. They had never seemed such a close and affectionate group.

I let the dogs loose. They leapt down from the ute and

went running in excited circles around him. He dropped to one knee; happy, I thought, to be in a group where he could be the focus of another sort and exhibit an easier and more exuberant affection. He hugged Tilly, then Jigger, who was jostling to be gathered in, and they licked at his face and hands. Perhaps they could smell the pig on him, or some other smell he carried that was whatever had passed between him and the three hundred pounds of malevolent fury, in beast form, that had come hurtling towards him in the blood-knowledge and small-eyed, large-brained premonition of its imminent death.

He looked up, with his arms round Tilly, who for the past eight years had shared so many of our games and excursions, and in her own way, with doggy intuition, so many of our secrets. I saw then what a relief it was to him that all this was done with at last, and done well.

He had wanted it to go well for his father's sake as much as his own; out of a wish, just this once and for this time only, to be all that his father wanted him to be. All that Glen wanted him to be as well, and Stuart, because this was the last time they would be together in this way. When he left at the beginning of the new year it would be for a life he would never come back from; even if he did, physically, come back.

Except for Braden himself, I was the only one among us, I thought, who knew this. And because I knew it, I felt, as he must have, the sadness that was in Wes McGowan's pride in him, and in what he had shown of himself in front of Henry Denkler and Matt Riley, whose good opinion the old man set such store on. Had it crossed his mind, I wondered, that Braden, even in this moment of being most immediately one with them, was already lost to him?

I glanced at Stuart. He knew Braden just well enough to see what was at stake for the boy in that other world he was about to give himself to, though not perhaps how commanding it might be, or how clearly Braden understood that there was no other way he could go.

Glen saw nothing at all. It was inconceivable to him that a fellow of Braden's sort, his brother, who had grown up in the same household with him, could imagine anything finer or more real than what had just been revealed to him: the deep connection between himself and these men he was with; his even deeper connection with that force out there, animal, ancient, darkly close and mysterious, which, when he had stood against it and taken upon himself the solemn distinction of cancelling it out, he had also taken in, as a new and profounder being.

What surprised me, and must have surprised Braden too, was the glow all this gave him. It was real, in a way I think that even he had not expected: the abundant energy surging through him that lit his smile when he glanced up at me, then gave himself, all overflowing warmth and affection, to the dogs.

An hour later, with Matt Riley's battered ute in front and Matt himself hanging out the cabin window to guide us, we bumped and lurched into the Valley. Which wasn't a valley in fact but a waterland of drowned savannah forest, reedy lagoons stained brownish in the shallows, sunlit beyond, or swampy places, half-earth, half-ooze, above which ti-trees stood stripping their bark or rotting slowly from the roots up. We parked beside an expanse of water wide enough to suggest a lake and with a good deal of leg-stretching, and expressions of satisfaction at the number of game birds in evidence, made camp, Matt directing.

Matt's precedence out here, I saw, had nothing to do with Braden's business with the pig or his 'professionalism'. It was something else. Very lightly ceded, the authority that Wes McGowan might have claimed as the getter-up of our party, or old Henry Denkler as its senior member and as mayor, had passed naturally, and with no need for explanation, to the younger man. And though no one had spelled it out I knew immediately what it was. I looked at Matt – at Jem too – with new eyes.

The land out here was Matt's grandmother's country, and the moment he entered it he had a different status: that was the accepted but unspoken ground of his authority. That and the knowledge of the place and all its workings that came with the land itself.

I had heard of this business of 'grandmothers'. The grandfathers were something else. Overdressed men with beards and side whiskers – farmers, saddlers, blacksmiths, proprietors of drapery shops and general stores – they had given their names to streets, towns, shires all over the North. You saw their photographs, looking sternly soulful and patriarchal, round the walls of shire halls and in mouldy council chambers; men who, in defiance of conditions so hard that to survive at all a man had to be equally hard in return (in defiance too of the niceties of law as it might be established fifteen hundred miles away, in Brisbane), had carved out of the rainforest a world we took for granted now, since it had all the familiar amenities and might have been here for ever.

In fact, they had made it with their bare hands, and with axes and bullock-wagons. Doing whatever had to be done to make it theirs in spirit as well as in fact. Brooking no question, and suffering, one guesses, no regrets, since such work was an arm of progress and of God's good muscular plan for the world. All that so short a time ago that Wes McGowan might well have been one of the children in long clothes you saw seated on the knee of one of those bearded ancients, or in the arms of one of the pallid women in ruched and ribboned silk who sat stolidly beside him flanked by her brood.

No one would ever have spoken of Matt Riley's 'grand-father'. That would have given something away that in those days was still buried where family history meant it to stay, in the realm of the unspoken. 'His grandmother's country' was a phrase that referred, without raising too precisely the question of blood, to the relationship a man might stand in to a particular tract of land, that went deeper and further back than legal posses-sion. When used in town it had 'implications', easy to pick up but not to be articulated. A nod to the knowing.

Out here, in the country itself, though what it referred to was still discreetly unspecified, it was actual. From the moment we climbed down out of the trucks and let the light of its broken waters enter us, and breathed in its sweetish water-smelling air, and took its dampness on our skins – from that moment something was added to Matt Riley, or given back; and he took it, with no sign of change in the quietness with which he went about things, or in his understated way of offering his own opinion or disagreeing with another's. He had re-entered a part of himself that was continuous with the place, and with a history the rest of us had forgotten or never known.

It was a place he both knew and was a stranger to; so deep in him that only rarely perhaps, save in sleep or half-sleep, did he catch a whisper of it out of some old story he had heard from one side of his family – the other would have a different story altogether – and which, the moment he stepped into it, became a language he understood in his bones and through the soles of his feet, though he had no other tongue in his head, or his memory, than the one we all spoke.

At home I had been shy of Matt — mostly, I think, because he was so shy of me. Out here things were different. All those afternoons in our kitchen when, with Eileen at the ironing board, I had sat at the table and drunk the milkshake she had stopped to make for me, and ate my biscuit or slice of cake, though we had barely addressed a word to one another, consti-tuted a kind of intimacy, out here, that could be drawn on and made to bloom. 'Com'on, son,' he'd tell me, 'I got somethin' you oughta take a look at.'

Alone, or with Braden, and always with Jem in tow, he would uncover for me some small fact about the world we were in — a sight or ordinary but hidden wonder that I might otherwise have missed. Brushing the earth away with a grimy hand, or delicately lifting aside a bit of crumbling damp, he would open a view into some other life there, at the grub or chrysalis stage, that in moving through several forms in the one existence was in progress towards miraculous transformation, and whose unfolding history and habits, as he evoked them in his grunting monosyllabic style, moved almost imperceptibly from visible fact into half-humorous, half-sinister fable.

He showed us how to track, to read marks in the softly disturbed earth that told of the passage of some creature whose size and weight you could calculate — sometimes from obser-vation, sometimes from a kind of visionary guesswork — by getting down close to the earth and attending, listening. The place was for him all coded messages; hints, clues, shining partic-ulars that once scanned, and inwardly brooded on, opened the way to another order of understanding and usefulness.

WE ate early, before it was dark, Matt choosing what should go into the pot and Jem doing the chopping and seasoning.

Afterwards, bellies full of the cook-up and of the damper Jem had made to soak up the last of the gravy, we sat on as the ghostly late light on the tree trunks faded, and the trees themselves stepped back into impenetrable dark. Slowly the world around us recreated itself as sound. The occasional flapping, off in the distance, of a night bird on the prowl, an owl or nightjar. Low calls. Bush mice crept in, and tumbled with a chittering sound in the undergrowth beyond the fire, lured perhaps by our voices, or by our smell, or the smell of the stew and Jem's damper, the promise of scraps. There was the splash, from close by in the lagoon, of waterfowl, the clicketing of tree frogs or night crickets, a flustering of scrub-turkey or some other shy bush creature that had been drawn to the light, here in the great expanse of surrounding darkness, of our fire.

We sat. Not much was said. Talk out here, at this hour, was not so much an exchange of the usual observations and asides as a momentary reassurance, subdued, unassertive, of presence, of company and speech. The few words, an occasional low laugh, mingled as they were with the hush and tinkle of bush sounds, lulled something in me as I lay stretched on one side on top of my sleeping bag, face to the flames, and led me lazily, happily towards sleep.

The one jarring note was Stuart.

He too said little. But often, when I glanced up, I would find his eyes on me, dark, hostile I thought, in the glow of the fire. His beard had grown. He looked a little mad. Sometimes, when I dropped some word into the conversation, I would hear him grunt, and when I looked up there would be a line of half-humorous disdain to his mouth that in the old days would have been a prelude to one of his outbursts of baffled fury.

Braden saw it too. But out here, Stuart kept whatever he was thinking to himself.

I stayed clear of him. Not consciously. But with Braden here it was easy to fall into the old pattern in which Braden and I were a pair and Stuart was on the outer. Perhaps he thought I had told Braden something – I hadn't. That I'd betrayed him in some way, and that we were ganging up on him. Then there was Matt Riley and the things he had to show. It simply happened that for the first two or three days we barely spoke.

IT was my job, first thing each morning, to take a couple of billies down to the edge of the lagoon and draw water for our breakfast tea. Usually Braden went with me, but that morning, when I rolled out of the blanket and pulled on my jeans, he was still sleeping. I sat to tie my bootlaces, waiting for him to stir. When he didn't I took the billies from beside the fire and set out. The grass was white with frost. Pale sunlight touched the mist that drifted in thin low banks above the lagoons. Cobwebs rainbowed with light were stretched between the trees, their taut threads beaded with diamond points that flashed and burned gold, then fiery red.

Later, in the heat of the day, the bush smell would be prickly, peppery with sunlight. Now it had the freshness in it of a sky still moist with dew.

I climbed down the weedy bank and trawled the first of the billies through the brownish water, careful not to go too deep. I heard someone behind me, and thought it was Braden, but when I looked up it was Stuart who was swinging his long legs over a fallen branch and glowering down at me.

'Hi, Angus,' he said, 'how's it goin'?' His tone had an edge to it. 'You havin' a good time out here?' He reached down and

I passed the first of the two billies up to him, then set myself to filling the second.

'Great,' I said. 'Great!'

'That's nice,' he said. He rested the billy on the log beside him. It sat there, balanced and brimming. 'I been hopin' to catch you an' have a bit of a talk,' he said at last. 'You been avoidin' me?'

I found it easier to ignore this than deny it.

'Aren't you goin' to ask me what about?'

'I suppose it's about Katie,' I said. I was wondering why, after so many weeks, he had broached the subject at last, and so directly. Did being out here make things different, relax the rules? Or was it that he had somehow come to the end of his tether? I emptied the second billy and for a second time drew it slowly across the surface of the lagoon. I had caught the little smile he had given me. Good shot, Angus. You got it in one. Satirical, I thought.

He waited for me to stop fooling with the second billy, then reached down and I handed it up to him.

'So,' he said, holding on to the handle but not yet taking its weight so that I was caught looking up at him, 'what do you know about all this, eh, Angus? What's happening? One minute everything was fine — you saw that. An' the next she's gone cold on me.'

'Honestly, Stuart, I don't *know* what's happened. She wouldn't say anything to me.'

He looked doubtful.

'I'm beat,' he said suddenly, taking the billy at last and hoisting it over to sit beside the other one on the log. I thought there were tears in his eyes. I was shocked.

'I just don't know what she wants out of me.'

'Stuart—'

'Yair, I know,' he said. 'I'm sorry, Angus.' He sniffled and brushed his nose with his knuckled fist. 'If you knew what it was like . . .'

I thought I did, though not from experience.

'The thing is,' he said, sitting on the low branch, his face squared up now, the cheeks under the narrowed eyes wooden, the eyes gazing away into himself, 'if this goes wrong it'll be the finish of me. For me it's all or nothing. If she would just have me − let *me* have *her* − it'd be all right − my life, I mean − hers too. If she won't I'm finished. She knows that, she must. I told her often enough. So why's she doing it?'

I found I couldn't look at him. We remained poised like that, the question hanging, the open expanse of water like glass in the early light. He got up, took one of the billies, then the other, and set off back to camp.

I sat on at the bank for a moment. Then I crouched down and splashed cold lagoon water over my face, then again, and again.

Stuart's misery scared me. My own adolescent glooms I had learned to enjoy. I liked the sense they gave me of being fully present. Even more the bracing quality I felt in possession of when I told myself sharply to stop play-acting, and strongly, stoically dealt with them. Did I despise Stuart because he was so self-indulgent? Was he too play-acting, but not alert enough to his own nature to know it? I preferred that view of him than the scarier one in which his desperation was real. I didn't want to be responsible for his feelings, and it worried me that out here there was no escape from him.

He tackled me again later in the day.

'You know, Angus,' he said mildly as if he had given the matter some thought and got the better of it, 'you could put in a good word for me. If there was the opportunity.'

We were standing together on a shoot, just far enough from the others not to be heard, even in the late-afternoon stillness.

Braden was with his father and Henry Denkler, a little away to the left. The air was still, the ground, with its coarse short grass, moist underfoot. Steely light glared off the nearby lagoon. The dogs, in their element now, had discovered in themselves, in a way that impressed me, their true nature as bird-dogs, a fine tense quality that made them almost physically different from the rather slow creatures they were at home. They were leaner, more sinewy.

'You could do that much,' he persisted, 'for a mate. We are mates, aren't we?'

I turned, almost angry, and found myself disarmed by the flinching look he gave me, the tightness of flesh around his eyes, the line of his mouth.

I was saved from replying by a clatter of wings, as a flock of ducks rose out of the glare that lay over the surface of the big lagoon and stood out clear against the cloudless blue. But it was too late. I had missed my chance at a shot and so had Stuart. The others let off a volley of gunfire and the dogs went crashing through the broken water to where the big birds were tumbling over in the air and splashing into the shattered stillness of the lake, or dropping noiselessly into the reeds on the other bank.

'Damn,' I shouted. 'Damn. Damn!'

'What happened?' Braden asked, when we stood waiting in a group for the dogs to bring in the last of the birds. 'Why didn't you fire?'

I shook my head, and Braden, taking in Stuart's look, must have seen enough, in his quick way, not to insist. The dogs were still coming in with big plump birds. There were many more of them than would go into the pot.

'Good girl, Tilly,' he called, and the dog, diverted for a moment, gave herself a good shake and ran to his knee. He leaned down, roughly pulled her head to his thigh and ruffled her ears. The strong smell of her wet fur came to me.

I spent the rest of the day stewing over my lost chance, exaggerating my angry disappointment and the number of birds I might have bagged, as a way of being so mad with Stuart that I did not have to ask myself what else I should feel. Braden and I spent the whole of the next morning with Matt Riley and Jem, but in the afternoon I came upon Stuart sitting on a big log a little way off from the camp, with a scrub-turkey at his feet. I stopped at a distance and spent a moment watching him. I thought he had not seen me.

'Hi,' he said. I stepped out into the clearing. 'What are you up to?'

'Nothing much,' I told him.

I settled on the log a little way away from him.

'Listen, Stuart,' I began, after a bit.

'Yair, I know,' he told me. 'I'm sorry.'

'No,' I said, 'it's not about yesterday. You've got to stop all this, that's all. She won't change her mind. I know she won't. Not this time.'

'Did she tell you that?'

'No. Not in so many words. But she won't, I know she won't. Look, Stuart, you should leave me out of it, that's what I wanted to say. I don't know anything so I can't help you. You've got to stop.'

'I see,' he said. 'That's pretty plain. Thanks, Angus. No, I mean it,' he said, 'you're right, I've been foolin' myself. I can see that now.'

'Look, Stuart–'

'No, you're right, it was hopeless from the start. That's what you're telling me, isn't it? That I might as well just bloody cut my throat!'

I leapt to my feet. 'Shut up,' I told him fiercely. 'Just stop all this. Bloody shut up!'

He was so shocked that he laughed outright.

'Well,' he said after a moment, with bitter satisfaction. 'Finally.'

What did *that* mean? He gave me a look that made me see, briefly, something of the means he might have brought to bear on *her*. But she was harder than I was. I knew the contempt she would have for a kind of appeal that she herself would never stoop to.

I stood looking at him for a moment. I did not know what more I could say. I turned and walked away.

'I thought you were on *my* side,' he called after me.

I had heard this before, or an echo of it. I looked back briefly but did not stop.

'I thought we were mates,' he called again. 'Angus?'

I kept walking.

I did know what he was feeling, but he confused me. I wanted to be free of him, of his turmoil. The nakedness with which he paraded his feelings dismayed me. It removed all the grounds, I thought, on which I could react and offer him real sympathy. It violated the only code, as I saw it then, that offered us protection: tight-lipped understatement, endurance. What else could we rely on? What else could *I* rely on?

I walked.

The ground with its rough tussocks was swampy, unsteady underfoot, the foliage on the stunted trees sparse and darkly colourless, their trunks blotched with lichen. I had no idea where I was headed or how far I needed to go to escape my own unsettlement. Little lizards tumbled away from my boots or dropped from branches, dragonflies hung stopped on the air, then switched and darted, blazing out like struck matches where the sun caught their glassy wings.

I walked. And as I moved deeper into the solitude of the land, its expansive stillness – which was not stillness in fact but an interweaving of close but distant voices so dense that they became one, and then mere background, then scarcely there at all – I began to forget my own disruptive presence, receding as naturally into what hummed and shimmered all round me as into a dimension of my own being that it had taken my coming out here, alone, in the slumbrous hour after midday, to uncover. I felt drawn, drawn on.

I had enough bush sense, a good enough eye for recording, unconsciously as I passed, the little oddnesses in the terrain – the elbow of a fallen bough, a particular assembly of glossy-leaved bushes that would serve as signposts on my way back – to feel confident I wouldn't get lost. I let Stuart, seated gloomily back there on his log, hugging his rifle, hugging even closer his dumb grief, fade from my thoughts, and moved deeper into the becalmed early-afternoon light, over spatterings of ancient debris, crumblings of dried-out timber. Slowly, all round and under me, an untidy grey-green world was continuously, visibly in motion. Ti-tree trunks unfurled tattered streamers; around their roots a seepage like long-brewed tea.

I walked, and the great continent of sound I was moving into recorded my presence, the arrival, in its close-woven fabric of light, sound, stilled or moving shadow, of a medium-sized foreign body, displacing the air a moment as it advanced, and confusing, with the smell of its sweat and the shifting of its breath, the tiny signals that were being picked up and trans-lated out there by a myriad forms of alien intelligence. I was central to it but I was also nothing, or close to nothing.

In the compacted heat and drowsy afternoon sunlight, I could have kept walking for ever, all the way to the Gulf. It was time, not space, I was moving into. Years it might be. And there was more of it – not just ahead but on all sides – than I could conceive of or measure.

There was no specific point I was heading for. I could stop now, turn back, and it would all still be here. It was myself I was moving into.

One day, far off down the years, I would come stumbling back in my body's last moments of consciousness and here it would be: crumbling into itself and dispersing its particles and voices, reassembling itself cell by cell in a new form that was also the old one remade. I had no need to go on and actually see it, the place where I would lie down in the springy marsh-grass, among the litter and mould, letting the grass take the impression of my weight, the shape of my body's presence, and keep it long after I was gone.

Away back, when I first heard about the Valley and let it form itself in my mind, I had thought that everything I found unsatisfactory in myself, in my life but also in my nature, would come right out here, because that is what I had seen, or thought I had, in others. Kids who had been out here, and whom I had thought of till then as wild and scattered, had come back settled in their own aggregation of muscle, bone and flesh, and in some new accommodation with the world.

Nothing like that had come to me. I was no more settled, no less confused. I would bring nothing back that would be visible to others – to my father, for instance. I had lost something; that was more like it. But happily. As I walked on into this bit of grey-green nondescript wilderness I was happily at home in myself. But in my old self, not a new one.

I don't know how far I had gone before I paused, looked around and realised I was lost. For the last ten minutes I had been walking in my sleep. The landscape of small shrubs and ti-tree I had been moving through was now scrub.

I consulted the sun and turned back the way I had come. Minutes later I looked again and changed tack. It was hot. I had begun to sweat. I took my shirt off, draped it round my neck, and set off again.

Five minutes more and I stopped, told myself sternly not to panic and, standing with my eyes closed and the whole landscape shrilling in my head, took half a dozen slow breaths.

THE shot came from closer than I would have expected, and from a direction — to my left — that surprised me. How had I gone so wrong? It was only when I had got over a small rush of relief that it struck me that after the first shot there had been no other. I quickened my pace, then began to run, my boots sinking and at times slipping on the swampy ground. When I arrived back at the clearing Stuart lay awkwardly sprawled, white-lipped and holding his shirt, which was already soaked, to his bloodied thigh.

'Hi, Angus,' he said, his tone somewhere between his old, false jauntiness and a dreamy bemusement at what had occurred and at my being the one who had arrived to find him.

'Better get someone. Quick, eh?'

He glanced down to where blood, a lot of it, I thought, was flooding through the flimsy shirt.

I fell to my knees, gaping.

'No,' he said calmly. 'Just run off as quick as you can, mate, and fetch someone. But be quick, eh? I'll be right for a bit.'

I wasn't sure of that. I felt there was something I should be doing immediately, something I should be saying that would make him feel better and restore things, maybe even cancel them out, and I was still nursing this childish thought as I sprinted towards the camp. Something I would regret for ever if he bled to death before I got back. *Was* he bleeding to death? Could a thing like that just happen, without warning, out of the blue?

In just minutes I had shouted my breathless announcement and we were back.

He was still sitting, awkwardly upright, his back against the log. I took in the rifle this time. It lay on the ground to his right. There was also the heap of dull black feathers that was a scrub-turkey. He was no longer holding the soaked rag to his outflung leg. A pool was spreading under him. He was streaming with sweat. Great drops of it stood on his brow and were making runnels down his chest.

'It's all right, Dad,' he said weakly when the old man and Matt and the others reached him. 'Bugger missed.'

It took me a moment to grasp that it was the bullet he was referring to.

They got his boot off and Matt slashed the leg of the scorched and bloodied jeans all the way to the crotch and worked quickly to apply a tourniquet. 'You'll be right,' he told Stuart. 'Bugger missed the main artery, you're a lucky feller. Bone too.' Blood was seeping out between his hands. There was a smell that made me squeamish. Seared meat. Stuart, bluish-white around the mouth, was raised up on his elbows and staring, fascinated by the throbbing out of the warm life in him. Like a child who has borne a bad fall manfully, but bursts into tears at the first expression of sympathy, he seemed close to breaking.

I was dealing with my own emotions.

I had seen Stuart stripped any number of times, in the

changing room at the pool, in the noise and general rough-house of the showers afterwards. A naked body among other naked bodies, with clear water streaming over it and a smell of clean soap in the air, is bracing, functional, presents an image too common to be remarkable or to draw attention to itself. But a single ravaged limb thrust out in the dirt, the soaked denim of the jeans that covered it violently ripped and peeled away, black hairs curling on the hollow of the thigh and growing furlike close to the groin, has a brute particularity that brought me closer to something exposed and shockingly intimate in him, to the bare forked animal, than anything I had seen when he stood fully naked under the shower. I was shaken. His jockeys, where they showed, sagged, and were worn thin and greyish. A trail of blood, still glistening wet, made its way down the long ridge of the shank bone.

Not much more than half an hour ago I had walked out on him. Exasperated. Worn down by the demands he put on me. At the end of my patience with his turmoil, the poses he struck, his callow pretensions to martyrdom. Now I was faced with a shocking reality. It was Stuart McGowan's blood I was staring at. What impressed me, in the brute light of day, was its wetness, how much there was of it, the alarming blatancy of its red.

He caught the look on my face, and something in what he saw there encouraged him back into a bravado he had very nearly lost the trick of.

'Angus,' he said. He might just have noticed me there in the tense crowd around him and recalled that I was the one who had found him. 'Waddya think then?' He managed a crooked smile, and his voice, though strained, had the same half-jokey, half-defensive tone as when on those early visits to my sleepout he had picked up one of my books and asked, 'So what's this one about?'

As if on this occasion too he were faced with a puzzle on which I might somehow enlighten him, and in the same expectation, I thought, of being given credit for the seriousness of his interest.

A smile touched the corner of his lips.

He was pleased with himself!

At being the undoubted centre of so much drama and concern. At having done something at last that shocked me into really looking at him, into taking him seriously. The wound was worth it, that's what he thought. All it demanded of him was that he should grit his teeth and bear a little pain, physical pain, be a man; he had all the resources in the world for that. And what he gained was what he saw in *me*. Which, when I got back, I would pass on to her, to Katie. When she was presented with the facts – that hole in his naked thigh with its raw and blackened lips, the near miss that had come close to draining him of the eight pints of rude animal life that was in him – she would have to think again and accept what she had denied: the tribute of his extravagant suffering, the real and visible workings of his pure, bull-like heart. He had done this for *her*!

'OK,' Matt Riley was saying. 'That's the best we can do for now.'

He got to his feet, rubbed his hands on the cloth of his thighs and told Jem: 'You – Jem – we'll need some sort of stretcher to get 'im to the truck. See what you can knock up.' Then, quietly, to Wes McGowan: 'The quicker we get 'im back to town now the better. It's not as bad as it looks. Bullet went clean through. Bugger'll need watchin', but.'

It took me a moment to grasp that what was being referred to this time was the wound.

In all the panic and excitement around Stuart, I had lost

sight of Braden. He was hunched on the ground a little way off, his back to Stuart and the rest, his head bowed. I thought he was crying. He wasn't, but he was shaking. I squatted beside him.

'You OK?' I asked. I thought he hadn't heard me. 'It's just a flesh wound,' I told him. 'Nothing serious. He's lost a bit of blood, but.'

He gave a snort. Then a brief contemptuous laugh.

Was that what it was? Contempt?

He thought Stuart had done it deliberately! I was astonished. But wasn't that just what I had assumed a moment back, when I told myself 'He's done this for her'?

I touched Braden lightly on the shoulder, then got up and turned again to where Stuart, wrapped in a blanket now and with his eyes closed, but still white-lipped and sweating, lay waiting for the pallet to be brought.

I told myself that it had never occurred to me that he would go so far. It was too excessive, too wide of what was acceptable to the code we lived by. An hysterical girl might do such a thing but not a man, not Stuart McGowan's sort of man. But at the edge of that I was shaken. Maybe what I thought I knew about people – about Stuart, about myself – was unreliable. I looked at Stuart and saw, up ahead, something that had not come to me yet but must come some day. Not a physical shattering but what belongs to the heart and its confusions, the mess of need, desire, hurt pride, and all the sliding versions of himself as lover triumphant, then as lover rejected and achingly bereft, that had led him to force things – had he? – to such lurid and desperate conclusions.

I considered again the nest of coppery hair he sported in the scoop of his underlip.

When it first appeared I had taken it, in a worrying way, as a dandified affectation, out of character with the Stuart I knew. I was less ready now with my glib assumptions. What did I know of Stuart McGowan's 'character' as I called it? Of what might or might not belong to it?

After a moment he opened his eyes, caught me watching, and in an appeal perhaps to some old complicity between us that for a good time now had been under threat, but which the shock of his near miss had re-established, he winked. Only when I failed to respond did it strike him that he might have miscalculated.

He struggled to one elbow, his head tilted, his brow in a furrow, and grinned, but sheepishly, as if I had caught him out in something furtive, unmanly. 'So how's tricks, Angus? How's it goin'?' he enquired. 'You OK?'

This time I did not turn my back on him, but I did walk away, even while I stood watching. Jem and Glen had come up with their makeshift stretcher, and Matt Riley and his father, with Henry Denkler directing, rolled him on to it, all of them quieting his sharp intakes of breath with ritual assurances, most of them wordless. For some reason, what I remember most clearly is the three-day grime on the back of Glen McGowan's neck as he bent to settle Stuart. And through it all, deep in myself, I was walking away fast into a freshening distance in which my own grime was being miraculously washed away.

Walking lightly. The long grass swishing round my boots as the sparse brush drew me on. Into the vastness of small sounds that was a continent. To lose myself among its flutings and flutterings, the glow of its moist air and sun-charged chemical green, its traffic of unnumbered slow ingenious agencies.

An hour later we had loaded up and were on our way home: Stuart well wrapped in an old quilt, laid out in the tray of the McGowans' ute with his father to tend him, Glen driving, and Henry Denkler, who seemed troubled and out of sorts, in the cabin beside him. Braden and I, seated high up on a pile of bedrolls and packs, rode in the back of Matt Riley's beaten-up ute with the guns, a mess of dogs and all our gear.

I sat, my back to the side of the truck, with Tilly between my knees, leaning forward occasionally to hug her to me, and receiving in return a soulful, brown-eyed look of pure affection. How straightforward animals are, I thought. As compared to people, with their left-handed unhappy agendas, their sore places hidden even from themselves.

I thought uneasily of Stuart, bumping about now in the other ute as it wallowed through waist-high grass down the unmarked track; still believing, perhaps, that Katie would be impressed by the badge of a near fatality he would be wearing when we got back.

Would she be? I didn't think so, but I could no longer be sure. She kept eluding my grasp. As Stuart had. And Braden.

I glanced across at him. He had pushed his hat off, though the cord was still tight under his chin, and his eyes were narrowed, his cheeks taut as he grasped the side of the ute with one hand to steady himself against its rolling and stared into space. After a moment, aware of my scrutiny, he turned, and for the first time in a while he smiled his old wry smile, which meant he had returned, more or less, to being relaxed again. Inside his own head. But not in a way that excluded my being in tune with him. I sat back, giving myself up to the air that came streaming over the cabin top as the ute emerged at last on to bitumen, turned north and put on speed.

We were less than thirty miles from home now. The land was growing uneven. Soon there would be canefields on either side of the steeply dipping road, dairy farms smelling of silage, and little smooth-crowned hills that had once been wooded and dark with aerial roots and vines, till the loggers and land-clearers moved in and opened all this country to the sky, letting the light in; creating a landscape lush and green, with only, in the gully breaks between, a remnant of the old darkness and mystery, a cathedral gloom where a smell of damp-rot lingered that was older than the scent of cane flowers or the ammoniac stench of wet cow flop, and where creatures still moved about the forest floor, or hung in rows as in a wardrobe high up in the branches, or glided noiselessly from bough to bough.

I must have nodded off. When I looked up, we were already speeding through settlements I recognised and knew the names of: wooden houses, some of them no more than shacks, set far back and low among isolated forest trees, the open spaces on either side of the bitumen strip narrowing so quickly that what there was of a township – a service station, a Greek milk bar and café – was gone again before you could catch the name on a signpost or register the slightly different smell on the air that signified settled life and neighbourliness.

I loved all this. But Katie was right. I too would leave. As she would, as Braden would.

He met my eye now and then, as the ute swung out to pass a slower vehicle and we had to reach for the side and hang on to steady ourselves, but I was less certain now that I could read his looks. He had already begun to move away.

The difference was, I thought, that he, like Katie, would not come back. But for me there could be no final leaving. This greenish light, full and luminous, always with a heaviness in it that was a reminder of the underlying dark – like the persistent memory, under even the most open of cleared land, of the ancient gloom of rainforests – was for me the light by which all moments of expectation and high feeling would in my mind for ever be touched. This was the country I would go on dreaming in, wherever I lay my head.

We were bounding along now. Sixty miles an hour. From the cabin of the truck, Jem Riley's voice, raw and a little tuneless, came streaming past my ear. 'Goodnight, Irene,' was what he was singing, 'I'll see you in my dreams.'

Braden took it up and grinned at me. I followed. A doleful tune, almost a dirge, full of old hurt, that people were drawn to sing in chorus, as if it were the sad but consoling anthem of some loose republic of the heart, spontaneously established, sustained a moment, then easily let go. Before we were done with the last of it the quick-falling tropical night had come. A blueness that for the last quarter of an hour had been gathering imperceptibly round fence posts and in the depths of trees had swiftly overtaken us, with its ancient smell of the land and its unfolding silence that was never silence. 'Goodnight,' we sang at full pelt, foolishly grinning, 'goodnight, goodnight, I'll see you in my dreams.'

Every Move You Make

Every Move You Make

—

WHEN Jo first came to Sydney, the name she heard in every house she went into was Mitchell Maze. 'This is a Mitchell Maze house,' someone would announce, 'can't you just tell?' and everyone would laugh. After a while she knew what the joke was and did not have to be told. 'Don't tell me,' she'd say, taking in the raw uprights and bare window frames, 'Mitchell Maze,' and her hostess would reply, 'Oh, do you know Mitch? Isn't he the limit?'

They were beach houses, even when they were tucked away in a cul-de-sac behind the Paddington Post Office or into a gully below an escarpment at Castlecrag. The group they appealed to, looking back affectionately to the hidey-holes and treehouses of their childhood, made up a kind of clan. Of artists mostly, painters, session musicians, film-makers, writers for the *National Times* and the *Fin Review*, who paid provisional tax and had kids at the International Grammar School, or they were lawyers at Freehills or Allen, Allen & Hemsley, or investment bankers with smooth manners and bold ties who still played touch rugby at the weekends or belonged to a surf club. Their partners – they were sometimes married, mostly not – worked as arts administrators, or were in local government. A Mitchell Maze house was a sign that you had arrived but were not quite settled.

Airy improvisations, or – according to how you saw it – calculated and beautiful wrecks, a lot of their timber was driftwood blanched and polished by the tide, or had been scrounged from building sites or picked up cheap at demolitions. It had knotholes, the size sometimes of a twenty-cent piece, and was so carelessly stripped that layers of old paint were visible in the grain that you could pick out with a fingernail, in half-forgotten colours from another era: apple green, ox-blood, baby blue. A Mitchell Maze house was a reference back to a more relaxed and open-ended decade, an assurance (a reassurance in some cases) that your involvement with the Boom, and all that went with it, was opportunistic, uncommitted, tongue-in-cheek. You had maintained the rage, still had a Che or Hendrix poster tacked to a wall of the garage and kept a fridge full of tinnies, though you *had* moved on from the flagon red. As for Mitch himself, he came with the house. 'Only not often enough,' as one of his clients quipped.

He might turn up one morning just at breakfast time with a claw hammer and rule at the back of his shorts and a load of timber on his shoulder. One of the kids would already have sighted his ute.

'Oh great,' the woman at the kitchen bench would say, keeping her voice low-keyed but not entirely free of irony. 'Does this mean we're going to get that wall? Hey, kids, here's Mitch. Here's our wall.'

'Hi,' the kids yelled, crowding round him. 'Hi, Mitch. Is it true? Is that why you're here? Are you goin' t' give us a *wall*?'

They liked Mitch, they loved him. So did their mother. But she also liked the idea of a wall.

He would accept a mug of coffee, but when invited to sit and have breakfast with them would demur. 'No, no thanks,' he'd tell them. 'Gotta get started. I'll just drink this while I work.'

He would be around then for a day or two, hammering away till it was dusk and the rosellas were tearing at the trees beyond the deck and dinner was ready; staying on for a plate of pasta and some good late-night talk then bedding down after midnight in a bunk in the kids' room, 'to get an early start', or, if they were easy about such things, crawling in with a few murmured apologies beside his hosts. Then in the morning he would be gone again, and no amount of calling, no number of messages left at this place or that, would get him back.

Visitors observing an open wall would say humorously, 'Ah, Mitch went off to get a packet of nails, I see.'

Sensitive fellows, quick to catch the sharpening of their partner's voice as it approached the subject of a stack of timber on the living-room floor, or a bathroom window that after eleven months was still without glass, would spring to the alert.

As often as not, the first indication that some provisional but to this point enduring arrangement was about to be renegotiated would be a flanking attack on the house.

'Right, *mate*,' was the message, 'let's get serious here. What about that wall?'

Those who were present to hear it, living as they did in structures no less flimsy than the one that was beginning to break up all around them, would feel a chill wind at their ear.

All this Jo had observed, with amusement and a growing

curiosity, for several months before she found herself face to face with the master builder himself.

JO was thirty-four and from the country, though no one would have called her a country girl. Before that she was from Hungary. Very animated and passionately involved in everything she did, very intolerant of those who did not, as she saw it, demand enough of life, she was a publisher's editor, ambitious or pushy according to how you took these things, and successful enough to have detractors. She herself wanted it all – everything. And more.

'You want too much,' her friends told her. 'You can't have it, you just can't. Nobody can.'

'You just watch me,' Jo told them in reply.

She had had two serious affairs since coming to Sydney, both briefer than she would have wished. She was too intense, that's what her friends told her. The average bloke, the average *Australian* bloke – oh, here it comes, *that* again, she thought – was uncomfortable with dramatics. Intimidated. Put off.

'I don't want someone who's average,' she insisted. 'Even an average Australian.'

She wanted a love that would be overwhelming, that would make a wind-blown leaf of her, a runaway wheel. She was quite prepared to suffer, if that was to be part of it. She would walk barefoot through the streets and howl if that's what love brought her to.

Her friends wrinkled their brows at these stagy extravagances. 'Honestly! Jo!' Behind her back they patronised and pitied her.

In fact they too, some of them, had felt like this at one time or another. At the beginning. But had learned to hide their disappointment behind a show of hard-boiled mateyness. They knew the rules. Jo had not been around long enough for that. She had no sense of proportion. Did she even *know* that there were rules?

THEY met at last. At a party at Palm Beach, the usual informal Sunday-afternoon affair. She knew as soon as he walked in who it must be.

He was wearing khaki shorts, work boots, nothing fancy. An open-necked unironed shirt.

Drifting easily from group to group, noisily greeted with cries and little affectionate pecks on the cheek by the women, and with equally affectionate gestures from the men – a clasp of the shoulder, a hand laid for a moment on his arm – he unsettled the room, that's what she thought, refocused its energies, though she accepted later that the unsettlement may only have been in herself. Through it all he struck her as being remote, untouchable, self-enclosed, though not at all self-regarding. Was it simply that he was shy? When he found her at last she had the advantage of knowing more about him, from the tales she had been regaled with, the houses she had been in, than he could have guessed.

What she was not prepared for was his extraordinary charm. Not his talk – there was hardly any of that. His charm was physical. It had to do with the sun-bleached, salt-bleached mess of his hair and the way he kept ploughing a rough hand through it; the grin that left deep lines in his cheeks; the intense presence, of which he himself seemed dismissive or unaware. He smelled of physical work, but also, she thought, of wood shavings – blond transparent curlings off the edge of a plane. Except that the special feature of his appeal was the rough rather than the smooth.

They went home together. To his place, to what he called 'The Shack', a house on stilts, floating high above a jungle of tree ferns, morning glory and red-clawed coral trees in a cove at Balmoral. Stepping into it she felt she had been there already. Here at last was the original of all those open-ended unfinished structures she had been in and out of for the past eight months. When she opened the door to the loo, she laughed. There was no glass in the window. Only a warmish square of night filled with ecstatic insect cries.

SHE was prepared for the raw, splintery side of him. The suncracked lips, the blonded hair that covered his forearms and the darker hair that came almost to his Adam's apple, the sandpapery hands with their scabs and festering nicks. What she could not have guessed at was the whiteness and almost feminine silkiness of his hidden parts. Or the old-fashioned delicacy with which he turned away every attempt on her part to pay tribute to them. It was so at odds with the libertarian mode she had got used to down here.

He took what he needed in a frank, uncomplicated way; was forceful but considerate – all this in appreciation of her own attractions. She was flattered, moved, and in the end felt a small glow of triumph at having so much pleased him. For a moment he entirely yielded, and she felt, in his sudden cry, and in the completeness afterwards with which he sank into her arms, that she had been allowed into a place that in every other circumstance he kept guarded, closed off.

She herself was dazzled. By a quality in him – *beauty* is what she said to herself – that took her breath away, a radiance that burned her lips, her fingertips, every point where their bodies made contact. But when she tried to express this

– to touch him as he had touched her and reveal to him this vision she had of him – he resisted. What she felt in his almost angry shyness was a kind of distaste. She retreated, hurt, but was resentful too. It was unfair of him to exert so powerful an appeal and then turn maidenly when he got a response.

She should have seen then what cross-purposes they would be at, and not only in this matter of intimacy. But he recognised her hurt, and in a way, she would discover, that was typical of him, tried out of embarrassment to make amends.

He was sitting up with his back against the bedhead enjoying a smoke. Their eyes met, he grinned; a kind of ease was re-established between them. She was moved by how knocked about he was, the hard use to which he had put his body, the scraps and scrapes he had been through. Her fingertips went to a scar, a deep nick in his cheekbone under the left eye. She did not ask. Her touch was itself a question.

'Fight with an arc lamp,' he told her. His voice had a humorous edge. 'I lost. Souvenir of my brief career as a movie star.'

She looked at him. The grin he wore was light, self-deprecatory. He was offering her one of the few facts about himself – from his childhood, his youth – that she would ever hear. She would learn only later how useless it was to question him on such matters. You got nowhere by asking. If he did let something drop it was to distract you, while some larger situation that he did not want to develop slipped quietly away. But that was not the case on this occasion. They barely knew one another. He wanted, in all innocence, to offer her something of himself.

When he was thirteen – this is what he told her – he had

been taken by his mother to an audition. More than a thousand kids had turned up. He didn't want the part, he thought it was silly, but he had got it anyway and for a minute back there, because of that one appearance, had been a household name, a star.

She had removed her hand and was staring.

'What?' he said, the grin fading. He gave her an uncomfortable look and leaned across to the night table to stub out his cigarette.

'I can't believe it,' she was saying. 'I can't believe this. I know who you are. You're Skip Daley!'

'No I'm not,' he said, and laughed. 'Don't be silly.'

He was alarmed at the way she had taken it. He had offered it as a kind of joke. One of the *least* important things he could have told her.

'But I saw that film! I saw it five times!'

'Don't,' he said. 'It was nothing. I shouldn't have let on.'

But he could have no idea what it had meant to her. What *he* had meant to her.

Newly arrived in the country, a gangly ten-year-old, and hating everything about this place she had never wanted to come to – the parched backyards, the gravel playground under the pepper trees at her bare public school, the sing-song voices that mocked her accent and deliberately, comically got her name wrong – she had gone one Saturday afternoon to the local pictures and found herself tearfully defeated. In love. Not just with the hard-heeled freckle-faced boy up on the screen, with his round-headed, blond pudding-bowl haircut and cheeky smile, his fierce sense of honour, the odd mixture in him of roughness and shy, broad-vowelled charm, but with the whole barefoot world he moved in, his dog Blue, his hardbitten parents who were in danger of losing their land, the one-storeyed sun-struck weatherboard they lived in, which was, in fact, just like her own.

More than a place, it was a world of feeling she had broken through to, and it could be hers now because *he* lived in it. She had given up her resistance.

On that hot Saturday afternoon, in that darkened picture theatre in Albury, her heart had melted. Australia had claimed and conquered her. She was shocked and the shock was physical. She had had no idea till then what beauty could do to you, the deep tears it could draw up; how it could take hold of you in the middle of the path and turn you round, fatefully, and set you in a new direction. That was what he could know nothing of.

All that time ago, he had changed her life. And here he was more than twenty years later, in the flesh, looking sideways at her in this unmade lump of a bed.

'Hey,' he was saying, and he put his hand out to lift aside a strand of her hair.

'I just can't get over it,' she said.

'Hey,' he said again. 'Don't be silly! It was nothing. Something my mother got me into. It was all made up. That stupid kid wasn't me. I was a randy little bugger if you want to know. All I could think about was my dick —' and he laughed. 'They didn't show any of that. Truth is, I didn't like myself much in those days. I was too unhappy.'

But he was only getting himself in deeper. Unhappy? He caught the look in her eyes, and to save the situation leaned forward and covered her mouth with his own.

FROM the start he famished her. It was not in her nature to pause at thresholds but there were bounds she could not cross and he was gently, firmly insistent. He did give himself, but when she too aggressively took the initiative, or crossed the line of what he thought of as a proper modesty, he would quietly turn away. What he was abashed by, she saw, was just what most consumed her, his beauty. He had done everything he could to abolish it. All those nicks and scars. The broken tooth he took no trouble to have fixed. The exposure to whatever would burn or coarsen.

A series of 'spills' had left him, at one time or another, with a fractured collarbone, three bouts of concussion, a broken leg. These punishing assaults on himself were attempts to wipe out an affliction. But all they had done was refine it: bring out the metallic blue of his eyes, show up under the skin, with its network of cracks, the poignancy – that is how she saw it – of his bones.

Leaving him sprawled, that first morning, she had stepped out into the open living room.

Very aware that she was as yet only a casual visitor to his world, and careful of intruding, she picked her way between plates piled with old food and set on tabletops or pushed halfway under chairs, coffee mugs, beer cans, gym socks, ashtrays piled with butts, magazines, newspapers, unopened letters, shirts dropped just anywhere or tossed carelessly over the backs of chairs. A dead light bulb on a glass coffee table rolled in the breeze.

She sat a moment on the edge of a lounge and thought she could hear the tinkling that came from the closed globe, a distant sound, magical and small, but magnified, like everything this morning. The room was itself all glass and light. It hung in mid-air. Neither inside nor out, it opened straight into the branches of a coral tree, all scarlet claws.

She went to the kitchen bench at the window. The sink was piled with coffee mugs and more dishes. She felt free to deal with those, and was still at the sink, watching a pair of rainbow lorikeets on the deck beyond, all his dinner plates gleaming in the rack, when he stepped up behind her in a pair of sagging jockey shorts, still half asleep, rubbing his skull. He kissed her in a light, familiar way. Barely noticing the cleared sink – that was a *good* sign – he ran a glass of water and drank it off, his Adam's apple bobbing. Then kissed her again, grinned and went out on to the deck.

The lorikeets flew off, but belonged here, and soon ventured back.

OVER the weeks, as she came to spend more time there, she began to impose her own sort of order on the place. He did not object. He sat about reading the papers while she worked around him.

The drawers of the desk where he sometimes sat in the evening, wearing reading glasses while he did the accounts, were stuffed with papers – letters, cuttings, prospectuses. There were more papers pushed into cardboard boxes, in cupboards, stacked in corners, piled under beds.

'Do you want to keep any of this?' she would enquire from time to time, holding up a fistful of mail.

He barely looked. 'No. Whatever it is. Just chuck it.'

'You sure?'

'Why? What is it?'

'Letters.'

'Sure. Chuck 'em out.'

'What about these?'

'What are they?'

'Invoices. 1984.'

'No. Just pile 'em up, I'll make a bonfire. Tomorrow maybe.'

★   ★   ★

SHE had a strong need for fantasy, she liked to make things interesting. In their early days together, she took to leaving little love notes for him. Once under the tea caddy, where he would come across it when he went out in the morning, just after six, to make their tea. On other occasions, beside his shaving gear in the bathroom, in one of the pockets of his windcheater, in his work shorts. If he read them he did not mention the fact. It was ages before he told her, in a quarrel, how much these love notes embarrassed him. She flushed scarlet, did not make that mistake again.

He had no sense of fantasy himself. He wasn't insensitive – she was often touched by his thoughtfulness and by the small things he noticed – but he was very straight-up-and-down, no frills. Once, when his film was showing, she asked if they could go and see it. 'What for?' he asked, genuinely surprised. 'It's crap. Anyway, I'd rather forget all that. It wasn't a good time, that. Not for me it wasn't.'

'Because you were unhappy?' she said. 'You told me that, remember?'

But he shut off then, and the matter dropped.

HE told her nothing about his past. Nothing significant. And if she asked, he shied away.

'I don't want to talk about it,' was all he'd say. 'I try to forget about what's gone and done with. That's where we're different. You go on and on about it.'

No I don't, she wanted to argue. You're the one who's hung up on the past. That's why you won't talk about it. What I'm interested in is the present. But all of it. All the little incidental happenings that got you here, that got *us* here, made us the way we are. Seeing that she was still not satisfied, he drew her to him, almost violently – offering her that, his hard presence – and sighed, she did not know for what.

HE had no decent clothes that she could discover. Shirts, shorts, jeans – workclothes, not much else. A single tie that he struggled into when he had an engagement that was 'official'. She tried to rectify this. But when he saw the pile of new things on the bed he looked uncomfortable. He took up a blue poplin shirt, fingered it, frowned, put it down.

'I wish you wouldn't,' he said. 'Buy me things. Shirts and that.' He was trying not to seem ungracious, she saw, but was not happy. 'I don't need shirts.'

'But you do,' she protested. 'Look at the one you've got on.'

He glanced down. 'What's wrong with it?'

'It's in rags.'

'Does me,' he said, looking put out.

'So. Will you wear these things or what?'

'I'll wear them,' he said. 'They're bought now. But I don't want you to do it, that's all. I don't *need* things.'

He refused to meet her eye. Something more was being said, she thought. I don't deserve them – was that what he meant? In a sudden rush of feeling for something in him that touched her but which she could not quite catch, she clasped him to her. He relaxed, responded.

'No more shirts, then,' she promised.

'I just don't want you to waste your money,' he said childishly. 'I've got loads of stuff already.'

'I know,' she said. 'You should send the lot of it to the Salvos. Then you'd have nothing at all. You'd be naked, and wouldn't be able to go out, and I'd have you all to myself.' She had, by now, moved in.

'Is that what you want?' he asked, picking up on her light-ness, allowing her, without resistance for once, to undo the buttons on the offending shirt.

'You know I do,' she told him.

'Well then,' he said.

'Well then what?'

'Well, you've *got* me,' he said, 'haven't you?'

HE had a ukulele. Occasionally he took it down from the top shelf of the wardrobe and, sitting with a bare foot laid over his thigh, played – not happily she thought – the same plain little tune.

She got to recognise the mood in which he would need to seek out this instrument that seemed so absurdly small in his hands and for which he had no talent, and kept her distance. The darkness in him frightened her. It seemed so far from anything she knew of his other nature.

SOME things she discovered only by accident.

'Who's Bobby Kohler?' she asked once, having several times now come across the name on letters.

'Oh, that's me,' he said. '*Was* me.'

'What do you mean?'

'It's my name. My real name. Mitchell Maze is just the name I work under.'

'You mean you changed it?'

'Not really. Some people still call me Bobby.'

'Who does?'

'My mother. A few others.'

'Is it German?'

'Was once, I suppose. Away back. Grandparents.'

She was astonished, wanted to ask more, but could see that the subject was now done with. She might ask but he would not answer.

THERE were times when he did tell her things. Casually, almost dismissively, off the top of his head. He told her how badly, at sixteen, he had wanted to be a long-distance runner, and shine. How for a whole year he had got up in the dark, before his paper run, and gone out in the growing light to train on the oval at their local showground at Castle Hill. He laughed, inviting her to smile at some picture he could see of his younger self, lean, intense, driven, straining painfully day after day towards a goal he would never reach. She was touched by this. But he was not looking for pity. It was the folly of the thing he was intent on. It appealed to a spirit of savage irony in him that she could not share.

There were no evocative details. Just the bare, bitter facts. He could see the rest too clearly in his mind's eye to reproduce it for hers. She had to do that out of her own experience: Albury. The early-morning frost on the grass. Magpies carolling around a couple of milk cans in the long grass by the road. But she needed more, to fix in a clarifying image the tenderness she felt for him, the sixteen-year-old Bobby Kohler, barefooted, in sweater and shorts, already five inches taller than the Skip Daley she had known, driving himself hard through those solitary circuits of the oval as the sunlight came and the world turned golden around him.

One day she drove out in her lunch hour to see the place. Sat in her car in the heat and dazzle. Walked to the oval fence and took in the smell of dryness. There was less, in fact, than she imagined.

But a week later she went back. His mother lived there. She found the address, and after driving round the suburb for a bit, sat in her car under a paperbark on the other side of the street. Seeing no one in the little front yard, she got out, crossed, climbed the two front steps to the veranda, and knocked.

There was no reply.

She walked to the end of the veranda, which was unpainted, its timber rotting, and peered round the side. No sign of anyone.

Round the back, there was a water tank, painted the usual red, and some cages that might once have held rabbits. She peeped in through the window on a clean little kitchen with a religious calendar – was he a Catholic? he'd never told her that – and into two bedrooms on either side of a hall, one of which, at one time, must have been his.

He lived here, she told herself. For nearly twenty years. Something must be left of him.

She went down into the yard and turned the bronze key of the tap, lifting to her mouth a cupped handful of the cooling water. She felt like a ghost returning to a world that was not her own, nostalgic for what she had never known; for what might strike her senses strongly enough – the taste of tank water, the peppery smell of geraniums – to bring back some immediate physical memory of the flesh. But that was crazy. What was she doing? She had *him*, didn't she?

That night, touching the slight furriness, in the dark, of his earlobe, smelling the raw presence of him, she gave a sob and he paused in his slow lovemaking.

'What is it?' he said. 'What's the matter?'

She shook her head, felt a kind of shame – what could she tell him? That she'd been nosing round a backyard in Castle Hill looking for some ghost of him? He'd think she was mad.

'Tell me,' he said.

His face was in her hair. There was a kind of desperation in him.

But this time she was the one who would not tell.

HE was easy to get on with and he was not. They did most things together; people thought of them as a couple, they were happy. He came and went without explanation, and she learned quickly enough that she either accepted him on these terms or she could not have him at all. Without quite trying to, he attracted people, and when 'situations' developed was too lazy, or too easy-going, to extract himself. She learned not to ask where he had been or what he was up to. That wasn't what made things difficult between them.

She liked to have things out. He wouldn't allow it. When she raged he looked embarrassed. He told her she was over-dramatic, though the truth was that he liked her best when she was in a passion, it was the very quality in her that had first attracted him. What he didn't like was scenes. If she tried to make a scene, as he called it, he walked out.

'It's no use us shouting at one another,' he'd tell her, though in fact he never shouted. 'We'll talk about it later.' Which meant they wouldn't talk at all.

'But I *need* to shout,' she shouted after him.

Later, coming back, he would give a quick sideways glance to see if she had 'calmed down'.

She hadn't usually. She'd have made up her mind, after a bout of tears, to end things.

'What about a cuppa?' he'd suggest.

'What you won't accept—' she'd begin.

'Don't,' he'd tell her. 'I've forgotten all about it.' As if the hurt had been his. Then, 'I'm sorry. I don't want you to be unhappy.'

'I'm not,' she'd say. 'Just – exasperated.'

'Oh, well,' he'd say. 'That's all right then.'

What tormented her was the certainty she felt of his nursing some secret – a lost love perhaps, an old grief – that he could not share. Which was there in the distance he moved into; there in the room, in the bed beside her; and might, she thought, have the shape on occasion of that ukulele tune, and which she came to feel as a second presence between them.

It was this distance in him that others were drawn to. She saw that clearly now. A horizon in him that you believed you alone could reach. You couldn't. Maybe no one could. After a time it put most people off; they cut their losses and let him go. But that was not her way. If she let him go, it would destroy her. She knew that because she knew herself.

There was a gleam in him that on occasion shone right through his skin, the white skin of his breast below the burn-line his singlet left. She could not bear it. She battered at him.

'Hey, *hey*,' he'd say, holding her off.

He had no idea what people were after. What she was after. What she saw in him.

FOR all the dire predictions among the clan, the doubts and amused speculations, they lasted; two people who, to the puzzlement of others, remained passionately absorbed in one another. Then one day she got a call at work. He had had a fall and was concussed again. Then in a coma, on a life-support system, and for four days and nights she was constantly at his side.

For part of that time she sat in a low chair and tuned her ear to a distant tinkling, as a breeze reached her, from far off over the edge of the world, and rolled a spent light bulb this way and that on a glass tabletop. She watched, fascinated. Hour after hour, in shaded sunlight and then in the blue of a hospital night lamp, the fragile sphere rolled, and she heard, in the depths of his skull, a clink of icebergs, and found herself sitting, half frozen, in a numbed landscape with not even a memory now of smell or taste or of any sense at all; only what she caught of that small sound, of something broken in a hermetic globe. To reach it, she told herself, I will have to smash the glass. And what then? Will the sound swell and fill me or will it stop altogether?

Meanwhile she listened. It demanded all her attention. It was a matter of life and death. When she could no longer hear it—

At other times she walked. Taking deep breaths of the hot air that swirled around her, she walked, howling, through the streets. Barefoot. And the breaths she took were to feed her howling. Each outpouring of sound emptied her lungs so completely that she feared she might simply rise up and float. But the weight of her bones, of the flesh that covered them, of the waste in her bowels, and her tears, kept her anchored – as did the invisible threads that tied her body to his, immobile under the crisp white sheet, its head swathed in bandages, and the wires connecting him to his other watcher, the dial-faced machine. It was his name she was howling. Mitch, she called. Sometimes Skip. At other times, since he did not respond to either of these, that other, earlier name he had gone by. Bobby, Bobby Kohler. She saw him, from where she was standing under the drooping leaves of a eucalypt at the edge of a track, running round the far side of an oval, but he was too deeply intent on his body, on his breathing, on the swing of his arms, the pumping of his thighs, to hear her.

Bobby, she called. Skip, she called. Mitch. He did not respond. And she wondered if there was another name he might respond to that she had never heard. She tried to guess what it might be, certain now that if she found it, and called, he would wake. She found herself once leaning over him with her hands on his shoulders, prepared – was she mad? – to *shake* it out of him.

And once, in a moment of full wakefulness, she began to sing, very softly, in a high far voice, the tune he played on the ukulele. She had no words for it. Watching him, she thought he stirred. The slightest movement of his fingers. A creasing of the brow. Had she imagined it?

On another occasion, on the third or fourth day, she woke to find she had finally emerged from herself, and wondered – in the other order of time she now moved in – how many years had passed. She was older, heavier, her hair was grey, and this older, greyer self was seated across from her wearing the same intent, puzzled look that she too must be wearing. Then the figure smiled.

No, she thought, if that is me, I've become another woman altogether. Is that what time does to us?

It was the night they came and turned off the machine. His next of kin, his mother, had given permission.

TWO days later, red-eyed from sleeplessness and bouts of uncontrollable weeping, she drove to Castle Hill for the funeral.

His mother had rung. She reminded Jo in a kindly voice that they had spoken before. Yes, Jo thought, like this. On the phone, briefly. When she had called once or twice at an odd hour and asked him to come urgently, she needed him, and at holiday times when he went dutifully and visited, and on his birthday. 'Yes,' Jo said. 'In June.' No, his mother told her, at the hospital. Jo was surprised. She had no memory of this. But when they met she recognised the woman. They *had* spoken. Across his hospital bed, though she still had no memory of what had passed between them. She felt ashamed. Grief, she felt, had made her wild; she still looked wild. Fearful now of appearing to lay claim to the occasion, she drew back and tried to stay calm.

The woman, Mitch's mother, was very calm, as if she had behind her a lifetime's practice of preserving herself against an excess of grief. But she was not ungiving.

'I know how fond Bobby was of you,' she told Jo softly. 'You must come and see me. Not today. Ring me later in the week. I can't have anyone at the house today. You'll understand why.'

Jo thought she understood but must have looked puzzled.

'Josh,' she said. 'I've got Josh home.' And Jo realised that the man standing so oddly close, but turned slightly away from them, was actually with the woman.

'I can't have him for more than a day or so at a time,' the woman was saying. 'He doesn't mean to be a trouble, and he'd never do me any harm, but he's so strong – I can't handle him. He's like a five-year-old. But a forty-year-old man has a lot of strength in his lungs.' She said this almost with humour. She reached out and squeezed the man's hand. He turned, and then Jo saw.

Large-framed and heavy-looking – hulking was the word that came to her – everything that in Mitch had been well-knit and easy was, in him, merely loose. His hands hung without occupation at the end of his arms, the features in the long large face seemed unfocused, unintegrated. Only with Mitch in mind could you catch, in the full mouth, the heavy jaw and brow, a possibility that had somehow failed to emerge, or been maimed or blunted. The sense she had of sliding likeness and unlike-ness was alarming. She gave a cry.

'Oh,' the woman said. 'I thought you knew. I thought he'd told you.'

Jo recovered, shook her head, and just at that moment the clergyman came forward, nodded to Mitch's mother, and they moved away to the open grave.

They were a small crowd. Most of them she knew. They were the members of the clan. The others, she guessed from their more formal clothes, must be relatives or family friends.

The service was grim. She steeled herself to stay calm. She had no wish to attract notice, to be singled out because she and Mitch had been – had been what? What had they been? She wanted to stand and be shrouded in her grief. To remain hidden. To have her grief, and him, all to herself as she had had him all to herself at least sometimes, many times, when he was alive.

But she was haunted now by the large presence of this other, this brother who stood at the edge of the grave beside his mother, quiet enough, she saw, but oddly unaware of what was going on about him.

He had moments of attention, a kind of vacant attention, then fell into longer periods of giant arrest. Then his eye would be engaged.

By the black fringe on the shawl of the small woman to his left, which he reached out for and fingered, frowning, then lifted to his face and sniffed.

By a wattlebird that was animating the branches of a low-growing grevillea so that it seemed suddenly to have developed a life of its own and began twitching and shaking out its blooms. Then by the cuff of his shirt, which he regarded quizzically, his mouth pouting, then drawn to one side, as if by something there that disappointed or displeased him.

All these small diversions that took his attention took hers as well. At such a moment! She was shocked.

Then, quite suddenly, he raised his head. Some new thing

had struck him. What? Nothing surely that had been said or was being done here. Some thought of his own. A snatch of music it might be, a tune that opened a view in him that was like sunlight flooding a familiar landscape. His face was irradiated by a foolish but utterly beatific smile, and she saw how easy it might be – she thought of his mother, even more poignantly of Mitch – to love this large unlovely child.

The little ukulele tune came into her head, and with it a vision of Mitch, lost to her in his own world of impenetrable grief. Sitting in his underpants on the floor, one big foot propped on his thigh. Hunched over the strings and plucking from them, over and over, the same spare notes, the same bare little tune. And she understood with a pang how the existence of this spoiled other must have seemed like a living reproach to his own too easy attractiveness. It was that – the injustice of it, so cruel, so close – that all those nicks and scars and broken bones and concussions, and all that reckless exposure to a world of accident, had been meant to annul. She felt the ground shifting under her feet. How little she had grasped or known. What a different story she would have to tease out now and tell herself of their time together.

The service was approaching its end. The coffin, suspended on ropes, tilted over the hole with its raw edges and siftings of loose soil. It began, lopsidedly, to descend. Her eyes flooded. She closed them tight. Felt herself choke.

At that moment there was a cry, an incommensurate roar that made all heads turn and stopped the clergyman in full spate.

Some animal understanding – caught from the general emotion around him and become brute fact – had brought home to Josh what it was they were doing here. He began to howl, and the sound was so terrible, so piteous, that all Jo could think of was an animal at the most uncomprehending extreme of physical agony. People looked naked, stricken. There was a scrambling over broken lumps of earth round the edge of the grave. The big man, even in the arms of his mother, was uncontrollable. He struck out, face congested, the mouth and nose streaming, like an ox, Jo thought, like an ox under the hammer. And this, she thought, is the real face of grief, the one we do not show. Her heart was thick in her breast. This is what sorrow is that knows no explanation or answer. That looks down into the abyss and sees only the unanswering depths.

SHE recalled nothing of the drive back, through raw unfinished suburbs, past traffic lights where she must dutifully have swung into the proper lane and stopped, her mind in abeyance, the motor idling. When she got home, to the house afloat on its stilts among the sparse leaves of the coral trees, above the cove with its littered beach, she was drained of resistance. She sat in the high open space the house made, feeling it breathe like a living thing, surrendering herself to the regular long expansions of its breath.

Against the grain of her own need for what was enclosed and safe, she had learned to live with it. What now? Could she bear, alone, now that something final had occurred, to live day after day with what was provisional, which she had put up with till now because, with a little effort of adjustment, she too, she found, could live in the open present – so long as it *was* open.

Abruptly she rose, stood looking down for a moment at some bits of snipped wire, where he had been tinkering with something electrical, that for a whole week had lain scattered on the coffee table, then went out to the sink, and as on that first morning washed up what was there to be washed. The solitary cup and saucer from her early-morning tea.

For a moment afterwards she stood contemplating the perfection of clean plates drying in the rack, cups turned downward to drain, their saucers laid obliquely atop. She was at the beginning again. Or so she felt. Now what?

There was a sock on the floor. Out of habit she retrieved it, then stood, surveying the room, the house, as you could because it was so open and exposed.

Light and air came pouring in from all directions. She felt again, as on that first occasion, the urge to move in and begin setting things to rights, and again for the moment held back, restrained herself.

She looked down, observed the sock in her hand, and had a vision, suddenly, of the place as it might be a month from now when her sense of making things right would already, day after day, imperceptibly, have been at work on getting rid of the magazines and newspapers, shifting this or that piece of furniture into a more desirable arrangement, making the small adjustments that would erase all sign of him, of Mitch, from what had been so much of his making – from her life. Abruptly she threw the sock from her and stood there, shivering, hugging herself, in the middle of the room. Then, abruptly, sat where she had been sitting before. In the midst of it.

So what did she mean to do? Change nothing? Leave everything just as it was? The out-of-date magazines, that dead match beside the leg of the coffee table, the bits of wire, the sock? To gather fluff over the weeks and months, a dusty tribute that she would sit in the midst of for the next twenty years?

She sat a little longer, the room darkening around her, filling slowly with the darkness out there that lay over the waters of the cove, rose up from the floaty leaves of the coral trees and the shadowy places at their roots, from around the hairy stems of tree ferns and out of the unopened buds of morning glory. Then, with a deliberate effort, she got down on her knees and reached in to pick up the match from beside the leg of the coffee table. Shocked that it weighed so little. So little that she might not recall, later, the effort it had cost her, this first move towards taking up again, bit by bit, the weight of her life.

Then, with the flat of her hand, she brushed the strands of wire into a heap, gathered them up, and went, forcing herself, to retrieve the sock, then found the other. Rolled them into a ball and raised it to her lips. Squeezing her eyes shut, filling her nostrils with their smell.

Then there were his shirts, his shorts, his jeans – they would go to the Salvos – and the new things she had bought, which lay untouched in the drawers of his lowboy, the shirts in their plastic wrappers, the underpants, the socks still sewn or clipped together. Maybe Josh. She had a vision of herself arriving with these things on his mother's doorstep. An opening. The big man's pleasure as he stroked the front of his new poplin shirt, the sheen of its pure celestial blue.

She sat again, the small horde of the rolled socks in her lap, the spent match and the strands of wire in a tidy heap. A beginning. And let the warm summer dark flow in around her.

War Baby

War Baby

—

CHARLIE Dowd spent the last weeks before he was inducted and went to Vietnam riding round town on a CZ two-stroke, showing himself off to people and saying goodbye.

It was August and cold: high dry skies, the westerlies blowing. He wore a navy blue air force greatcoat of his father's, who had been a Spitfire pilot in the war. It was belted and double-breasted with wide lapels, and when you turned the collar up your ears were covered. The skirts were so long that what Charlie saw in the long wardrobe mirror in his room (he'd been reading *War and Peace*) was a French cavalry officer in the Napoleonic Wars in flight from Cossacks. Anticipating his first day in camp he had been down to Sam Harker and had his hair cut short on top and shaved at the sides. When he stood and contemplated himself in the mirror, he really looked the part.

He had a routine. He got up late, ate the breakfast his aunt made for him, which doubled as lunch, then sat for a couple of hours in warm winter sunlight in the window of the pub. Always in the same place, looking out across the veranda rails to the median strip of the town's one main street, with a schooner of beer at his elbow on the chocolate-brown sill, and beside it, as a way of making himself at home, his pen, his wallet, the paperback he was reading, and the makings of the roll-your-owns he liked to smoke – papers, Drum tobacco in a plastic wrap, and an oblong tin not much bigger than a matchbox that contained the simple mechanism for turning them out. He took trouble over this, giving the roller a practised spin between fore-finger and thumb, and when he ran his tongue along the edge of the paper, putting just enough spit into it for the spill to be dry but perfectly, almost professionally, sealed. He smoked a little, read a little, wrote in his notebook.

He was keeping notes. Not a diary exactly, just random thoughts. As they came to him in the drowsy sunlight in the slow early session after midday, and as they took off, the moment he began to set them down, and led him into all sorts of unpre-dictable and shadowy places where he was pleased to roam. Bemused speculations.

If he tired of writing, and had no book at hand, he would read the contents of his wallet: his library card and driver's licence, several torn-off corners of a notepad or newspaper with names and phone numbers on them that he could barely deci-pher, ads from magazines that he must have thought, when he folded them small and tucked them away in one of his wallet's many pockets, might one day come in useful. With a cigarette at his lips, the sun on his hands, a crease between his brows, he would give these exhibits his solemn attention, as if this time he might catch, in the evidence they offered of unful-filled needs and momentary promises, some reflection of himself that till now had subtly eluded him.

Occasionally when he looked up he would find upon him the pink-rimmed, rheumy eyes of one of the old-timers, pensioners and retired tradesmen or storekeepers, who were the regulars of this hour: thin-faced, silent fellows with elongated ears and noses who had been turned out of the house by their daughters or daughters-in-law, and towards two or two thirty in the afternoon dropped in, very formally attired in coat and hat, for a beer and whatever talk might be going. In the early days one or two of them had enquired from a distance what he was writing. They seemed ready to start a conversation. Charlie put his pen down and let them go on.

It wasn't really a conversation. What they wanted was to tell him their story – well, not him exactly, anyone would have done.

He listened. That they had a story, and took it for granted they did, confirmed him in the assumption that he too had one. But he was glad when they drifted off at last and went back to their beer, and after a time they ceased to be curious about him. He had become one of them.

They were becalmed at the end of their lives, that's what he saw, and he was becalmed in the middle of his, but nearer the beginning. Waiting out these last days as if they were an enforced holiday, which was why his aunt let him sleep till past midday and did not complain, as she would have done earlier, when the breakfast she made him was also his lunch.

Afternoons had always been a trouble to him, going right back to when he was little and had to take a nap each day beside his mother on a high double bed in their cool spare room. He would play afterwards on the lino and watch his mother laugh on the phone or do her nails on the back veranda, or with her skirt hoiked up and her bare feet propped on the rail, sit tanning herself while the radio played, 'Music, music, music', and willie wagtails switched about on the grass.

Time passed slowly after midday, before tea. That's what he had found. The air grew thicker. There was a weight that dragged. It had something to do with the clouds, loaded at times with thunder, that at that hour gathered and rolled in over the Range. Summer or winter, it made no difference: trees, houses, grass, sky – the whole world seemed to be waiting only for the coming on of dark.

Lately, that quality he had felt of a whole world hanging on what was to come, nightfall, had become the keynote of his own existence. He had waited. First for his birthday to come around, then for his name to come up. He was waiting now for the last days to pass before his induction. All that time had been a mixture in him of restless impatience for each day to dawn and pass, and a kind of inertia which, if he had not deliberately taken a hand, would have made a sleepwalker of him, just when he needed to be most fully awake.

The truth was that Vietnam, and his going, was the certainty he had needed to give his life direction; to close off an open and indeterminate future where he might have gone on stumbling about in a maze that had no end. He was going. He would see action – the phrase brought a prickle of excitement to his skin that scared and at the same time gravely enlivened him. Meanwhile, though others need not see it in this light, he had organised a small carnival for himself.

Around four in the afternoon, with the sun gone from the sill where his empty beer glass sat – he never had more than two – he set out on his rounds.

HIS arrival on their doorstep puzzled some people. They had not seen him in a while; in some cases, a long while. They did not immediately recognise the crop-headed boy in uniform greatcoat who loomed in the door frame as if he had come to deliver something official, and stood smiling and stamping on the doormat in the assurance of being invited in. They had difficulty remembering who he was.

They did remember at last – and would have known the name anyway, because of his grandfather – but could not guess why on earth he had called, and why, when he settled, his long legs extended, the skirts of the greatcoat open like dark wings, he looked from one to another of them with so much wide-eyed alertness – in expectation of what, they wondered.

More than puzzled, some of them were embarrassed. But Charlie wasn't. He knew very well what he was after. He wanted to know, before he went away, what impression his having lived here for a whole twenty years had made on people. Not much, he guessed. But that was just the point. They would remember his going. They would remember that he had come to say goodbye.

One or two of them were old friends of the family who had known him when he was little and whom his aunt had mentioned. They were surprised to see him after so long but soon made him feel at home.

In other cases they were fellows a little older than himself who, two or three years back, had been on the school swimming team with him but could not, when he turned up now, come up with his name.

'Who did you say he was?' he heard a girl whisper out in the kitchen while he sat alone in the front room with a round-eyed baby and the TV. 'Have I met him? Was he at the wedding?'

In households where he had, for a time, been the schoolfriend of a son or daughter now lost to the city, it was recalled that he had always been odd – old-fashioned they had called it then; a consequence of his having no one to bring him up but his grandfather and an old-maid aunt.

Well, he was even odder now. The way he had of just sitting and looking. With his ears sticking out above the lapels of his greatcoat. And the greatcoat itself. What was that? What was that about?

For all his affability, some older men looked him over and were put off. They had been to a war themselves. They hadn't gone around making a song and dance of it, parading about in what looked like fancy dress. He was young of course, but no younger than they had been. Young people these days made too much of themselves. That came from the sort of pop music they listened to, and from the TV. Life for them was all play-acting, dressing up. Sideburns, old double-breasted suits and striped collarless shirts they'd raked up from a deceased uncle's lowboy or picked up cheap at the St Vincent de Paul's. Fleecy-lined bomber jackets, and if the leather was cracked and worn so much the better. Camouflage battledress and other fads. Sergeant Pepper Band uniforms!

In a way that would never have occurred to them at that age, this feller was making a show of himself, and enjoying it too. What gave him the right to prance around drawing attention to himself?

All this would have surprised Charlie.

He *was* enjoying himself, and it was true, he did want to be noticed. But play-acting? He was on his way to Vietnam. Wasn't that real enough? There had been a ballot, a lottery. The world had cast him one of its backhanded prizes, and since he had no notion himself of what his life was to be, he had accepted it. Not passively, but without complaint. He'd let a roll of the barrel decide things. Given himself over to hazard, to chance. In a spirit, as he thought, of existential stoicism.

The war itself, when he got to it, would present hazards of a different sort. He had seen something of that. Body bags, statistics, fellows who brought back, in one way or another, a good deal less of themselves than they had taken away. He had no illusions. But chance in that case was tempered with something else. Something you yourself brought to the bar.

Guts. A feeling for where to put your foot down and where not. The good-luck charm of life itself – the one you were intended for. He believed, though none of this, of course, had yet been tested, that he was the possessor of all three.

Beyond that you could present yourself as you wanted to be seen and then try to live up to it. With a rough outline in your head of a story, you could do everything in your power to act it out; to incorporate the accidents that hit you into its form, as he had incorporated the lottery and his conscription. Later parts of it, in his case, included Paris, which he definitely saw himself visiting one day, a language or two he meant to pick up, a wife of course – he had a whole list of things he'd barely started on. He had already read *War and Peace*, but he had not, as yet, fired a gun or been up in a plane. He had never tasted Tokay, or champagne or oysters, or slept with a girl or been further from home – this small town tucked into a hollow behind the Range – than Brisbane once on a rugby trip while he was at school: he had been sick, both ways, on the coach. But he was young, and believed, even with Vietnam up ahead, that he had time.

He had discovered in the eyes of others, beginning with his grandfather, an affectionate wish that all things should go well with him. It was partly out of a desire to extend to as many people as possible the privilege of exercising their large goodwill towards him that he appeared on so many doorsteps of what was still, for the time being, his own little world.

ONE of the places he liked to go was a household where he *was* known; the family of his best friend Brian Whelan, who at the end of the previous year had decided on university and was away now in Brisbane.

The Whelans had known him since he was ten years old. The difference, when he went there now, was that Brian was gone and his sister Josie, who was three years older and had been away, was back. It was Josie who had opened the door to him when, after a six-month absence, he turned up one weekday around five in the afternoon, a little light-headed from the two beers he had drunk and with his hair, and the hairlike filaments of the greatcoat, touched with tiny droplets of moisture, silvery and weblike from the drizzling rain he had driven through.

'Well, look what the cat dragged in,' Josie announced to the lighted room behind her as he stood stamping on the threshold.

It was three years or more since he had last seen her. She had changed. She was thinner with longer hair. But her voice had not changed. It still had its edge of dismissive irony.

She had never really liked him, that's what he felt. His closeness to Brian had shut her out. He had never intended that and was sorry for it. He wished now that he had known her better and that she was more pleased to see him.

'Come in, love,' Mrs Whelan called.

In a little while there were mugs of tea and his favourite Tim Tams. The greatcoat was draped over the back of a chair.

'I'm going to Vietnam,' he announced.

'Oh,' Mrs Whelan said, and Josie, who was standing with her back against the sink, made a huffing sound.

'Brian's older than you,' Mrs Whelan said after a bit. 'Isn't your birthday in March, love?'

'May,' he told her.

'Yes,' she said, 'Brian's is February the ninth.'

What she meant was that Brian's birthdate had put him in a previous ballot, he was safe. She held out the plate of Tim Tams, as if offering him a small consolation, and when Charlie saw it he wanted to laugh. He had, he felt, grasped so clearly what was in her mind.

Lately he had found himself looking at the world – at people – as if he had developed another sense, beyond the usual five, for what was happening around him, for what was being said. Listening, really listening, was a kind of looking. For the way a glance passed from one person to another, or a soft mouth was compressed into a hard line, as Josie's was now, or cheeks were momentarily sucked in. As often as not that was where the real conversation was being conducted.

The younger boys of the family, Luke and Jack, came crashing into the room. They were eleven and fifteen. Barefooted, in out-at-elbow woollies, they had been tempted in by his arrival – and the promise of Tim Tams – from practising hoops at the basketball ring where he and Brian had spent long afternoons just a year ago.

'I've seen you riding,' Luke told him. His eyes went to the greatcoat.

Jack, the older boy, laughed, as if this intended more than it said.

'CZ,' Luke said admiringly.

The greatcoat and the bike, that's what they saw.

What Josie saw was a warmonger.

'I suppose you're proud of yourself,' she accused, 'going off to blow a lot of women and children to pieces who've never done you any harm.'

He was surprised by her vehemence, but when he looked he saw that her eyes were bright with something different.

'Leave Charlie alone now,' her mother told her. 'Have another Tim Tam, love.'

'Can I?' Luke asked.

'He's had two already,' the older boy protested.

'Don't be a tittle-tat,' his mother told him.

'Well, he has!'

'She's a real Tartar, eh?'

This, proudly, came from the father, who had just stepped in from work and overheard the scene. 'Good to see you, son.'

He shook Charlie's hand, and they stood a moment in what might have been manly solidarity while Josie scowled.

'He's going to Vietnam,' Luke told his father.

'Hmmm,' Mr Whelan said.

He gave Charlie another look and accepted the mug Josie was passing him.

'Well,' he said gravely, 'I suppose someone's got to go. Good on you, son.'

'No they don't,' Josie insisted.

'Josie's been on demos' – this was Luke again – 'in Sydney.'

'That's enough, Luke,' his mother told the boy.

But Josie was not so easily silenced. She gave them her opinion of various politicians, local and overseas, and in no uncertain terms stated her convictions about wars in general, men, and this war in particular.

'I told you she was a Tartar,' her father said with a laugh, and Charlie wondered what side he was on. 'Hope you've got your crash helmet handy.'

Charlie was amused. He enjoyed being so immediately the centre of attention here, and the little sensual kick he got from her high colour and excitement. He'd never looked at Josie in this light. She had always been simply 'Brian's sister'. But there was something as well that confused him. All this talk of politics, all these fierce convictions.

He had no convictions himself and did not consider what he was about to do as involving him in 'politics'. There was nothing in the notebook about that. His going or not going concerned only himself. It had to do with where he stood with the world and what it had put in his way, the claims *that* made on him. With how he saw himself and wanted others to see him. With what he could live with. Maybe – though he believed this would not be demanded of him – with what sort of death he might make.

Josie's insistence that what really mattered was some larger question of right or wrong made nothing of all that. And made nothing too – this is what affronted him – of his presence here, a little heated as he was by all the sensations of the moment and the turmoil of these last weeks. As if his life, *his* life, the one he felt so strongly pulsing through him, was of no account.

'You've got no imagination,' Josie accused.

'And you have, I suppose,' he shot back. Surprising himself.

'That's it, son,' Mr Whelan laughed. 'You speak up for yourself.'

'Enough of a one,' Josie told him mildly.

Charlie tried not to show how angry he felt. The implication was that his rude good health, his youth, his high spirits, put some things that she saw with blinding clarity beyond his comprehension. That something boyish and crudely warlike in him, male bravado, the rush of hormonal mayhem, made him insensitive to the price that others would have to pay – women and the old, and little helpless terrified kids – so that his brand of swagger and mindlessness could have its way. He felt acutely, under her gaze, the bunched muscles of his shoulders in the old school sweater and eased them a little.

But the fact was, he did see these things, and no less clearly perhaps than she did. He *knew* about blood. His own, just at the moment, was very much present to him, in his forearms and wrists, in the veins of his neck. He meant to keep it there. But also, if he could, to preserve his honour as well. That was *his* argument.

It involved words it would have embarrassed him to use. Things that could be thought, and warmly felt, but not stated. There was no way he could lay claim – or not openly – to so much for himself. But he was sorry just the same that she had not seen it.

There were ways in which she too was insensitive – and she didn't see that either.

Still, all this intrigued him. He kept coming back.

'A glutton for punishment, eh, son?' was how Mr Whelan put it.

AT home in his grandfather's house they never argued about politics. They never argued about anything. If his grandfather and his aunt had convictions he had never heard them. His aunt's view was that some things, most things as it turned out, were better left unsaid, and Charlie had learned to see the point of this, having learned early that a good deal that went unsaid was too cruel, or too painful, for speech. The unspoken, in his grandfather's house, had mostly to do with his father.

Charlie had few memories of his father, and none of them substantial. The earliest was a character called Charlie that his mother and aunt spoke of in passionate whispers, and ceased to discuss the moment he appeared. He had assumed at first that they were speaking of him (he must have been three years old) and wondered what he had done that they should be so disturbed; his aunt so angry, his mother so weakly tearful. Only over time did it come to him that *this* Charlie, whose shadow fell so darkly over the house, was his father. Who had, it seemed, once more *failed* them − but mostly himself − and whom his aunt sometimes defended, and sometimes his mother, but never both at the same time and never in front of his grandfather.

Sometimes, when his grandfather laid a hand on his shoulder and asked sadly: 'So how's it going, Charlie? How are they treating you?' he understood that it was not really him that his grandfather was speaking to but that other, who once, before he failed them all, had also been young, and had not yet discovered, or not yet revealed, that failure was what he was inevitably heading for. His father seemed frighteningly present then in his own name and skin.

There was a photograph on the piano in the front room of a young man in RAAF uniform and cap, much the same age as Charlie was now and bearing a resemblance to him that Charlie found unsettling. He looked out of the frame with such a guileless sense of his own presence and future that Charlie, on those occasions when he was led to take a good hard look, felt − along with curiosity and a shy affection for this stranger who was so uniquely close to him − a pang of doubt about his own too easy optimism.

No hint of failure there, or of failings either. What clung to the image was the romance of a period when his father had been a hero fired with a belief in his own physical survival into a time to come. It was in this spirit, it seemed, that he had got hold of Charlie's mother; the suggestion being that she had been deceived.

But perhaps, Charlie thought, she had wanted to be. And wasn't his father also deceived? By a belief that the high spirits that had swept him up, and the high action he had been involved in, were an aspect of his own nature rather than of the times; were in *him* rather than in the air, and could be confidently extended. And that the old weakness in him had been burned away. By a boyish delight in immediate danger and the nerve with which, in mission after mission, he had met it and come through.

Charlie was inclined to identify with this youthful warrior, and had developed, from what he knew of his own doubts and confusions – his own anxiety about getting what he was, or might be, out into a world that was so undependable and chancy – an understanding, a sympathy even, for what might have gone wrong in the man, though he did not mean to repeat it.

Perhaps the dramatic excitements of that brief year of scrambles and dogfights and ditchings had exhausted what was in him. He had made demands on his spirit that he could meet only once, and could not match under other, more ordinary circumstances.

But then he had never seen, as his mother had – his aunt, too, perhaps – what weakness was *like* close up; the sly deceits and fierce self-justifications that were the daily accompaniment of it.

The clearest sense he had of his father's actual presence was of standing – he must have been six – at his father's grave.

Men in dark suits, their hats clasped to their chest, hair plastered to their skulls and sweating, stood on the far side of the grave and all around it, looking hard at him and frowning. The ladies at their side wore gloves and were also looking, but their eyes were hidden under wide-brimmed hats that they were allowed to keep on.

It was hot. The midsummer sky was a blanched yellow-white, and the gum trees at the edge of the cemetery shimmered as if they were not real trees at all, only their reflection in water.

He stood very still, trying not to shift his feet, but could not tell if he was standing the right way, and thought he must be doing it wrong, which was what made people over there look at him so hard, and frown.

He had frequently been encouraged by his aunt to be a good little soldier in the matter of grazed elbows and bloodied knees, and plasters that had to be ripped off, but no one had told him how it would be at his father's funeral and how he should stand.

His grandfather was close behind him. His hand, blotched, with lumpy veins, rested on his shoulder, and occasionally drew him in to the soft belly and the hot smell of his woollen suit.

His mother and his aunt were on the other side of him, his aunt crying. He had never thought of his aunt as a woman who cried.

His mother cried very often, and noisily. She was what his aunt called theatrical. When his father met her, in London, she had been on the stage. Being theatrical was something, later, when his mother was gone, that he would be severely warned against; as he was against being, like his father, weak – it was the double inheritance he must constantly fight against.

But at his father's funeral his mother did not cry, she simply stood, and he thought of her later as having already left, as he understood by then she must already have decided to do. So that what he recalled of that day was his aunt's tears, the weight of his grandfather's hand on his shoulder, and the dry, peppery smell of the bush, along with a ladies' smell of talcum powder and sweat.

The white gravestones all around pulsed with light and might have been preparing to rise straight up like rockets. Which was just what was required, he thought, to free him from the scrutiny of the strangers over there and the need to hold himself so strictly to attention. Then suddenly the trees on the skyline exploded. Dozens of snow-white, sulphur-crested cockatoos flocked skyward, the noise of their shrieking so fierce, so like the sound of souls in torment, that all the people turned their heads.

That was his father's funeral. His father had always been absent in one way. Now he was absent in another. And beginning then, at the edge of the open grave, so was his mother. She went home to her family in England. From where she rang regularly twice each year, on his birthday and at Christmas, long distance, tearfully. And sent presents in elaborate wrappings that his aunt resented and referred to, though never to him, as 'extravagant'.

He had heard often enough from his grandfather that every man had his justifications, though one did not have to believe that they were always good; and since every man clearly meant every woman too, he wondered what his mother's might be. For having left him – temporarily at first, then permanently – in the charge of his grandfather and aunt.

Had she already given him over so completely to them and what they had to offer that she felt her own claim was weak, and that by taking him with her she would deprive him of more than she could give – even in the matter of love? Was he unlovable? Did he remind her too much of his father? Was she simply — he felt the implication of this in his aunt's silence on the matter — *weak*?

The word hung in the air so often, though unspoken like so much else, because his grandfather, and even more his aunt, were so fond of the word 'strong'.

He felt the house was full of watchers. Not just his grandfather and aunt, but those presences, invisible but by no means to be underestimated, who were watching *them* — which was as far as his grandfather went in the matter of religion.

But all this meant was that the forces under whose watchful gaze they were living — who missed nothing, he came to feel, and were pitilessly demanding — had no names, no faces, and were difficult therefore to get a hold on, to approach and reason with. No doubt they too had their justifications, impossible to challenge.

He wondered sometimes, since his grandfather did not actually refer to them, how he had got so clearly into his head, and so early, that they were there. As palpably there as the furniture — big old-fashioned dining chairs with high backs, ample seats, solid legs, bedroom suites with mirrored wardrobes and dressing tables — that his grandfather had had made in Brisbane, and which, as newly-weds, his grandparents had brought up here after the First World War.

He reminded himself that his father too had grown up among these heavy presences. Perhaps it was the furniture, and the shadow it cast, that had alarmed his mother and driven her from the house.

These were the perplexities and childish conclusions of a lively seven-year-old. But a dozen years later he had got no further with them.

SOMETIMES, in the early afternoon, he rode out to the edge of town and spent an hour or two with Cliff Hodges, who had sold him the CZ and was prepared to take it back again when he left.

Cliff was twenty-four. An easy-going fellow and a big drinker on Friday and Saturday nights, he was popular with the girls. Married women mostly, if his own stories were to be believed. Charlie was never sure he did believe them, but it didn't matter. Cliff glowed so convincingly in the aura of them.

He was a mechanic. He worked out of a corrugated-iron shed on a lot where two giant pepper trees grew out of broken concrete. A dozen oil drums and some old car parts, now gone to rust, were piled against a fence that seemed to be held up only by the woody rose bush, all outbursts of yellow buds and creamy, extravagant blooms, that climbed in and out of its grainy slabs.

Charlie looked forward to the afternoons he spent out here; his back to the corrugated-iron wall of the shed, his long legs thrust out before him, while Cliff, sprawled out of sight, flat on his back under the car he was working on, put easy questions to which he gave his own wry answers, or launched into a live-wire account, all crude but colourful riffs and clownish avowals of contrition, of his latest night out with the boys. The desultory nature of these exchanges, the easy pace, which included a good many silences, none of them heavy as elsewhere with the unsaid, was tonic. Charlie laughed. He let go.

Very little that passed between them was personal. What they shared were the formal rituals of taking an engine apart and putting it together again, which Charlie, under Cliff's instruction, had quickly grasped and become expert in. The dexterity it involved, the easiness about getting your hands mucky, the masculine talk punctuated with *shit, fuck, come on you bitch, give*, which was the almost musical accompaniment to this, led naturally, while the fingers worked delicately with wires and screws, to discussion of that other area of male expertise where the parts were anatomical. Charlie was less expert here but once again looked to Cliff's instruction as a likely way ahead.

Later in the afternoon it was the Beach Boys or Cream or Hendrix that filled the air between them, when Cliff, at a point of exasperation with some bit of machinery that would not yield to him, took time out, and they sat side by side with a mug of hot coffee to warm their hands, and floated — mostly on drags of the good grass Cliff had access to.

What Charlie found so appealing in these afternoon hours was that they led nowhere and could have no consequence. Two years from now, when he got back, Cliff would be just the same, or he would be married with a kid and would be the same anyway. And *he* would have Vietnam behind him. Because he had chosen that, and all that it involved and would bring. To mark him; mark him off. To set the seal on a certain way of living that a man could choose, and which Cliff had *not* chosen and might never know. It was a difference between them that was already in operation, because in spirit he was already gone. It gave him, despite his being so much younger, and quite without experience in some matters, an advantage here that Cliff recognised and did not resent.

'Rather you than me, boy,' Cliff had said after a pause when Charlie first made his announcement.

The respect, a matter of taking him seriously, Charlie thought, had come about later. A kind of concern for him too, which in Cliff's case took a particular form.

'We better set you up with a girl, eh? Before you go and get your collateral blown off.' This was a reference, witty to an extent that surprised Charlie, to a Dylan song they were fond of.

So far it had gone no further than that, the offer. In the meantime they sat with their backs to the wall and took in the music along with the grass.

The nice thing, around Cliff, was that there was no need to hurry.

So he came to the last days. He had a strong sense, as he made his rounds, of other people stopping, in the ordinary flow of their lives, to make room for him. He had made that much at least of an impression. Perhaps it was simply that they knew it would soon end: that he would in a few days now be gone. They could afford to grant him room.

He had no illusions. The moment he was no longer here their lives would flow on again without him; not because they did not care but because that's the way it is, the way we are.

He felt he existed in a space which, the moment he stepped out of it, would close behind him, and he began practising; in mind stepping out, then looking back at the space he had filled for a little with his warmth and watching it cool and give up all sign of his presence.

This sort of thinking was new to him. That there might be in you a ghostly quality of your own absence even when you were most warmly there; when you were most conscious of your long, blunt-ended fingers flattened against a mug of scalding tea, your breath visibly blowing across the earthenware rim, your smile and your last words hanging in the silence. And their eyes on you, also smiling, and telling you how substantially present you were.

He would glance briefly towards the greatcoat tossed over the back of a chair, its thick serge bunched and shapeless. His father's greatcoat. Which he had commandeered for a bit. And where was his father?

He shrugged, and the cough he gave was half a chuckle.

It was an uncomfortable feeling only for a moment. The mug was warm against the soft flesh of his palm. The coffee or tea, when he lowered his head to hide his confusion, and sipped, was hot in his mouth.

There was a design of painted flowers on the tiles behind the sink in the Whelans' kitchen: detached yellow petals round a dob of red, with a green stem and two symmetrical green leaves – the kind of flower he remembered painting when he was first at school, the flower a five- or six-year-old paints. Not a real flower, one you've seen – they're too difficult, too complicated and raggedy. The stripped-down *idea* of a flower. The one from which all other flowers might have evolved.

The rightness of these flowers, each one planted in the centre of its tile and repeated all over the bit of wall, pleased him in a way he could not have explained, and centred him for a moment, but only for a moment, in a space of his own.

One afternoon, when he was leaving the Whelans, Josie followed him out to where his bike was parked under the overhanging canopy of a camphor laurel.

She dawdled, and he wondered, as he sat astride the CZ, at a hesitancy in her that was unusual and which, for all the little crease between her brows, softened her features and brought her close, in a way that created a soft feeling in him as well.

It was a time of day when everything was in suspense. The light high up in the sky just yielding to the first smokiness of dark. A hint of night-time coldness in the air. Birds restless in the grass and beginning to flock low now over the neighbouring roofs. He waited.

Josie too had an offer to make. What she had access to, if he wanted, was a line of safe houses. In Sydney. He could, even at this point, refuse to go, declare himself an objector – and people down there, good people, would pass him on from one house to another till the war was over.

He listened quietly. To the agitation of birds. To some boys off in the distance, shouting as they kicked a ball about.

'How would I get there?' he asked. Not because he might actually do it but out of curiosity, to catch himself briefly in the light of an unexpected possibility. 'To Sydney, I mean.'

'I could arrange it,' Josie told him. He was impressed by her intensity. 'There's an organisation.'

He nodded but remained sceptical. She made it sound like the underground during the War. It had the air of a game.

What was no game was where *he* was going.

'I'll think it over,' he told her, turning his head to where the voices of the footballers were raised in a triumphant shout. She touched the sleeve of the greatcoat. 'No, I will,' he assured her, 'I'll think about it. I really will.'

But he wondered that she should have seen so little of what was in him. When his last visit came and he gave her his answer, feeling clumsy though he tried not to be – they were once again in the half-dark under the camphor laurel tree – she was silent and did not try to persuade him, though she accepted none of his 'reasons'. What he could not tell her was that since the ballot was announced his life had had a shape. He could see himself. He had begun to see, in the events he had organised for himself, the outline of what he was to be.

She kissed him lightly to one side of his mouth and turned back into the house.

He sat a moment – he was not reconsidering – he had never in fact considered – before he kicked the bike into sputtering life and went roaring off.

The other proposition that had been put to him, Cliff's offer to set him up with a girl, he did accept. He was shy, he found, about such matters, even with Cliff, and feared afterwards that he had not hit the right note between throwaway ease and the sort of eagerness that might have been expected of red-blooded youth when he told Cliff, 'What you said that time – you know, about a girl – I've been thinking, and I'd really appreciate it.' Cliff seemed to have forgotten his offer. They agreed, however, to meet up at the pub on his last night.

HE arrived on time but missed Cliff, who had already been there and left. He bought a beer, talked to one or two people, but after half an hour pushed his way out again and took a slow ride around town.

It was Saturday night. Everyone was out. He felt an odd affection for the place now that he was about to leave it, though it had nothing to recommend it really and he was eager to go.

The usual Saturday-night crowd of fellows and their girls was milling round the entrance to the Pictures, which was all lit up; the girls with hair buffed and lacquered, a little top-heavy in their miniskirts and skintight sweaters, the boys trying not to look dressed up, but dressed up just the same in camou-flage battledress or motorcycle jacket and cord flares. Some with long hair, one or two with the beginnings of a beard. A good many of those who were still at school, or worked in banks or stores, had short hair with just the sideburns left to thicken.

Charlie felt distanced from them. He rode slowly, scanning the crowd, then did a circuit of the local War Memorial.

Groups of lone youths sat on the backs of benches in the low-walled park there, and smoked or skylarked; others stood leaning against the cars parked along the kerb, making remarks to the passers-by that flared up on occasion into shouting matches. But on the whole a fairground atmosphere prevailed.

He stopped and shouted across to a group of fellows he recognised from school.

'I'm looking for Cliff Hodges,' he called. 'Anyone seen Cliff Hodges?'

'You seen him?' one of them asked another.

The boy pursed his lips.

'We haven't seen him,' the first boy called. 'Try the pub.'

Charlie drove off, did another slow circuit of the park. He felt let down, decided to look in again at the pub, just in case.

An hour later he was still there. He hadn't found Cliff but had got into conversation with a fellow he'd known at primary school when they were eleven.

Still reddish-blond and freckled, Eddie McPhee was not much bigger than he had been then. Charlie towered over him. He was an apprentice jockey at a local stables. For a good two hours before Charlie met up with him he had been drinking vodka and orange and Charlie decided now to join him. He was very noisy and argumentative, but so slight and pallidly childlike that none of the fellows he picked on thought it honourable to hit him. The worst they did was tell him to get lost and walk away, which made him all the madder. After his second vodka Charlie found this extraordinarily amusing.

He remembered Eddie as a kid who couldn't spell and was always getting whacked across the palm with a ruler. He had grown up cocky and sure of himself. This surprised Charlie but impressed him too. He began to feel happily light-headed, then elated, then affectionately grateful to Eddie for having at this point reappeared out of his primary-school years to take him on a long loop backwards that he might otherwise have missed.

'Remember that bastard Hoyland?' Eddie shouted. This was

the wielder of the ruler. 'Remember Frances Jakes?' She was a girl who, at twelve, had had the most enormous tits. I'm really enjoying myself, Charlie thought. Too bad about Cliff.

When the pub closed, he redeemed his overcoat from a bar stool where he had abandoned it and offered Eddie a lift back to the stables on the other side of town.

It was after midnight, and cold. What he was aware of, as they rode between the houses down deserted street after street, was the closeness of the stars overhead and the distance between his hands on the handlebars of the bike and his head, where it just managed to stay put at the top of his body. This made the business of keeping the bike upright – and steering it through space with the cold night air pouring over them, and the bitumen, with its starry sheen, ribboning out before and behind – a skill that for all its familiarity approached the miraculous. If anyone was looking down from up there, he thought, how amazing all this must look. And us too. How amazing *we* must look!

'I'm fucken freezing,' Eddie shouted in his ear, crouched behind the wall of his back.

'Yahwee!' Charlie shouted in return and, aiming at the stars, he jerked the bike upward so that for a moment they sailed along on one wheel.

HE woke, feeling stiff and sorry for himself, as the first light was coming. His head was heavy, still thick with sleep, his mouth dry. He couldn't think for a moment where he might be, swaddled in the bulkiness of the greatcoat, its collar round his ears.

There was a sharp ammoniac smell. Ah! Eddie! The stables.

He saw the wooden walls of the stall then. Sat up in straw. Heard the snuffling close by of horses.

Eddie, in thick socks and greyish longjohns that sagged at the knees, was already upright, pulling a sweater over his head. 'I gotta go,' he explained.

'I'll go with you,' Charlie told him and got to his feet.

Eddie sat to pull on his boots. Charlie discovered he was still wearing his.

They staggered out into the pearly light, unbuttoned, and standing side by side took a good long piss, watching it stream and puddle between the pebbles in the yard. Eddie hitched up his pants and went back inside. Charlie walked up and down, hands deep in the pockets of his greatcoat, which was still unbuttoned, his head and shoulders drawn inside the collar, hunched in on the warmth of himself. 'Jesus,' he hissed.

He couldn't believe how cold it was out here. There was a bluish frost on the paddock; on the fence post, where it had split and hardened, a glint of ice.

'Here,' Eddie said when he reappeared, 'give us a hand with these.'

He was weighed down with a load of gear. Charlie allowed him to heft a pouched bag over his shoulder that weighed a ton. He released a hand from his pocket to steady it. They went out of the yard, where the CZ rested against the fence, and down a gravel drive beside a slip-rail fence towards the highway. Other figures loomed up in the misty light.

'Is it always as cold as this?' Charlie asked.

Eddie had almost disappeared under the load he was carrying. 'Yair. You never fucken get used to it!'

They came to a T-junction. There was no traffic. Horses were being brought up in a long line; silvery shadows in the misty half-light, their hooves making a hollow sound on the bitumen. They might have been packhorses setting out across a conti-nent. Charlie was reminded of a troop of soldiers – or was it

Indians? – out of some black-and-white movie. Something unfamiliar anyway, not part of his world. Yet here it was, and routine to Eddie, who was grumping along at his side. Just another Sunday morning.

If I hadn't missed Cliff last night, and the girls, Charlie thought, I wouldn't know all this was here. How much else was there, he wondered, that he wouldn't have time now to discover?

He felt a little cloud of doubt, of depression, puff up in him. But just then the sun broke through, touching the grass on either side of the road, and with its sudden warmth came a strong earth smell, comfortingly dark, along with the rankness of the horses.

He dumped the bag. 'I should get going,' he said.

Eddie, standing beside him at the fence, was absorbed now with what was happening out in the paddock.

'Yair, good,' he said in an absent voice. 'See you round.'

He continued to stare out into the distance.

Charlie, standing for a moment, felt the pull of Eddie's absorption. In a world. In work. There was so much liveliness in the way the horses pranced about, proud and full of themselves and their power, the air blowing white from their nostrils, light rippling on their coats. When he turned and walked back briskly to where the CZ was parked, he felt in himself some of the energy they moved with, the touch of coming warmth in the air, the beginning excitement of realising that this was it, it had arrived. The day.

AT home he showered, got his few things together.

He was very much aware, in a sentimental way, that these would be his last moments, for a while at least, in this room.

It had been his for the whole of his life. Its view, into the branches of an old liquidambar, was one of the first he could recall, the luminous green of its star-shaped leaves in the early-morning light, the way it went gold then rusted at the end of May, then crisped and yielded to a faint line of hills; bluish, but sometimes with the red of the sun behind them, and a flash as it was sucked down and disappeared behind their blackness.

He stood now looking out over the sill. There was just an instant when it struck him – repeating an episode from a conventional Boy's Own story – that he could still climb over the sill, grab one of those branches, swing to the ground ten feet below and be away. But where to? To Josie and the limbo, the dangling interim, of a series of safe houses?

He turned back into the room. He had slept here virtually every night of his life for almost twenty years. Seven full years that would make in all, of being laid out here in a state of suspension, colouring its darkness with his dreams. Its walls bore the record, meagre as it might be, of the dedications and brief enthusiasms of his passage – it too seemed brief – from childhood to wherever he had arrived at now of imperfect manhood. When he closed the door on it, it would remain here, complete to a point, while four thousand miles away the same body that had trusted itself each night to unconsciousness, and done its daily push-ups here on the polished floor, and sat at the desk sweating over the binomial theorem and making its way through *Sons and Lovers* and the *Iliad* and *War and Peace*, would be putting itself through a new set of experiences, as yet unimaginable, which it might or might not at last get back from.

He hung the greatcoat in the wardrobe – the period of that particular uniform was over – and closed the door, then stood and examined himself, hair still wet from the shower, in the mirror.

He had expected these last weeks to resolve in some way

the puzzle of what he was – they had not. To provide something, caught from others, that he could take away and hang on to, refer back to, measure himself against.

He opened the door of the wardrobe and looked again at the greatcoat on its hanger, bulky and familiar. He buried his nose in it. The odour of mothballs had faded over the weeks. There was another smell now, not quite familiar. Was *that* him?

Once more he closed the wardrobe door and, avoiding his image, sat for a moment, hands placed lightly on his knees, very quiet and still, on the edge of his bed, the way the characters do in a Russian novel before a journey. Then went out to where his aunt, in her dressing gown, was just coming from the bathroom.

She kissed him, laying her hand very gently to his cheek. It was so unusual, the touch of her fingers added to the regular, rather formal kiss, that it came to him with a little start of reality, which those last moments in his room had not quite produced, that he was actually going.

They were quiet at breakfast, though no more than usual. His grandfather complained, which *was* unusual, of a neighbour's dog, which had kept him awake half the night, he insisted, with its barking – growing, as he went on, more and more aggrieved, then angry.

What Charlie saw, his aunt too, was that he really *was* angry, though not with the neighbour. And not with me either, Charlie said to himself, but with the fact that I am going. Maybe even with the war. But nothing of this – the war, his going or not going – had ever been discussed between them, and he wondered why. He had simply taken it for granted that if his number came up he would go, and that his grandfather and aunt, however they might fear for his safety and miss him, would expect him to, because it was the *strong* thing to do. Wasn't that what they had always been looking for in him? A sign that the moral weakness, or whatever it was that had made his father run, and had then brought him back again destroyed by his own hand, had passed him over. Now, when they shook hands on the veranda step and he felt himself briefly hugged and pushed away, his grandfather's anger, or sorrow, suggested something shocking: that in his own unaccustomed weakness, the old man might be willing to accept even a lack of strength in this last of his line if he could be kept home and safe from harm.

'Look after yourself, boy,' was what he said.

His aunt kissed him. Again her fingertips. Soft on his cheek.

And that, on a quiet Sunday morning in August 1968, was how Charlie Dowd went to a war.

THREE years later he was back, almost unscathed and nearly two stone heavier, an ex-sergeant, released to take up civilian life where he had left off – after a period of adjustment, of course.

The house he had left was much changed. His grandfather had died the previous year and the first thing his aunt did was suggest that he move into his grandfather's room, which had been cleared and cleaned and was the best room in the house.

He declined. Though his own room now felt small, he preferred, by keeping it, to make the point that his stay was to be temporary. Till he got on his feet, worked out what he wanted to do with himself.

His aunt did not press him. Her enquiries into his plans were tactful and oblique. So were her attempts, which amused him – he thought of Cliff – to set him up with girls. *Nice* ones.

In fact, he had no need of help in this direction but for the moment was taking things, in this area as in all others, slowly.

The world he had come back to struck him as being very different from the one he had known. More relaxed in some ways, more strenuous in others, and his aunt's life was a measure of it.

It wasn't simply that she no longer had her father to care for, his exacting standards to meet. She no longer had *him* – and only now did he understand how much of her life had been devoted to fulfilling what his mother, by leaving, had passed to her in the way of duty, and of affection too. He was shocked now at what it might have cost her, and abashed at how little of this he had appreciated or shown gratitude for, perhaps because she made so little of it herself. He had scarcely considered her then in separation either from his grandfather or himself. He saw, now that things were more equal between them, that she was a woman with her own interests, and was in her own way interesting. She had a sharp eye when it came to the affairs of the town and her various friends; a sharp tongue too, now that her father was not here to monitor it. They got on well together. She still worried about him but did not fuss.

She had had the kitchen, which had been an old-fashioned place of leadlight cupboards and scrubbed-wood draining boards, fitted out with a good deal of Laminex and stainless steel. A skylight filled the whole space with the kind of light that would once have been considered dangerous, in the way of fading curtains or exposing the lurking places of ineradicable grime.

There were no curtains now, and little fear of grime. The archway into the dining room had been removed and the new space furnished with pieces of a spare 'modern' design – bold fabrics, pale wood. Hard, he thought, for the old presences to find harbour in a world that was so shadowless and bright.

He wondered where his aunt had found in herself such a capacity for lightness. Had it always been there, waiting to establish itself the moment the old man was gone? A refutation, long unspoken, of his world of solid truths?

Charlie was surprised, but he enjoyed surprise. It was one of the small surprises his own nature had yielded him in recent years.

She was made wary, he saw, by his experiences. Since he offered no account of them and gave no outward sign of how they had touched him, she had had to make them up out of horrors she had read about in the papers or seen on TV. That he did not need to talk about what he had seen, and did not bring to breakfast with him the smell of napalm or of the night sweats that must accompany his dreams, was not in itself a reassurance. Neither was his lack of visible wounds. His father too had come home without wounds.

What worried her was what might be there in his head. Deep-hidden, unspoken. In the meantime they took refuge, both, since he proved to be such an obedient pupil of her rules, in good-humoured banter and routine.

But neither of them any longer believed in rules. That's what he saw. The new rule was to pretend they did, while knowing perfectly well, on each side, that the other did not.

But perhaps, he thought, she never had. Maybe that was another of the ways in which, over the years, he had misread her.

HE developed his own routine: got up late, did odd jobs around the yard that he found oddly satisfying – putting new palings into the back fence, climbing up on to the roof to replace a length of guttering. He read, sat with his hands in his lap idling an hour away on the new couch in front of the TV. Took long walks along the roads that led out of town.

Walking, he found, set just the right pace for the sort of thinking he had to do; and watching people at their ordinary occupations, in a world where the commonest source of disruption was the weather, comforted him – he didn't mind the tedium of it.

People talked about the weather in a way he had never noticed till now. As if they looked to the sky for *relief*. For a mild irruption into their lives of chance or change that might at one time have come from the gods, but in the clear assurance now that the worst it could produce was a fistful of hail.

'Looks like it might rain,' men who stood behind a fence with a pair of shears would call across to him – entire strangers.

It was a way of invoking a link between them within a dispensation so easily admissible on both sides, and so large and all-embracing, that no answer was required.

It was in such moments that he felt closest to being home.

Sometimes, on one of his walks, he dropped in at the pub and, feeling like an old-timer himself these days, settled in his old place by the window with a beer.

He recognised one or two of the old fellows sitting alone in the sunlight, but had changed too much for them to see in him the thin-shouldered youth in the air force greatcoat who had once sat scribbling in his notebook at the sill.

He no longer wore the greatcoat or had a notebook with him, and in a general doing-over in which the whole place had been subjected to progress, the sill was no longer chocolate-coloured but a spanking white.

But when he looked across, the boy was still there, his wallet and the little machine for producing roll-your-owns, which he had long since abandoned, on the sill before him. Urgently, solemnly setting down his thoughts. Looking up. Biting the end of his pen. Writing again. Thoughts. Endless lists. Impossible now to get back into that boy's head.

Tenderly curious, he had gone in search of the notebook, but had hidden it so well from others who might stumble across it in his absence that he could not find it himself.

Occasionally a phrase came back to him, or an item from one of the lists, and he blushed, then found himself feeling oddly, indulgently protective of his former self. He had been so full of the easy belief that his thoughts, and the careful formulation of them, mattered. Perhaps it was better that the notebook was lost.

But the boy continued to haunt him. There in silhouette against the light of the window, or as a slighter sharer of his own more solid flesh. Which he shared now with other presences as well. Ghosts he carried in him who saw things in their own way.

What they felt, what they had seen, formed a glow around his own feelings that on occasion confused him and was the chief reason why he kept clear of old friends. He did not know how to present himself to them or what he had to present. In the other lives that now haunted him he had lived a different history, lighter or darker than the one he had brought home and could show.

As for the boy at the sill, the tenderness he felt for him was of a brotherly kind; blood-closeness, but with an element, as well, of distance.

It wasn't a question of innocence, or the loss of innocence – he found these days he could no longer talk in such terms, and people who did made him angry.

There were fellows he had come across 'up there' who were, in a childlike way, unknowing; others who, again like children, seemed unmarked by the evil they had come up against. The first was just that – childishness. The second, maybe, a form of grace. We lose whatever innocence we might have laid claim to the moment we are drawn into that tangle of action and interaction, of gesture and consequence, where the least motion on our part, even the drawing of a breath, may so change things that another, close by or far off, will be nudged just far enough out of the clear line of his life as to be permanently impaired.

That, so Charlie would have written now, if he still had his notebook and thought it worth the effort of setting down, was the price of living. To that extent, no man is innocent. As for the loss of innocence, how could you lose what you'd never had? He had never claimed to be innocent. Only alive.

Ah, thoughts. Thoughts.

He saw himself as a man who, whole as he might look, in that he had no wound to show, had come back just the same with a limb missing, a phantom limb that continued to putrify.

Or with fragments of shrapnel in his flesh that sent metal detectors into electronic fits, whether others had ears for it or not.

Or bearing on his breath spores from the soil of a disorderly and darkly divided country where for two whole years he had taken the infected air into his lungs, so that that too – along with the dulled habit of boredom, the unnatural excitements and dreams he had been dragged through, the brutal descents into degradation and a blundering despair without hope of renovation – had come home with him, in selves who had their own other and haunting lives to live.

It scared him at times that one of these ghostly selves who now sheltered in him might speak up and send a conversation skidding in some new and terrible direction. He would have to deal then with a look on the face of whatever companion he had found of startled incomprehension, as if with no warning a mask had slipped.

So he watched himself. Watched *them*. These others who had set up in him, who insisted at times on drawing attention to themselves and had motives that were not his own.

The need to be heard was theirs, not his. He had no wish to discuss what he had been witness to, and there was no way of doing it anyway. So he did not mention that he had been to the war.

Some people knew it already. They did not mention it either. Embarrassed for him, and for themselves, in case it led to argument. There was a lot of argument on the subject, but only, up here, on the TV, which had smuggled itself now into every household all up and down the country, where it dominated the front room like a child overexcited by the power to say at last the once unsayable.

Up here an older decorum prevailed. People had as little appetite as ever for open dispute.

He thought of Josie and wondered how deep she was now in her hostility to the war, and her disappointment with fellows, like him, who had been duped into going. But he wasn't sure of that – of having been duped. He had had no illusions. The experience had offered itself, that's all, and he had accepted. He did not disagree with the arguments he heard against the war, and his aunt, he suspected, was fiercely opposed to it, though she did not say so. He picked this up from the line of her profile as they sat watching the news together. Her sharp little glances to see how he was taking it. She was afraid of offering some insult to what he had 'been through'.

He recognised this and was touched. Her fierceness, he knew, was on his behalf. She meant to protect him. But it was too late for that.

What affronted him was not the opinions he heard but the gap between their glib abstractions and what he himself had come across in the way of fact: the heaviness of a soaked pack and mud-caked army boots; grime, dank sweat, the death smell of bloated corpses; the incessant tense preoccupation with keeping all the parts of a body that was suddenly too large, and could not effectively be hidden, clear of the random brute agents of destruction that kept hurtling in from every direction; death-dealing but indifferent. For whom you, warm and intelligently alive as you might be, were no more than another object in their path, though the roar with which they came at you was specific and the collision, when it came, so wet and personal.

On the few occasions when people did argue he turned his back. He had only his experience – combustive actualities – to offer, and they weren't an argument. He screwed his mouth shut and sat sullen over his beer.

The wall of silence he felt between himself and others, which he refused to breach, was noise of a kind they could not even begin to conceive: so dense with the scream of metal and the lower but distinguishable screams of men, with the splash of heavy objects through oil-slicked swamp, and night calls out there in the stilled other world of nature that might be birds but might also be the location signals of a waiting enemy, and with heartbeats and the thump-thump of rotor blades, that not even the music he liked to listen to, and which his aunt thought unnecessarily loud, could block out.

WEEKS passed. He drifted.

In the month before he left things had been like this. He had felt the same way. Detached. Floating. But those days had not been entirely aimless. They had a fixed termination; he had known then what he was moving towards. Now he did not.

And he himself had been different, not simply younger. With a different sense of where he might look for enlightenment. Intrigued still by the spectacle of his own existence, and open to every clue he might pick up – a look here, a passing comment there – of what he might be. Still making himself up out of what others saw in him. Or wanting to. Because it was easier than looking too clearly into himself.

He had tried that too, but it was confusing. What he had found there was contradictory, or the evidence was in a code he could not crack.

Was he wiser now?

Not much, he thought.

What he had learned in the heat of action was useful only in moments of extremity, of violent confrontation. The pressures now were soft, the dangers more insidious because not deadly. Or not immediately so.

His aunt went easy on him, was not demanding. She had become sociable and went out a good deal, leaving his meals on a plate in the fridge with a note telling him how they should be heated. The notes were jaunty, an easier and more playful form of communication than talk, and became more so as the weeks rolled on.

He ate alone in the kitchen with the radio playing, for the comfort of some other voice in his head than his own, which wearied him, or in the new lounge in front of the news.

He ate slowly, trying not to let the images that flashed from the TV connect with his own low-level anger; which was more like a taste in his mouth that no other could quite displace than an emotion, a subtle disturbance of his vision that bled the world of vividness and gave everything he looked at a yellow tinge.

He watched a group of young men in battledress run hunched

and stumbling towards a medevac chopper that swayed and tilted. Its blades churned the fetid air, whipped up a tornado of smashed grass stalks and twigs. He felt a damp heat on his skin. Found he was sweating.

He watched a bunch of young men, much the same age as in the previous clip, but in T-shirts and jeans and with young women among them – and some older women too, not unlike his aunt, grey-haired, in glasses – push hard against a line of uniformed police. Banners hung askew above their heads, like thought bubbles in a cartoon. All capitals, all pointing in the same direction. The young men, animal spirits fiercely mobilised in a violent forward movement, were engaged in their own version of war. And the enemy?

He ate. Chewing slowly. Swallowing it down.

'You know,' his aunt remarked one morning at breakfast, 'there's some money. You haven't asked, but it's yours, you know, whenever you want it.'

'I don't need it yet,' he told her.

'Well,' she said, not pressing, 'it's there. Just ask when you do.'

On another occasion: 'Have you thought of getting in touch with your mother?'

This surprised him. He looked up, but could not tell from her eyes – she glanced quickly away – what she was thinking. Did she want him to or not?

'No,' he said. 'I can barely remember what she looks like.'

This wasn't quite true.

'She thinks you're angry with her.'

'I'm not,' he said. 'Not any more. There are too many other things. Anyway, I try not to be angry at all. It does no good.'

'You're right,' she said, but seemed unconvinced.

'Do you keep in touch then?'

'Not regularly. But there *is* a tie. Your father–'

She foundered, unwilling to go further, and he was glad –
he did not want her to. He wanted, just for a moment, to think
of himself as a free agent, no ties – or at least to tell himself
he had none. The ties, such as they were, he could pick up
later. When he was ready. When.

'She's moved to Aberdeen,' his aunt told him.

'Aberdeen!'

The word fell into the room out of nowhere. He knew
where Aberdeen was, he could see it on the map, but had never
expected to have any connection to it. Hadn't thought of his
connections as being so worldwide. He gave a little laugh, more
a snigger perhaps, and his aunt looked alarmed.

'I can't imagine her,' he said, 'in Aberdeen,' and laughed again.

It denied, of course, what he had already claimed. That he
had no clear picture of her at all. And what did he know of
Aberdeen?

HE walked. From one end of town to the other. Walking was
another form of thinking – or maybe *un*thinking – in which
the body took over, went its own way and the mind went with
it; the ground he covered, there and back, measurable only by
the level of quietude he had arrived at, and the change, when
he came out of himself, in the atmosphere and light.

One of the places he liked to go when the weather was fine
was to a river park at the far end of town. Willow-fringed along
the brown, rather sluggish stream, it was featureless save for an
elaborate rotunda of timber and decorative wrought iron that
was unusual in that it offered more in the way of fantasy than
you got in other parts of town, and a children's playground
where, in the afternoon, mothers brought their kids to climb,
swing and roll about in a sandpit. He liked to sit high up in

the bandstand, where he had a good view over the expanse of park and an oval beyond, and lose himself in a book.

Towards the end of January it rained for three days. He stopped his walks and stuck to the pub.

Finally the rain gave up, though the air remained saturated. There were still heavy clouds about and the ground was soggy underfoot. He took his usual walk out towards the river. And the park when he came to it was a place transformed. Great sheets of water broke the green of its surface, and hundreds of seagulls had flocked in, bringing with them the light of ocean beaches and of the ocean itself. They were crowding the shores of the newly formed ponds: huge white creatures that had made their way a hundred miles from the coast to translate what had been one kind of landscape into something entirely other. The children had deserted the swings and ladders of the playground and were chasing about among the big birds, delighted by the novelty they presented, the news they had brought – not just of another world, but of a world inside the one at their feet that they had scarcely dreamed of.

He too felt the miracle of it. It was as if a breath of fantasy, that had existed as no more than an unlikely possibility in the lightness and whiteness of the bandstand, had recreated itself as fact in these hundreds of actual bodies, independent organisms and lives, that were shifting about over the green or making brief flights across the expanse of silvery, sky-lit water.

What he felt in himself was an equal lightness, that reflected, he thought, the persistence out there in the world, of the unexpected – an assurance that nothing was final, or beyond surprise or change. The dry little park had transformed itself into a new shore, but the force he felt in touch with was in himself. It was as if he had looked up from a book he was lost in and found that what his eyes had conceived of on the page was shining all round him.

Half a dozen children were chasing along the banks, delighted that by rushing at them they could drive the big birds skyward, half expecting perhaps to find in themselves the power to join them and go heavily circling and gliding. One small boy, unready to challenge the birds as the others were doing, stood stranded on the sidelines. He was maybe five years old. Skinny with pale reddish hair. Doubtful but tempted.

Charlie stood looking at him, and the boy, aware of it, turned to meet Charlie's gaze, drawing his underlip in, which only made his moist eyes rounder.

'Magic,' Charlie told the boy with a laugh, and made a sweep with his arm that sent a dozen birds streaming aloft.

The boy's mouth fell open, and Charlie saw in the look of sudden enlightenment in his eyes that the child had taken the word literally, as a claim on Charlie's part to be the presiding genius here who had turned a bit of the local and familiar into something extraordinary, and for a moment Charlie actually felt a breath of what the child's belief had accorded him.

A girl of ten or eleven appeared, also skinny but more vigorously red-headed than the boy. She took him sternly by the hand.

'Kelvin,' she scolded in a whisper, 'you know you're not allowed!' Fiercely protective, she cast a baleful look in the direction of the stranger who had been *speaking* to him. But the boy, suddenly defiant, broke away, and with arms outspread launched headlong into a flock of gulls, which lifted with excited shrieks and went flapping past his head. Glancing back a moment to make sure that he was the one who had been the actual cause of this commotion, he tilted his arms like outstretched wings and made another rush among the birds.

Charlie turned away, lightly amused. But he would think of this inconsequential moment afterwards as being for him the end of one thing and the beginning of another, though which element in it, if any, had been decisive he would never know: the translation of the park to another shore; the boy Kelvin's mistaken belief that, like a conjuror at a children's party, he had produced all this shifting light, all these plump white bodies, out of his sleeve; the sister's defiance of him as a dangerous stranger. Perhaps it was all these in odd collusion with one another, or in collusion with something in himself that had been waiting for just this concatenation of small events to touch it awake and open a way to the future. Or something else again that he had no possibility of bringing to consciousness. Some chemical change in him even more miraculous at one level, though ordinary and explicable at another, than the appearance overnight, out of nowhere as it were, of a thousand sea creatures so far from the sea.

Walking home he had no sense that anything momentous had occurred. He was aware only of his immediate mood; an amusement that continued to work on him, quiet but quickening, and a glimpse – for the moment it was no more than that – of how small the pressures might be that determine the sum of what is and what we feel, the fugitive deflections and instinctive blind gestures that might be the motor of change.

He did not know as yet that there *was* a change. Only that it was possible, and that the agents of it could be small. But that, for the moment, was enough.

Towards Midnight

Towards Midnight

—◆—

WHAT came to her ear was the hovering close by of mechanical wings, that had come, she thought, to carry her off. In her dream-state she felt only the relief it would be to pass the weight of her body, light as it now was, to some other agency.

The wings beat closer. She started awake, and the familiar objects of her upstairs sitting room, as if a second earlier she might have surprised them in a temporary absence, settled back into place.

The TV screen was dancing, white with static. It was after midnight. For a good hour and a half, it seems, she herself had been absent. She reached for the remote. But the sound out of her dream persisted. It was the clatter of the filter boxes in the pool two levels below. A breeze must have sprung up. She stirred herself, gathered up her things.

But against the blue Tuscan night the cypress tops in the window were as still as if they were painted.

She stepped out on to her terrace and, half hidden in

shadow, peered down through the darkness of pomegranate and bay. Someone was down there, swimming. All she could make out were the streamers of light at his shoulders, and when he came, too quickly, to the end of a length, the heap of silvery bubbles he left as he tucked over into the turn. Up and down he went, in a dozen powerful strokes, and the pool, which for so many weeks had lain heavy and still in the heat, under a mantle of olive florets, drowned midges, beetles paddling in clumsy circles, expanded and contracted like a living thing.

If Gianfranco was here, or one of her sons, Tommy or Jake, what a ruckus there'd be! They'd feel bound to go down and shout at the fellow. Chuck him out.

Well, she wasn't going to try that. She was alone in the house, a kilometre from the village. No neighbours in calling distance. But she felt no particular alarm. Only surprise, and a kind of delight at the unexpectedness of it, exhilaration in the presence of so much effort. As if she had got herself hooked up to some new chemical – neat starlight – that glowed in her veins and quickened her awareness of her own body, but as a thing alive and part again of the living scene.

With her elbows propped on the parapet of her terrace, she watched – hard to say for how long – and was taken out of herself, till at the end of a length like any other he did not tumble into a turn, but with his head streaming moonlight came to his feet, and in the same agile movement sprang on to his splayed hands, heaved himself up, and was out.

No one she recognised.

A sturdy peasant type, in a bathing slip that might have been red.

She stepped back in case he glanced up and caught her there. But he was too absorbed for that. Standing with his arms forced back hard behind him, fingers linked, he did half a dozen stretching exercises, dipping his head swiftly like a bird; then straightened and moved out of sight under the pergola.

The pool, meanwhile, had settled to clear moonlight again.

She felt let down, as if he had taken with him part of the night and what was vital to it. Was it over? Was that it?

She stood peering into the darkness of the pergola. He must have gone already, through one of the gaps in the fence. The fence had gaps, but there were so many brambles along its length, and the bank was so steep, that they hadn't bothered to have it mended. Was he really gone?

A gust of fragrance came on the air, then thinned and came again. So strong! Her lime tree.

Out of sight on the other side of the house, and taller now than the house itself, its scent was so overpowering on these warm May nights that in her mind she could actually see the great dark mass of it looming against the stars.

How good it is to be here, she thought, at just this moment. With the moon resting like that on the tip of a cypress, the air freighted with the scent of *tiglio*, the clear bright notes of the nightingale dropping so precisely into place, off in the dark. It was a moment, she thought, when all things were just as they should be. Not a degree lighter or heavier or louder or more intense.

Ah, her swimmer!

Wearing rough workman's trousers but still bare-chested, he moved to the edge of the pool and stood there towelling his hair with his T-shirt; then, rather dreamily, began to dry his chest.

He might have looked up then and seen her. She drew back. But something else had caught his attention.

He was gazing out over the wall of bay to the hills with

their swathes of blue-black *macchia*. Looking, perhaps, for where
the nightingale was dinning from its post in the olive grove,
establishing, note on note, its claim to territory.

There, she could have told him. Further to the left. Down
there.

He turned his head as if he had heard, but in the wrong
direction. Then kneeling, laced his sneakers and, with the soaked
T-shirt across his shoulders, ducked down beside the fence and
was gone.

She continued to stand. Looking at the place where he had
vanished, but with no sense of being left. Rather of remaining,
of being here and in possession of all this. The place. The hour.
Most of all, of herself.

The moon, which just a moment ago had been straw-
coloured, when she looked at it now was paling, as if it had
been subjected to immersion in some fast-working chemical.
Again the scent of lime came to her, and with it the quickening sense of a whole world astir and on the move. Small
nocturnal creatures, destructive in fact — but so what — were
nosing in around the fleshy roots of her iris. A cat was on the
prowl — or was it a fox? Other lives, intent on their interests.
Invisibly close and companionable.

She felt settled, wonderfully so. And by a situation that on
another occasion or in a different mood might have alarmed
her. Why hadn't it? She did not know and did not need for
the moment to ask. What she needed now was to tumble into
her bed and sleep.

SHE was alone because she chose to be. Later it might not be
possible, she knew that, but for the time being she could manage,
and it was what she preferred. She had worked through her

period of rage and hard words, but wasn't sure she could trust herself, just yet, with others.

Each night at seven she boiled herself an egg or heated a pan of soup, and at half past, right on the dot, Gianfranco rang. She was comfortably settled in her routine.

No, she told him, everything was fine, just fine. Marisa came to clean each morning. Corrado looked after the *orto* and the pool.

Gianfranco, she knew, was nodding, but what she could hear in his silence, even at this distance, was the terrible humming of anxiety in him, the fear that there was something – there was always *something* – that she was holding back. She raged up and down beside her kitchen cupboards, the receiver tight in her fist. But her voice, when she spoke was soothing (or so she hoped).

'No, no,' she cooed. 'Gianfranco! Darling! I'm perfectly OK, I promise I am. Stop fussing.'

She gave a little laugh that was meant to assure him that this, like all the other things he fretted over – the boys, his office, money, the house – was nothing, he was being silly.

He said goodnight, made her promise to ring if there was the slightest problem, the least change.

Then waited, as he always did, for her to reconsider and tell him the bad news. She refrained. And in fact there *was* none.

At last, on his third goodnight, he rang off.

She gave a subdued scream of a theatrical kind – seeing herself in a jokey, self-dramatising way helped to keep up her spirits – and sat down hard on a stool.

But it was over. She was alone again. Free. The whole night before her.

She thought sometimes that she would like it if Tommy was here; Jake, her second son, was mid-Atlantic somewhere on someone's yacht. There were afternoons when she found herself gazing out of her window and wishing she could just call down to the terrace, where, his mobile on the glass-topped table within easy reach, Tommy would be lazing on a daybed. She would get him to come up then and put on one of the Roy Orbison albums she liked to listen to only when he was here. Or wishing that she would look up, having caught a scent, and find him there in the doorway of her room, filling its space with his hungry presence.

What she meant was, she would like it for about *five minutes*. Any longer and she would discover all over again the things about this favourite child that exasperated and enraged her.

The way he stalked about, clutching his mobile like a small instrument of torture. Waiting pathetically for someone to call.

And when he gave in at last, and himself did the calling, the way he pursed his lips at the thing, as if it was a mouth; arguing with his ex-wife and sounding so mild and reasonable, or sweet-talking some girl he'd picked up on the train. Then, the moment he hung up, going glowery and dark again, casting about, like the bewildered four-year-old she saw so clearly at times in the big unhappy man, for some mischief he could get up to that would make someone pay.

Somebody, it didn't matter who.

She had been paying for more than thirty years.

Well, she could do without that just for the moment. What she needed, just for the moment, was solitude, and blessèd, blessèd routine.

THREE days each week she went up to Siena for her chemo. They taped a plastic bubble like a third breast to the soft flesh below her shoulder and it fed mineral light into her at a slow run. The nausea it left her with was like space sickness. As if they were minerals from another planet, changing her slowly into a space creature who would be free at last of the ills of earth.

Well, she knew what *that* was code for!

Between visits she wore a holster packed with a flattish canister that for twenty-four hours a day played with the weather of her body – its moods, her dreams; filling her mouth with the taste of metals straight off the periodic table, getting her ready for the thing itself – the taste of earth.

For Siena she had a driver from the village and a big old Audi. Soft-leathered, air-conditioned. She sat in magisterial coolness, closed off from the straw-coloured, treeless hills, the vine rows where the grapes, as yet, were like hard little peas, but swelling, swelling towards October.

At intervals along the highway, black girls in six-inch heels toting fake Gucci handbags paced up and down in the dust. Some of them in skintight leather miniskirts, others in gold lurex pants tight at the ankle. In the middle of nowhere! With nothing in sight but oakwoods or a distant viaduct, they paced elegantly up and down beside the hurtling traffic, in a tide of ice-cream sticks, paper cups, dried acacia blossom. She watched them from the closed-off sanctuary of the car, and sometimes, to pass the time, kept count. On long car journeys in her Queensland childhood, she and her brother had watched for white horses. The appearance in the timeless Tuscan landscape of opulent, overdressed black girls seemed no less marvellous.

They came from as far away as Cape Verde and Sierra Leone, these girls, and drove out here in taxis to wait for the long-distance lorry drivers. Their managers (or so she had heard) were women: big African mammas who were also witches and used old-country spells to keep them in fear of their lives, or their children's lives, but to be doubly sure held their passports

– a modern touch. In bodies that seemed entirely their own, and giving no hint of being fearful or enslaved, they walked up and down as if the dirt under their heels were the paving stones of some fashionable piazza in Florence or Milan.

She watched them. Hard not to envy, whatever the facts, the grace and assurance they brought to this new version of pastoral.

Till one of the lorries, with a whine of its air brakes, came powerfully to a halt, and the driver – the god – stepped down.

Her own body was *not* her own. In some moment of ordinary distraction, while she was on her knees in the rose bed pulling up weeds, or waiting idly for the kettle to boil, her mind God knows where, her body had taken a wrong turning, gone haywire, and now did exactly as it pleased. It was like being in the hands of a loony housebreaker who did not have your interest at heart. Who had moods and notions of his own. Was savagely perverse, and curious to see how far he could push you. And was there at every moment, making his obscene, humiliating demands. To get away from him she read, or rather, reread. Chasing up old friends in the pages of her favourite books to see how she or they had changed over the years, or to rediscover, with a little shock of affection, the earlier self who at sixteen or thirty had first been touched by them.

Effi Briest, who was in favour of living, poor girl, but had no principles. Mrs Copperfield, one of the two Serious Ladies, who had always wanted to go to pieces. Gratefully she went back to them. And found herself, towards midnight, with her book in her lap and her glasses at the end of her nose, listening impatiently for the familiar clap-clap of the filter boxes and the arrival of her intruder.

SHE knew now who he must be.

There were woods on the far side of the village. The men who worked there these days, cutting and stacking logs, came from Eastern Europe. Poles or Yugoslavs. They had rooms in the village and sat around playing cards outside the bar. She had seen them riding through the square on top of a truck piled with firewood, their muddy boots dangling. He would be one of those. She didn't need to know which one or to see him close. She liked the idea of his being a stranger in the further sense of his having other words in his head, when she looked down and saw him gazing out over the hills, for *owl*, *fence*, *distance*. Of there being nothing between them but his body, either in vigorous action down there in the pool or in dreamy repose; which he did not know was being watched, and in the long hour before he made his appearance, impatiently waited for.

He came every night, not always at the same hour. Sometimes earlier – a surprise! – mostly later. There would come the clatter of the filter boxes as he brought the pool to life, and with it the quickening of her heart, which laughed quietly as she took her book up again and pretended for a moment to go back to her reading. Then she would rise, draw her robe about her, and step out on to the terrace.

SIPPING her coffee each morning she caught glimpses of the pool as it shimmered and flashed between the leaves, an electric, unnatural blue. Housemartins, in their furious hunger, would be swooping for insects that danced in swarms on its surface, taking the pool's reflected light in flushes on their underbodies. The air, down there, as it heated, would be sharp with the scent of bay.

She might have gone down to lie for a little on one of the sunbeds. It was still cool at this hour and she would get down easily enough. But where would she find the strength to climb back again?

As they moved deeper into June, the afternoons grew fiery, she could not sleep. Elbows on the parapet of her terrace, sipping cold tea, her thoughts went to a young man, Justin Ferrier, who, fifteen years before, had come out from England to be her summer help in the garden.

The son of a business contact of Gianfranco's, he was the same age as Jake and just down from Eton. Hard-working, sociable, the perfect guest.

Unused to their southern habits, he had spent long afternoons, under the low bronze sky, at work on an old 350cc motorbike he had acquired from a mechanic in the next village and set up like an idol on the terrace below her window.

Sometimes, when it was too hot to sleep, she would lean over the parapet and chat to him while he squatted like a child in his open sandals and worked, or simply rested there on her elbows and watched. Drawing back at times in dazzled embarrassment at the intensity with which, under his flop of sunbleached hair, he devoted all his shining attention to the mucky business of laying out on sheets of yesterday's *Repubblica* all the dismantled parts of the god he worshipped: chain, gears, greaseslicked carburettor, screws.

He'd put his stamp on the summer – even Jake and Tommy felt that. Whenever they talked of it later it was always 'the year Justin was here'.

Because it would have seemed shameful to shout or call one another names in front of him, they had, for a whole two months, been on their best behaviour, playing just the sort of nice *per bene* family he believed them to be.

Her friend Jack Chippenham, Chipper, was with them and had immediately been smitten. He had made a big play for the boy – but in a jokey way, as if it was accepted, a part of that summer's special mood, that they should all be a little in love with him.

She and Chipper had grown up together. They had met at a birthday party in Toowoomba when they were still at school. Chipper, at sixteen, was already in possession of things – style, a humorous take on the world, and himself and others – that she had only begun to be aware of. 'You saved my life,' she told him on that first occasion. Meaning that without him the party would have been a write-off. He had been doing it, in different ways, ever since.

Justin, like everyone Chipper set his sights on, was charmed, and was charming in return. He let Chipper drive him across to Monteriggione and Sinalunga to expensive meals, and to the summer discos all up and down the coast. There was nothing in it, of course, she knew that. But when Chipper's attentions began to be so obvious that even Gianfranco noticed, she took him aside and gave him a good talking to. After all, she was *in loco parentis* here. She actually said that: *in loco parentis*.

Chipper's response was to pretend astonishment. That she should turn out, in her old age, to be so moralistic. And humourless. It was the second charge that hurt.

And he was right. The boy enjoyed being made a fuss of, and why not? He knew just how to handle such things. There was no harm in it. But the next day, while they were having drinks before lunch, she suggested to Justin that he might like to bring his girlfriend Charlotte out, and for the rest of the summer Charlotte too worked in the garden, and they had a tent in the olive grove.

'Uh-huh,' Chipper had said. 'Nice.' He might have been

referring to the sip he had taken from the Bloody Mary she had just passed to him.

Maintaining *his* sense of humour right to the end.

One morning, to amuse the young people, as she thought of them, she raked out a dress she had kept from their Rome days twenty years before, a sleeveless low-waisted Yves Saint Laurent that came just to the knee, and which, when she tried it on, still miraculously fitted. After consulting the mirror in her room she had gone down to where they were sunbathing beside the pool – Justin, Chipper, the girl – and was flattered that the young people, when they glanced up, did not at first recognise her.

Justin had had to take his sunglasses off, and she could tell that he was seeing her as if for the first time.

'Oh my, my,' Chipper had said, and Yes, she was saying to herself as she stood there transformed, here I am at last, this is the *real* me.

The dress, which was of dark green silk, fitted like a secret skin. The fashion of that particular year had been made for her. It had been her moment, her season. Which she had stepped back into as if it had never passed.

Well, it had of course. It was Chipper who got gallantly to his feet, took her hand and led her, while the others applauded, through her one celebratory twirl.

Poor Chipper! It was, after all, Chipper that this memory had been moving towards. He was dead. Six years ago in San Francisco.

'I'm not sorry,' he had written, just before the end, 'to have wasted my time on such an agreeable planet.'

THE last days of June came on. One night of intense moon-light, when the whole landscape, fields, vineyards, river meadows, the densely wooded surrounding hills, had the glow of midday in some other part of the universe, she realised that for several evenings now she had not heard what she thought of as the embodiment of so much silvery stillness, the bright little hammer-strokes and exuberant volleys of the nightingale. He had said 'Enough' and was gone.

Standing behind her parapet, in the hard shadow of the terrace, she was even more aware of her swimmer, who had not. A small blessing, but one, she knew, that must also have its term. One night soon he would come to his feet at the end of a length and that would be that. All unknowing, she would wait the next night and he would not appear. And the next. Till she was used once again to getting through the midnight hours without him. But for the moment — maybe for the last time — he was here. The disturbance he made as he rocked the water, which was all tilted planes of moonlight and dark, set the filter boxes dancing and beating the air just as she had first heard it. Like the arrival of wings.

Back and forth he hurled himself. Effortless, the body its own affair. Weightless. As if there was no limit to the energy that powered it. As if the breath it drew on might have no end.

Elsewhere

Elsewhere

——

WHEN Debbie Larcombe died she had not been home to her family for nearly three years. Her father decided at once that he would go down to Sydney for the funeral, which was already arranged. There was no suggestion of her being brought back to Lithgow. Her sister Helen couldn't go. She had the children. So Harry's son-in-law, Andy Mayo, would go with him. The two men worked together down the mine and were mates.

Andy was a steady fellow of thirty-three. He'd been to Sydney once, with a rugby team, when he was nineteen. The prospect of driving down and seeing something of the Big Smoke excited him, but he felt he should disguise the fact. After all it was a funeral. 'Are you sure?' he asked Helen, who was kneeling at the bathtub bathing their youngest.

'It's only for the day,' she told him. 'And Dad would like it. I'd be worried about him going down all on his own.'

She paused at her work and said for the third or fourth time, 'It's so sudden! I can hardly believe it.'

Andy, stirred by a rush of tenderness, but also of tender sensuality, brought his fingertips to a strand of hair, damp with steam, that had stuck to the soft white of her neck. Responding, she leaned back for a moment into the firmness, against her nape, of his extended forefinger and thumb, which lightly stroked.

He'd barely known Debbie; in fact he'd met her only twice. She had already left home when he arrived on the scene. After training college at Bathurst she had taught in country towns all up and down the state and had ended up at Balmain, in Sydney. She was four years older than Helen.

The one occasion they'd spent any time together – he had sat up late with her on the night of her mother Dorothy's funeral – Andy had been impressed but had also felt uneasy. She was nothing like Helen, except a little in looks – same nose, same big hands. Keen that she should see him as more than the usual run of small-town fatheads and mug lairs she had known before she left, but unpractised, he was soon out of his depth. They'd gotten drunk together – she was quite a drinker – and he was the one, being unused to spirits, who had ended up fuzzy-headed.

She sat with her legs crossed and smoked non-stop. Her legs were rather plump, but the shoes she wore, which had thin straps across the instep, were very fashionable-looking. Expensive, Andy thought. Though in no way glamorous, she was a woman who took trouble with herself.

The impression he'd got was that she moved in a pretty fast crowd down there, and some of what he caught on to of what Balmain was, and the people she knew – poets and that – and the fact that she lived now with one poet, and had been the girlfriend earlier of another, excited him. He had had very little of that sort of excitement in his own life.

He'd been a football player, good but not good enough. At

sixteen he'd gone down the mine. Married at twenty. That there
was another life somewhere he had picked up from the magazines he saw and the talk, some of it rough, of fellows who got
down to the city pretty regularly and had much to tell. In
Debbie, he had, for an hour or so, felt the breath of something
he had missed out on. Something extra, something more. Now
she was dead.

At thirty-six, some woman's problem. An abortion he guessed,
though Helen had done no more than raise a suspicion and
the old man of course knew nothing at all. So far as Harry
knew, all Debbie had been was a high-school science teacher.

It hadn't struck Andy till now, but everything he'd heard of
Debbie's doings had come from Helen and he wondered how
much more she knew than she let on. Out of loyalty to Debbie
no doubt – but also, he thought, to protect him from a side of
herself that might be less surprised by Debbie's way of life, and
less disapproving of it, than she pretended.

He felt, vaguely, that here too he had missed out. There
was something more he hungered for, and occasionally pushed
towards, that Helen would not admit. Because for all the twelve
years they had passed in the closest intimacy, she did not want
him to see in her the sort of woman who might recognise
or allow it.

THE drive down was uneventful. Harry was silent, but that
wasn't unusual. They were often silent together.

All this, Andy thought, must be hard on him. He'd never
asked himself how Harry felt about Debbie's being away. Proud
of her, certainly, as the only one of them who had got enough
of an education to make a new life for herself. Sad to see so
little of her. Worried on occasion. Now this.

Andy followed these thoughts on Harry's behalf – he was fond of Harry – then followed his own.

Which sprang from the lightness he felt at having a day off like this in the middle of the week. The sunlight. The high white clouds set above open country. The freedom of being behind the wheel. The freedom too – he felt guilty to be thinking this way – of being off the hook, away from home and its constrictions. And along with all that, the exhilaration, the allure, of a faster and more crowded world 'down there' that he would finally get to see and feel the proximity of.

He was surprised at himself. Here he was, a grown man, twelve years married, two kids, seated side by side with his father-in-law, both of them in suits on the way to a funeral, and he might have been seventeen, a kid again, he was so full of expectation at what the day might offer. In some secret place where the life in him was most immediately physical, he still clung to a vision of himself that for a time back there had seemed golden and inextinguishable. He thought he had dealt with it, outgrown it, let it go, and without too much disappointment replaced its bouts of extravagant yearning with the reality of small prospects, work, the life he and Helen had made together. And now this.

He was surprised, ashamed even. What would Harry think? But not enough, it seemed, to subdue the flutter he had felt in his belly the moment the idea of the trip came up, or the heat his body was giving off inside the suit.

THEY arrived early. To kill the time they drove out to Bondi and sat in the car eating egg hamburgers in greasy paper and watching the surf.

Boardriders miraculously rose up and for long moments kept

their balance on running sunlight, then went down in a flurry of foam.

Mothers, their skirts round their thighs, tempted little kiddies too far past the waterline for them to run back when the sea, in a rush, came sparkling round their feet. Surprised beyond tears, they considered a moment, then squealed with delight.

Andy thought of his girls. He should bring them down here, show them the ocean. They hadn't seen it yet. He had only seen it one other time himself.

On their rugby trip they had come down here in the dark, half a dozen of them, seriously pissed, and had chased about naked on the soft sand after midnight, skylarking, taking flying tackles at each other, wrestling, kicking up light in gritty showers, then stood awestruck down at the edge, watching a huge surf rise up like a wall, and roar and crash against the stars.

He glanced sideways now to see what Harry was making of it, this immense wonder that at every moment surrounded them.

'That's South America out there,' Harry informed him. 'Peru.'

As if, by narrowing your eyes and getting the focus right, you might actually see it.

Andy narrowed his eyes. What his quickened senses caught out there was the outstretched figure of a long-bodied woman under a sheet, thin as a veil, slowly turning in her sleep.

THE funeral was a quiet affair, with everyone more respectable-looking than Andy had expected, though the fellow who gave the service, which wasn't really a service – no prayers or hymns – was jollier than is normal on such occasions. He talked of Debbie's life and how full it had been. How full of life *she* had

been, and how they all liked her and what a good time they'd
had together.

He did not refer to the fact that she was actually here, screwed
down now inside the coffin they'd carried in.

Andy himself was acutely aware of that. It made him uncomfortably hot. He pushed a finger into his collar and eased it a
bit, but felt the blood swelling in the veins of his neck.

It was the bulk of his own body he felt crammed into a
coffin. How close the lid would be over his head. And how
dark it must be in there when the chapel all around was so
full of sunlight and the pleasantness of women in short-sleeved
frocks, and a humming from the garden walks outside, of bees.
The big-boned woman he'd spent a night drinking vodka with
seemed very close: the heaviness of her crossed legs in the
expensive-looking shoes, and her determination, which he had
missed at the time but saw clearly now, to outdrink him. He
wondered what shoes she was wearing in there. Then wondered,
again, what Harry was thinking.

Harry looked very dignified in his suit and tie. Andy had
last seen him in it at Dorothy's funeral, a very different affair
from this. It was hard to tell from the straightness of him, and
the line of his jaw, what he might be feeling. Andy looked more
than once and could not tell.

It's his daughter, he thought. He's the father. Someone ought
to have mentioned that.

But there was no talk of Debbie's family at all. Didn't they
have families, these people? Or was it that they thought of
themselves as a family? He couldn't work it out, their ties to
one another – wives and husbands, mothers and fathers.

Still, it went well. People listened quietly. One or two of the
women cried. People laughed, a bit too heartily he thought, at
the speaker's jokes. They were private jokes that Andy did not

catch, and he wondered what Harry thought of *that*. A couple of poems were read, by an older fellow with a ponytail who seemed to be drunk and swallowed all his words. When the curtains parted and the coffin tilted and began to slide away, there was music.

At least that part was like a funeral. Except that the music was another fellow singing to a guitar: Dylan's 'Sad-eyed Lady of the Lowlands'. Andy cast a glance at Harry and laid his hand for a moment on the soft pad of his father-in-law's shoulder, but Harry gave no sign.

THEY drove for nearly half an hour to the wake, through heavy traffic, the city dim with smoke but the various bits of water they crossed or saw in the distance – the Harbour – brightly glinting. They stopped at a phone box and he called Helen, who was full of questions he found it hard to answer. He had really called – the idea occurred to him towards the end of the service – so that Harry could speak to her.

When Harry took the phone he walked away from the box and stood on the pavement in the sun, and only once looked back to see how things were going.

It was hot in the sun. Too hot for a suit. He was sweating under the arms and in the small of his back. Most of the passers-by wore jeans and T-shirts. It was a run-down neighbourhood of old factory buildings, with a view of wharves stacked with containers, and on the dirty waters of the bay a busy move-ment of ships.

He took his jacket off, hooking his finger into the collar and letting it trail over his shoulder.

He felt easier back in his own loose body, though he continued to sweat. He rolled his shirtsleeves, but only halfway.

At last Harry appeared. He pursed his lips and nodded, which Andy took as an indication that the talk with Helen had gone well. Well, that was something. When they got back into the car he remained silent, but his silence, Andy thought, was of a different kind. More relaxed. Something had broken.

When they got to the house and found a parking place, Harry, who had not removed his jacket, stood waiting for Andy to resume his. Which he did, out of respect. For Harry. For the fact that Harry thought it was the right thing to do.

The front door of the house was open and a crush of people, all with drinks in hand, spilled out on to the narrow veranda that ran right across the one-storeyed cottage and down on to the footpath. They pushed through, conspicuous, Andy thought, in their suits. People looked and raised an eyebrow. Maybe they think we're cops, Andy thought. It made him smile.

The hallway, which ran right through to the back door, was crowded. It was noisy in the small rooms with their tongue-and-groove walls, so noisy you could barely hear yourself speak. Music. Voices.

'Debbie's brother-in-law,' he shouted to a fellow who gave him a beer, and offered the man his hand. The man took it but looked surprised.

'Debbie's father,' he explained when, with just a glance, the fellow looked to where Harry was standing, towering in fact, in his pinstriped double-breasted suit, against the wall.

The fellow was fifty or so, in a black skivvy, and bearded, with a chain and a big clanking medal round his neck.

'Well, cheers,' he said, looking uncertain.

'Cheers,' Andy replied, raising the can.

He took a good long swig of the beer, which was very cold and immediately did something to restore him – his confidence, his interest. He looked around, still feeling that he stuck out here like a sore thumb; so did Harry. But that was to be expected.

This was *it*. Elsewhere. He was in the middle of it.

But he wished Harry would relax a bit. Trouble was, he didn't know what to do or say that would help. He had to tell himself again that Harry was a man standing in the hallway of a house full of people shouting at one another over a continuous din of party music, at his daughter's wake. He felt protective of Harry, most of all of Harry's feelings, but he also wanted to range out. All this represented a set of possibilities that might not come his way again. His own impatience, the itch he felt to move away, be on his own, see for himself what was going on here, seemed like a betrayal.

'Listen,' he said to a woman who was pushing past with two cans of beer in her hand and a fag hanging from the corner of her mouth. 'Where can I get a drink for my mate?' He jerked his head in Harry's direction. 'He's Debbie's father,' he told her, lowering his voice.

The woman looked. 'Agh!' she said. 'Here, take one a' these.' Then, with lowered voice and a stricken glance in Harry's direction, 'I didn't know that was Debbie's father.'

'It is,' he told her. 'I'm her brother-in-law.'

He took the beer, thanked her, then carried it over to Harry. They stood together, side by side in the hallway, and drank.

'Thanks, mate,' Harry told him.

ANDY stood, taking in the changing scene. People pushing past to the front door and the veranda. Pausing to greet others. Joking, laughing. More guests kept arriving, some with crates of beer. He still hadn't said more than a word or two to anyone else, but felt a rising excitement. He would move out and get into it in a minute. He was very willing to be sociable. It was just a matter, among these people, of how to make a start.

He was curious, considering the mixture, about who they were, how they were related to Debbie and came to be here, and increasingly confident, looking around, of what he himself might have to offer. He caught that from the eye of some of the girls – the women – who went by. Things were developing.

He had another beer, then another, lost track of Harry, got involved with one group, then a second – but only at the edge. Just listening.

He drifted out to the kitchen, where people were seated around a scrubbed-pine table stacked with empties and strewn with scraps. Others leaned against the fridge and the old-fashioned porcelain sink. He leaned too.

No one paid any attention to him, though they weren't hostile. They just went on arguing.

Politics. Though it wasn't really an argument either, since they all agreed.

He stepped past them to a little back porch with three steps down to a sloping yard, grassy, the edges of it, near the fence, thick with sword fern in healthy clumps. It was getting dark.

There was a big camphor laurel tree, huge really, and a Hill's Hoist turning slowly in the breeze that he felt, just faintly, on his brow, and clothes pegged out to dry that no one had bothered to bring in. They were hung out just anyhow. Not the way a woman would do it.

He watched them for a while: the shirts white in the growing darkness, filling with air a moment, then collapsing; the tree, also stirring, filling with air and all its crowded gathering of leaves responding, shivering. He too felt something. Something familiar and near.

He thought of Helen. Of the girls. He did not want the feeling of sadness that came to him, which had been there all day, he felt, under the throb of expectation, and which declared itself now in the way these clothes had been hung out, the tea towels all crooked, the shirts pegged awkwardly at the shoulder so that the sleeves hung empty and slack.

Back in the hallway he got talking to a very young woman in a miniskirt, hot pink, with a tight-fitting hot-pink top and a glossy bag over her shoulder, and glossy cork-heeled sandals, her toenails painted the same hot pink as her lips and clothes. He hadn't seen her at the funeral. She had just arrived. He introduced himself. 'I'm Debbie's brother-in-law,' he told her, but without making it sound, he hoped, like a claim.

The girl took a sip from her glass and looked up at him, all eyelashes. 'Who's Debbie?' she asked, genuinely stumped.

He opened his mouth but felt it would be foolish to explain. Still, he was shocked.

A little later he found himself engaged with another woman, older and very drunk, who in just minutes began pushing herself against him. He was a bit drunk himself at this stage. Not very drunk, but enough to go where his senses took him. He stood with his back against a wall of the crowded hallway and the woman pushed her knee between his thighs in the thick woollen suit and her tongue into his mouth. Her fingers were in his hair. He was sweating.

She undid a button on his shirt, put her nose in. 'Ummm,' she murmured, '*au naturel*, I like it. Where have they been keeping *you*?' When they broke briefly to catch their breath he glanced around in case Harry was close by.

All this now was what he had expected or hoped for, but he was surprised how little of the initiative was his. Somewhere in the back of his head, as the woman urged her tongue into it and her hand went exploring below, he was repeating to himself: 'I'm Debbie's brother-in-law. She's dead, this is her wake.' Since he had arrived in this house he was the only one, so far as he knew, who'd volunteered her name.

Things were going fast down in his pants, the woman luxuriously leading. He liked it that for once someone else was making the moves. A small noise struggled in his throat. No one around seemed to care, or even to have noticed. He wondered how far all this was to go, and saw that he could simply go with it. He was pleased, in a quiet, self-congratulatory way, that this was how he was taking it.

The woman drew her head back, looked at him quizzically, and smiled. 'Umm,' she said, 'nice. I'll be back.' Then, fixing her hair with a deft hand, she disengaged; gently, as he thought of it, set him down. He was left red-faced and bothered, fiercely sweating.

He dealt with his own hair, a few flat-handed slaps, discreetly adjusted things below. He felt like a kid. What was he supposed to do now? Wait for her to come back? Follow? He leaned against the wall and stared at the plaster ceiling. His head was reeling. He decided to stumble after her, but she was gone in the crowd and instead he found Harry, squatting on a low three-legged stool that was too small for him, his thumb in a book.

'Harry?'

Harry glanced up over the big horn-rimmed glasses he used for reading. He looked like a professor, Andy thought with amusement, but could not fathom his expression. Harry handed him the book.

It was a poetry book. There were more, exactly like the one he was holding, on the shelf at Harry's elbow, with the gap between them where he had pulled this one out. Andy shifted his shoulders, rubbed the end of his nose, consulted Harry. Who nodded.

Andy rubbed his nose again and opened the book, turning one page, then the next. *To Debbie*, he read on a page all to itself. All through, he could see, her name was scattered. Debbie. Sometimes Deb.

He was puzzled. Impressed. The book looked substantial but he had no way of judging how important or serious such a thing might be, or whether Harry, in showing it to him, had meant him to see in it a justification or an affront. It was about things that were private, that's what he saw. But here they were in a book that just anyone could pick up.

He turned more pages, mostly so as not to face Harry. Odd words jumped out at him. 'Witchery' was one – he hoped Harry hadn't seen that one. In another place, 'cunt'. Right there on the page. So unexpected it made his stomach jump. In a book of poetry! He didn't understand that. Or any of this. He snapped the book shut, and moved to restore it to the shelf, but Harry reached out and took it from him.

Andy frowned, uncertain where Harry's mind was moving. Using both hands, Harry eased himself upright, slipped his glasses into one pocket of his jacket, forced the book into another, and turned down the hallway towards the front door.

Andy followed.

So it was over, they were leaving. It struck Andy that he had never discovered whose house this was.

'You need to say goodbye to anyone?' he asked Harry.

'Never bloody met anyone,' Harry told him.

Outside it was night-time, blue and cool. Some people on the steps got up to let them through. One of them said, 'Oh, you're leaving,' and another, 'Goodbye,' – strangers, incurious about who they might be but with that much in them of politeness or affability.

They found the car, and Andy took his jacket off and tossed it into the back seat. Harry retained his.

They drove across bridges, through night traffic now. Past water riddled with red and green neon, and high tower blocks where all the fluorescent panels in the ceilings of empty offices were brightly pulsing.

After a bit, Harry asked out of nowhere, 'What's a muse? Do you know what it means? A muse?'

'Amuse?' Andy asked in turn. 'Like when you're amused?' He didn't get it.

'No. A – muse. M–U–S–E.'

Andy shook his head.

'Don't worry,' Harry told him. 'I'll ask Macca. He'll know.'

Andy felt slighted, but Harry was right, Macca would know. Macca was a workmate of theirs, a reader. If anyone knew, Macca would. But the book in Harry's pocket was a worry to Andy. He hoped Macca wouldn't uncover *too* much of what was in it. He'd seen enough, himself, to be disturbed by how much that was personal, and which you might want to keep that way, was set down bold as brass for any Tom, Dick or Harry – ah, Harry – to butt in on. He didn't understand that, and doubted Harry would either.

Suddenly Harry spoke again.

'She was such a bright little thing,' he said. 'You wouldn't credit.'

Andy swallowed. This was *it*. A single bald statement breaking surface out of the stream of thought Harry was adrift in – which was all, Andy thought, he might ever hear. He kept his eyes dead ahead.

What Harry was thinking of, he knew, was how far that bright little thing he had been so fond of, all that time ago, had moved away from him, how far he had lost track of her.

He had his own bright little girl, Janine. She was ten. He felt sweetly bound to her – painfully bound, he felt now, in the prospect of inevitable loss. She too would go off, go elsewhere.

At the time Harry was recalling, Andy thought, he would have been a young man, the same age I am now. He had never thought of Harry as young. There was a lot he had not thought of.

He glanced at Harry. Nothing more would be said. Those last few words had risen up out of a swell of feeling, unbearable perhaps, that Harry was still caught up in, but when Andy looked again – the look could only be brief – he got no clue.

A wave of sadness struck him. Not only for Harry's isolation but for his own. He was fond of Harry, but they might as well have been on different planets.

'Have a bit of a nap if you like,' he told Harry gently. 'You must be buggered. I'll be right.' What he meant, though Harry would not take it that way, was that he wanted to be alone.

In just minutes Harry had sunk down in the seat, letting the seat belt take his weight, and had followed his thoughts deeper, then deeper again, into sleep. Andy focused on the road ahead, his hands resting lightly on the wheel. Free now to follow his own thoughts. Not thinking exactly. Letting the thoughts rise up and flow into him. Flow through him.

Something had come to him back there and changed things. When? he wondered. In the noisy hallway? Where in a world that was so far outside his experience, and among people whose lives were so different from his own, he'd given himself over to what might come? No, he'd been fooling himself, and he blushed now, though no one but himself would ever know about it. Earlier than that.

His body, which knew better than his slow mind, set him back in the bluish dusk of that back porch.

For a moment there he had been out of things, looking down from high up into a quiet backyard. A camphor laurel tree, its swarming leaves lifted by a quickening of the air. The same breeze touching shirts pegged awkwardly on a line, filling them with breath. Then like fingers in his hair. It was something in those particular objects that had struck him. Something he felt, almost grasped, that was near and familiar.

Or it was a way of looking at things that was in himself. That *was* himself. A lonely thought, this – the beginning, perhaps, of another kind of loss, though his own healthy resilience told him it need not be.

He drove. The road was straight now, a double highway running fast through blue night scrub. Under banks of smoky cloud a rounded moon bounced along treetops. He put on speed and felt released. Not from his body – he was more aware than ever of that, of its blockiness and persistence – but from the earth's pull upon it. As if, seated here in this metal capsule, knees flexed, spine propped against tilted leather, it was the far high universe they were sailing through, and those lights off to the side of the ribboning highway – small townships settled down to the night's TV, roadside service stations all lit up in the dark, with their aisles of chocolate biscuits and potato crisps – were far-flung constellations, and Harry, afloat now in the vast realm of sleep, and he, in a lapse of consciousness of a different kind, had taken off, and weightless as in space or in flying dreams, were flying.

Mrs Porter and the Rock

Mrs Porter and the Rock

—

THE Rock is Ayers Rock, Uluru. Mrs Porter's son, Donald, has brought her out to look at it. They are at breakfast, on the second day of a three-day tour, in the Desert Rose Room of the Yullara Sheraton. Mrs Porter, sucking voluptuously, is on her third cigarette, while Donald, a born letter writer who will happily spend half an hour shaping and reshaping a description in his head, or putting a dazzling sheen on an ironical observation, is engaged on one of the airy rockets, all fizz and sparkle and recondite allusions, that he can barely wait, once he is out of town, to launch in the direction of his more discerning friends. In a large, loose, schoolboyish hand, on the Sheraton's rich notepaper, he writes:

To complete the scene, only the sacred river is missing, for this resort is surely inspired by the great tent city of Kubla Khan. Nestling among spinifex dunes, it rises, like a late vision of the impossible East, out of the rust-red sands, a postmodern Bedouin encampment, all pink and apricot turrets and slender aluminium poles that hum and twang as they prick the skyline. Over the walkways and public spaces hover huge, shadow-making sails that are meant to evoke, in those of us for whom deserts create a sense of spiritual unease, the ocean we left two thousand miles back.

So there you have it. The pitched tents of the modern nomads. That tribe of the internationally restless who have come on here from the Holy Land, or from Taos or Porto Cervo or Nepal, to stare for a bit on an imaginable wonder – when, that is, they can lift their eyes from the spa pool, or in pauses between the Tasmanian Salmon and the Crème Brûlée . . .

Mrs Porter is here on sufferance, accepting, with minimal grace, what Donald had intended as a treat. Frankly she'd rather be at Jupiter's playing the pokies. She takes a good drag on her cigarette, looks up from the plate – as yet untouched – of scrambled egg, baked beans and golden croquettes, and is astonished to find herself confronting, high up on the translucent canopy of the dining-room ceiling, a pair of colossal feet. The fat soles are sloshing about up there in ripples of light. Unnaturally magnified, and with the glare beyond them, diffuse, almost blinding, of the Central Australian sun. She gives a small cry and ducks. And Donald, who keeps a keen eye on her and is responsive to all her jerks and twitches, observing the movement but not for the moment its cause, demands, 'What? What's the matter? What is it?'

Mrs Porter shakes her head. He frowns, subjects her to worried scrutiny – one of his what's-she-up-to-now looks. She keeps her head down. After a moment, with another wary glance in her direction, he goes back to his letter.

Mrs Porter throws a swift glance upward.

Mmm, the feet are still there. Beyond them, distorted by fans of watery light, is the outline of a body, almost transparent – shoulders, a gigantic trunk. Black. This one is black. An enormous *black* man is up there wielding a length of hose, and the water is red. The big feet are bleeding. Well, that's a new one.

Mrs Porter nibbles at her toast. She needs to think about this. Between bites she takes long, sweet drags on her cigarette. If she ignores this latest apparition, she thinks, maybe it will go away.

Lately – well, for quite a while now – she's been getting these visitations – apparitions is how she thinks of them, though they appear at such odd times, and in such unexpected guises, that she wonders if they aren't in fact *re*visitations that she herself has called up out of bits and pieces of her past, her now scattered and inconsiderate memory.

In the beginning she thought they might be messengers – well, to put it more plainly, angels. But their only message seemed to be one she already knew: that the world she found herself in these days was a stranger place than she'd bargained for, and getting stranger.

She had wondered as well – but this was only at the start – if they might be tormentors, visitors from places she'd never been, like Antarctica, bringing with them a breath of icebergs. But that, she'd decided pretty smartly, was foolish. Dulcie, she told herself, you're being a fool! She wasn't the sort of person that anyone out there would want to torment. All *her* apparitions did was make themselves visible, hang around for a bit, disturbing the afternoon or whatever with a sudden chill, and drift off.

Ghosts might have been a more common word for them – she believes in ghosts. But if that's what they are, they're the ghosts of people she's never met. And surely, if they were ghosts, her husband Leonard would be one of them.

Unless he has decided for some reason to give her a miss.

She finds this possibility distressing. She doesn't particularly want to see Leonard, but the thought that he could appear to her if he wanted and has chosen not to puts a clamp on her heart, makes her go damp and miserable.

All this is a puzzle and she would like to ask someone about it, get a few answers, but is afraid of what she might hear. In the meantime she turns her attention to Donald. Let the feet go their own way. Let them just go!

Donald looks sweet when he is writing. He sits with one shoulder dipped and his arm circling the page, forever worried, like a child, that someone might be looking over his shoulder and trying to copy. His tongue is at the corner of his mouth. Like a sweet-natured forty-three-year-old, very earnest and absorbed, practising pot-hooks.

Poor Donald, she thinks. He has spent his whole life waiting for her to become a mother of another sort. The sort who'll take an interest. Well, she *is* interested. She's interested, right now, in those feet! But what Donald means is interested in what interests him, and she can't for the life of her see what all this stuff *is* that he gets so excited about, and Donald, for all his cleverness, can't tell her. When she asks, he gets angry. The questions she comes up with are just the ones, it seems, that Donald cannot answer. They're too simple. He loses his cool – that's what people say these days – but all that does is make him feel bad, and the next moment he is coming after her with hugs, and little offerings out of the *Herald* that she could perfectly well read for herself, or out of books! Because she's made him feel guilty.

This capacity she appears to possess for making grown men feel guilty – she had the same effect on Donald's father – surprises her. Guilt is not one of the things she herself suffers from.

Duty. Responsibility. Guilt. Leonard was very strong on all three. So is Donald. He is very like his father in all sorts of ways, though not physically — Leonard was a very *thin* man.

Leonard too would have liked her to take an interest. Only Leonard was kinder, more understanding — she had almost said forgiving. It wasn't her fault that she'd left school at thirteen — loads of girls did in those days, and clever men married them just the same. Leonard was careful always not to let her see that in this way she had failed him; that in the part of his nature that looked out into the world and was baffled, or which brought him moments of almost boyish elation, she could not join him, he was alone.

She was sorry for that, but she didn't feel guilty. People are what they are. Leonard knew that as well as she did.

Donald's generation, she has decided, are less willing to make allowances. Less indulgent. Or maybe that is just Donald. Even as a tiny tot he was always imposing what he felt on others. His need to 'share', as he calls it, does have its nice side, she knows that. But it is very consuming. 'Look at this, Mum,' he would shout, his whole tiny body in a fury. 'You're not *looking*! *Look!*'

In those days it would be a caterpillar, some nasty black thing. An armoured black dragon that she thought of as Japanese-looking and found particularly repulsive. Or a picture of an air battle, all dotted lines that were supposed to be machine-gun bullets, and jagged flame. Later it was books — Proust. She'd had a whole year of that one, that *Proust*. Now it was this Rock.

High maintenance, that's what they called it these days. She got that from her neighbour, Tess Hyland. Donald was high maintenance.

'What's up?' he asks now, seeing her dip her shoulder again and flinch. 'What's the matter?'

'Nothing's the matter,' she snaps back. 'What's the matter yourself?'

She has discovered that the best way of dealing with Donald's questions is to return them. Backhand. As a girl she was quite a decent tennis player.

She continues to crouch. There is plenty of space up there under the cantilevered ceiling, no shortage of space; but the fact that twenty feet over your head the splayed toes of some giant black acrobat are sloshing about in blood is not an easy thing to ignore, especially at breakfast. She is reminded of the roofs of some of the cathedrals they'd seen – with Leonard it was cathedrals. They visited seven of them once, seven in a row. But over there the angels existed mostly from the waist up. You were supposed to ignore what existed below. They hung out over the damp aisles blowing trumpets or shaking tambourines. Here, it seems, you did get the lower parts and they were armed with hosepipes. Well, that was logical enough. They were in the southern hemisphere.

Donald is eyeing her again, though he is pretending not to. They are all at it these days – Donald, Douglas, Shirley. She has become an object of interest. She knows why. They're on the lookout for some sign that she is losing her marbles.

'Why aren't you eating your breakfast?' Donald demands.

'I am,' she tells him.

As if in retaliation for all those years when she forced one thing or another into their reluctant mouths – gooey eggs, strips of limp bread and butter, mashed banana, cod-liver oil – they have begun, this last year, to torment her with her unwillingness to do more than pick about at her food. When Donald says, 'Come on now, just one more mouthful,' he is reproducing, whether he knows it or not, exactly the coax and whine of her own voice from forty years ago, and so accurately that, with a sickening rush, as if she had missed a step and fallen through four decades, she finds herself back in the dingy, cockroach-infested maisonette at West End that was all Leonard was able to find for them in the Shortage after the war. The linoleum! Except in the corners and under the immoveable sideboard, roses worn to a dishwater brown. A gas heater in the bathroom that when she shut her eyes and put a match to it went off like a bunger and threatened to blast her eyebrows off. Donald in his high chair chucking crusts all over the floor, and Douglas hauling himself up to the open piano, preparing to thump. To get away from that vision she's willing even to face the feet.

She glances upward – ah, they're gone! – then away to where an oversized ranger in a khaki uniform and wide-brimmed Akubra is examining the leaves of a rainforest shrub that goes all the way to the ceiling. For all the world as if he was out in the open somewhere and had just climbed out of a ute or off a horse.

'You shouldn't have taken all that,' Donald is saying – she knows this one too – 'if all you're going to do is let it sit on your plate.'

Dear me, she thinks, is he going to go through the whole routine? The poor little children in England? What a pain I must have been!

In fact, she doesn't intend to eat any of this stuff. Breakfast is just an excuse, so far as she is concerned, for a cigarette.

But the buffet table here is a feature. Donald leads her to it each morning as if it was an altar. Leonard too had a weakness for altars.

This one is garishly and unseasonably festive.

A big blue Japanese pumpkin is surrounded by several smaller ones, bright orange, with shells like fine bone china and pimpled.

There are wheatsheaves, loaves of rye and five-grain bread, spilled walnuts, almonds, a couple of hibiscus flowers. It's hard to know what is for decoration and what is to eat.

And the effect, whatever was intended, has been ruined because some joker has, without ceremony, *unceremoniously*, plonked his saddle down right in the middle of it. Its straps all scuffed at the edges, and with worn and frayed stitching, its seat discoloured with sweat, this saddle has simply been plonked down and left among the cereal jars, the plates of cheese, sliced ham and smoked salmon, the bowls of stewed prunes, tinned apricots, orange quarters, crystallised pears . . .

But food is of no interest to her. She has helped herself so generously to the hot buffet not because she is hungry and intends to eat any of this stuff but so she'll have something to look at. Something other than *it*.

It is everywhere. The whole place has been designed so that whichever way you turn, it's there, displaying itself on the horizon. Sitting out there like a great slab of purple-brown liver going off in the sun. No, not liver, something else, she can't think quite what.

And then she can. Suddenly she can. That's why she has been so unwilling to look at it!

She is seven, maybe eight years old. Along with her friends of that time, Isobel and Betty Olds, she is squatting on her heels on the beach at Etty Bay in front of their discovery, a hump-backed sea creature bigger than any fish they have ever seen, which has been washed up on this familiar bit of beach and is lying stranded on the silvery wet sand. Its one visible eye, as yet unclouded, which is blue like a far-off moon, is open to the sky. It is alive and breathing. You can see the opening and closing of its gills.

The sea often tosses up flotsam of one kind or another. Big

green-glass balls netted with rope. Toadfish that when you roll them with a big toe puff up and puff up till you think they'd burst. But nothing as big and sad-looking as this. You can imagine putting your arms around it like a person. Like a person that has maybe been *turned* into a fish by a witch's curse and is unable to tell you that once, not so long ago, it was a princess. It breathes and is silent. Cut off in a silence that makes you aware suddenly of your own breathing, while the gulls rise shrieking overhead.

They have the beach to themselves. They sit there watching while the tide goes out. No longer swirling and trying to catch your feet, it goes far out, leaving the sand polished like a mirror to a silvery gleam in which the light comes and goes in flashes and the colours of the late-afternoon sky are gaudily reflected.

And slowly, as they watch, the creature begins to change – the blue-black back, the golden belly. The big fish begins to throw off colours in electric flashes. Mauve, pink, a yellowish pale green, they have never seen anything like it. Slow fireworks. As if, out of its element, in a world where it had no other means of expression, the big fish was trying to reveal to them some vision of what it was and where it had come from, a lost secret they were meant to remember and pass on. Well, maybe the others had grasped it. All she had done was gape and feel the slow wonder spread through her.

So they had squatted there, all three, and watched the big fish slowly die.

It was a fish dolphin, a dorado, and it had been dying. That's what she knew now. The show had been its last. That's why she didn't want to look at this Rock. Just as she wouldn't want to look at the fish dolphin either if it was lying out there now. No matter what sort of performance it put on.

She finds herself fidgeting. She stubs out the last of her cigarette, takes up a fork.

'*My mother*,' Donald writes to his friend Sherman, offering yet another glimpse of a character who never fails to amuse, '*has for some reason taken against the scenery. Can you imagine? In fact it's what she's been doing all her life. If she can't accommodate a thing, it isn't there. Grand as it is, not even Ayers Rock stands a chance against her magnificent indifference. She simply chain-smokes and looks the other way. I begin to get an idea, after all these years, of how poor old Leonard must have felt.*

'*The hotel, on the other hand, has her completely absorbed. She devotes whole mealtimes to the perusal of the menu.*

'*Not that she deigns to taste more than a bite or two. But she does like to know what is there for the choosing.*'

He pauses and looks up, feeling a twinge at having yet again offered her up as a figure of fun, this woman who has never ceased to puzzle and thwart him but who still commands the largest part of his heart. He knows this is odd. He covers himself by making her appear to his friends as a burden he has taken on that cannot, in all honour, be thrown off; an endless source, in the meantime, of amusing stories and flat-footed comments and attitudes.

'What would Dulcie think of it?' his friends Sherman and Jack Anderson say, and try, amid shouts of laughter, to reproduce one of her dead ordinary ways of looking at things, without ever quite catching her tone.

She eludes them – 'One for you, Dulcie,' Donald tells himself – as she has for so long eluded him.

He watches her now, fork in hand, pushing baked beans about, piling them into modest heaps, then rearranging them in steep hills and ridges, then using the prongs of the fork to redistribute them in lines and circles, and finds himself thinking of the view from the plane window as they flew in from Alice: a panorama of scorched, reddish rock that must have been created, he thinks, in a spirit of wilfulness very like his mother's as she goes now at the beans.

He smiles. The idea amuses him. His mother as demiurge.

He continues to watch, allowing the image to undergo in his head the quiet miracle of transformation, then once more begins to write.

MRS Porter sits in the tourist bus and smokes. Smoking isn't allowed of course, but there is nobody about. She has the bus to herself. She has no qualms about the breaking of rules.

The bus is parked in the shade but is not cool. Heated air pours in at the open window, bearing flies. She is using the smoke to keep them off. Outside, the earth bakes.

To her left, country that is flat. Orange-red with clumps of grey-green spiky bushes. *It*, the Rock, is a little way off to her right. She does not look.

People, among them Donald, are hauling themselves up it in relays; dark lines of them against the Rock's glowing red. Occasionally there is a flash as the sun bounces off a watch or a belt buckle, or a camera round someone's neck. Madness, she thinks. Why would anyone want to do it? But she knows the answer to that one. Because it's *there*.

Except that for most of the time, it hadn't been – not in her book. And what's more, she hadn't missed it, so there! When they drew maps at school they hadn't even bothered to put it in! She had got through life – dawdling her way past picket fences, barefoot, in a faded frock, pulling cosmos or daisies through the gaps to make bouquets, parsing sentences, getting her teeth drilled, going back and forth to the dairy on Saturday mornings for jugs of cream – with no awareness whatsoever that this great lump of a thing was sitting out here in the middle of nowhere and was considered sacred.

She resents the suggestion, transmitted to her via Donald, that she had been missing out on something, some other – dimension. How many dimensions are there? And how many could a body actually cope with and still get the washing on the line and tea on the table?

That's the trouble with young people. They think everything outside their own lives is lacking in something. Some dimension. How would they know, unless they were mind-readers or you told them (and then you'd have to find the words, and they'd have to *listen*), what it felt like – that little honey-sack at the end of a plumbago when it suddenly burst on your tongue, or the roughness of Dezzy McGee's big toe when he rubbed it once on her belly while she was sunbaking at the Townsville Baths. 'Waddabout a root, Dulce?' That's what he had whispered.

She laughs, then looks about to see if anyone has heard, then laughs again. Eleven she was, and Dezzy must have been twelve. Blond and buck-toothed, the baker's boy.

All that seems closer now than this Rock ever was. Closer than last week.

Plus a butcher-bird her uncle Clary owned that was called Tom Leach after a mate he'd lost in France. Which was where – a good deal later of course – she lost Leonard. It could whistle like a champ. And a little stage set, no bigger than a cigar box, that belonged to Beverley Buss's mother, that consisted of a single room with walls that were all mirrors, and little gold tables and chairs, and a boy in silk breeches presenting to a girl in a hooped skirt a perfect silver rose. It played a tune, but the mechanism was broken so she never got to hear it. She had pushed her face so close once, to the tiny open door, that her hot breath fogged up all the mirrors, and Beverley Buss had said, 'Look, Dulce, you've made a different weather.'

Cancer. Beverley Buss, she'd heard, had died of cancer. Beverley McGowan by then.

She had loved that little theatre, and would, if she could, have willed herself small enough to squeeze right in through the narrow doorway and join that boy and girl in their charmed life that was so different from her own barefooted one – she bet *that* girl didn't have warts on her thumb or get ringworm or nits – but had managed it only once, in a dream, and was so shocked to be confronted with herself over and over again in the seven mirrors, which were only too clear on that occasion, that she burst into tears and had to pinch herself awake not to die of shame in front of such a perfect pair.

So what did this Rock have to do with any of that?

Nothing. How could it? It wasn't on the map. It wasn't even on the *list* – there was a list, and you had to find out where the names belonged and mark them in. Capes, bays, the river systems, even the ones that ran only for a month or two each year. You marked them in with a dotted line. But this Rock that everyone makes such a fuss of now wasn't on the list, let alone the map. So there!

It certainly wasn't on *her* map. Her map, in those days, was five or six cross-streets between their weatherboard, her school, the open-air pictures where coloured people sat on the other side of a latticed partition, and the Townsville Baths. Later, in Brisbane after the war, it was the streets around West End as she dragged Douglas and pushed Donald, up to the shops and then back again in the boiling sun, her route determined by the places where you could get a stroller over the kerb.

Big grasshoppers would be chugging past, and at nesting

time you had to watch out for magpies. Nothing to see on the way. A stray dog sniffing then lifting its leg in the weeds round a lamp-post. Roadmen at work round a fenced-off hole. A steamroller laying a carpet of hot tar, and that smell, burning pitch or hellfire, and the fellers in army boots and shorts at work beside it, most of them leaning on shovels or sitting on one heel with a fag hanging from their lip, waiting for the billy to boil over a pile of sticks. The tar smell thinning at last to the peppery scent that came through a paling fence. Dry stalks in a spare allotment.

Sometimes she stopped off to have morning tea with her only friend at that time, a Chinese lady called Mrs Wau Hing.

Mrs Wau Hing had a cabinet in her front room made of carved cherrywood, with shelves and brackets and appliquéd ivory flowers, chrysanthemums and little fine-winged humming-birds. It was beautiful. Though you wouldn't really know what to do with it. Mrs Wau Hing called it decorative.

Mrs Wau Hing called *her* Blossom (which was silly really, but she liked it) and gave her chicken in garlicky black sauce to take home, which Leonard said was 'different'. Too different for her, but never mind, it was the thought.

What pleased her was the fine blue-whiteness of the bowl her friend sent it home in, with its design of pinpricks filled with transparent glaze.

When she went out barefoot in her nightie to get a glass of water at the kitchen sink, there it was, rinsed and shining in the wooden rack along with her own familiar crockery.

So what did the Rock have to do with any of that? Or with the stone she had in her kidneys in 1973?

These days, mind you, it's everywhere. Including on TV. Turns up dripping with tomato sauce as a hamburger, or as a long red-clay mould that starts to heave, then cracks open, and when all the bits fall away there's a flash-looking car inside, a Ford Fairlane – stuff like that. Its red shadow turned into a dingo one night and took that baby.

Suddenly it has plonked itself down in the middle of people's lives like something that has just landed from outer space, or pushed up out of the centre of the earth, and occupies the gap that was filled once by – by what? She can't think. Movie stars? Jesus? The Royal Family? It has opened people's minds – this is Donald again – in the direction of the *incommensurable*. What a mouthful! It is exerting an *influence*. Well, not on her it isn't! She gives it a quick dismissive glance and takes another deep drag on her Winfield.

Cathedrals. With Leonard it was cathedrals. As soon as the war was over and the big liners were on the go again he started planning their trip. They made it at last in 1976.

Cathedrals. Great sooty piles at the end of crooked little streets, more often than not with something missing, like the veterans they made a space for, *mutilés*, on every bus.

Or on islands. Or high up on cliffs. Leonard's eyes went all watery just at the sight of one of them and she felt him move quietly away.

He wasn't religious in a praying way. When Leonard got down on his knees each morning it was to polish his boots – Nugget boot polish was what he believed in. The smell of it hung about in the hallway long after he had taken his brief-case and hat and run off to the tram. But with cathedrals, she'd decided, it was the gloom that got him. Which had been brewing there for centuries, and connected with some part of his nature she recognised, and felt soft towards, but had never felt free to enter. She associated it with the bald patch on top of his head, which you only saw, or *she* did, when he got down on his knees in the hallway on a sheet of newspaper, and held one boot, then the other, very lovingly to his heart, and stroked it till it shone.

She felt such a surge of tenderness for him then. For his reliability, his decency. And for that bald spot, which was the one thing she could see in him that he couldn't, a hidden weakness. That's the sort of thing that got her. But cathedrals, no thanks!

When she did manage to feel something, other than a chill in her bones that was like creeping death, was if the organ happened to be playing, or the sun, which was rare enough, was dropping colours from a stained-glass window on to the stony floor, in a play of pink and gold.

As for the proportions, as Leonard called them, well, she didn't go in for height, she decided; all *that* gave you was a crick in the neck. What she liked was distance. A good long view towards the sunset, or at a certain soft hour at home, towards an empty intersection, and if you got a glimpse of something more it would be the way the hills blurred off into blueness beyond the last of the flashing roofs. You would feel small then, in a way she found comforting.

What really put her off was when Leonard, half lying in one of the pews, with the guide laid open in his lap and his arms extended along the wooden back, rolled his eyes up, like suffering Jesus or one of their Catholic saints. Where, she wondered, had he got *that* from? As far as she knew he was a Methodist.

As they moved on from Cologne to those others – the French ones – she'd taken against the cathedrals, started to really resent them. The way you can resent a teacher (that Miss Bishop in third grade for instance) who has got a set against you and decided you're a dill, or some little miss at the bank.

She had never had to worry, as some do, about other women, but she'd felt then that Leonard was being stolen from her. The moment they pushed through the doors and the cold hit her heart, she felt the change in him. Lying awake at his side in poky rooms, she would stare up at the ceiling and have to prevent herself from reaching out to see if he was still there.

She began to feel a kind of dread. The sight of yet another of those Gothic monsters looming up out of a side street and opening its stone arms to him was more than she could face.

But when it happened it wasn't in a cathedral but in one of the hotels, and for two days afterwards she sat waiting in the room beside their ports, eating nothing, till at last Donald arrived to reclaim her and take his father home.

'It's something you should *see*,' Donald had told her, speaking of this Rock.

'Why?'

'Because you should, that's all.'

'You mean before I die,' she said, and gave a rough laugh.

It's what Leonard had said. 'I want to see Cologne Cathedral before I die.' But after Cologne he had got in another six.

'Are there any more of these things?' she asked of the Rock. 'Or is there just the one?'

Donald gave her a hard look. He wondered sometimes if she wasn't sharper than she let on.

She had come out here to please him. He was easily pleased and she knew that if she didn't he would sulk. It was a break as well from the unit, and from having to show up at Tess Hyland's every afternoon at five thirty – the Happy Hour – and listen to her complaints about the other owners and what the dogs were doing to her philodendrons.

Tess Hyland had been a convent mouse from Rockhampton when, in all the excitement after the war, she was recruited by UNRWA and went to work in the DP camps in Europe, then spent twenty-five years as a secretary at the UN in New York, where she had picked up a style that included daiquiris at five thirty in the afternoon and little bits of this and that on 'crackers'.

Five thirty, the Happy Hour. Personally it was a time she had always hated, when a good many people might think seriously of cutting their throat.

She would also miss out, just this once, on babysitting her three grandchildren, Les, Brett and Candy, on a Saturday night, and her drive in the back seat of Douglas's Toyota on Sunday afternoon.

They had given her a room out here with an en suite, and the menu, even at breakfast, was 'extensive'. It was only three nights.

THE first thing she'd done when Donald left her alone in the room was to have a good go-through of the cupboards. She didn't know what she was looking for, but people, she knew, were inclined to leave things, and if there was a dirty sock somewhere, or a suspender belt or a used tissue, she wouldn't feel the place was her own.

The drawers for a start. There were two deep ones under the table where they had put her port, and two more at the end of the long cupboard. When you opened the cupboard a light came on. There was a good six feet of hanging space in there, with a dozen or so good hangers. Real ones, not fixed to the rail so you couldn't walk off with them like the ones in France.

But all that hanging space! All those shelves and drawers! Who had they been expecting? Madame Melba? How many frocks and matinee coats and smart little suits and jackets would you have to have, how many hankies and pairs of stockings and undies, to do justice to the facilities they had provided? She had brought too little. And even that, when she opened her port and looked at it, seemed more than she would need. And why were there two beds? Both *double*.

In the fridge, when she looked, and in the bar recess above, was all you would need to put on a good-sized party: cans of VB, bottles of Carlsberg, Cascade, champagne, wicker baskets packed like a Christmas hamper with Cheezels, crisps, Picnic and Snickers bars and tins of macadamia nuts and cashews.

So what am I in for? she wondered. Who should I be expecting? And what about those double beds?

Casting another panicky glance in the direction of so many tantalising but unwelcome possibilities, she fled to the en suite and snicked the lock on the door.

The whole place gleamed, you couldn't fault them on that. Every steel bar and granite surface gave off a blinding reflection. There was a band of satiny paper across the lid of the lav. You had to break it to use the thing. Like cutting the ribbon on a bridge.

You could crack your skull in here. That's what she thought. Easily. It was so shiny and full of edges. Or fall and break a hip.

She settled on the rim of the bath and considered her predicament. Just stepping into a place like this was a *big risk*.

Suddenly she saw something.

On the floor between the gleaming white lav and the wall was a cockroach, lying on its back with its curled-up legs in the air. It could hardly be the victim of a broken hip, so must have died of something the room had been sprayed with, that was safe for humans – well, it had better be! – but fatal to cockies and such. She got down on her knees and took a good look at it.

Cockroaches, she had heard, were the oldest living creatures on earth. Survivors. Unkillable. Well, obviously you could kill individuals like this one, but not the species. They would outlast anything. Even a nuclear explosion. She sat back on her heels and considered this.

The cockie statistics were impressive, but when it came to survival you couldn't beat people, that was her view. People were amazing. They just went on and on. No matter how poor they were, how pinched and cramped their lives, how much pain they had, or bad luck, or how unjust the world was, or how many times they had been struck down. Look at Mrs Ormond with her one breast and that husband of hers who was always after the little boys. Look at those fellers in Changi and on the Railway – Dezzy McGee had been one of those. Look at that cripple you saw down at the Quay, in a wheel-chair with his head lolling and the snot running down into his mouth. Living there – sleeping and all – in a wheelchair, with no other shelter, and young fellers running in off the ferries in relays to wheel him into the Gents and put him on the lavvie and clean him up afterwards at one of the basins. Look at the derros with their yellow beards and bare, blackened feet, shifting about among the suits in Martin Place. They were all up and moving – well, not that one in the wheelchair – pushing on to the next day and the next and the one after, unkillable, in spite of the bombs and the gas chambers, needing only a mouthful of pap to live on, like those Africans on the TV, and the least bit of hope. Hanging on to it. To life and one another.

She took the cockroach very gingerly by one of its brittle legs, used the side of the bathtub to heave herself upright, went through to the bedroom, and tossed it out into a garden bed. Something out there, ants or that, would get a meal off it. Good luck to them!

But when she turned back to the room and saw the wide-open empty cupboard with its blaze of light she regretted it.

She could have thrown the cockroach in there. A dead cock-roach was all right. It wouldn't have disturbed her sleep. Not like a dirty sock.

She closed the cupboard door and squinnied through a crack to see that the light was off, then sat very quietly on one of the beds. Then, after a moment, shifted to the other.

She was saved by a light knocking at the door. Donald. Afternoon tea. But when she came back the problem was still there. All that cupboard space, the second bed.

She did what she could by distributing her belongings in as many places as possible – one shoe in one drawer, one in another, the same with her undies, her four hankies and the things from her handbag: lipstick, a little hand mirror, an emery board, half a roll of Quick-Eze, a photograph of Donald and friends from the Arts Ball in Shanghai, another of Les, Brett and Candy in school uniform. But it looked so in-adequate after a moment or two, so hopeless, that she gathered everything up again, put it back into her handbag, then repacked her port and left it to sit there, all locked and buckled, on the rack, as if only her unclaimed luggage had arrived in the room, and she as yet had acquired no respon-sibilities. Then she stretched out fully clothed on one of the beds and slept.

'WHAT now?'

Donald had lowered the novel he was reading and was watching her, over the top of his glasses, slide down, just an inch at a time, between the arms of the yielding silk-covered lounge chair. They were in one of the hotel's grand reception rooms after dinner.

'What now what?' she demanded.

'What are you doing?'

'Nothing,' she told him. 'Getting comfortable.'

Dim lighting, the lampshades glowing gold. Outside the beginnings of night, blue-luminous. The long room suspended out there in reflection so that the lounge chairs and gold-legged glass-topped tables floated above a carpet of lawn, among shrubs that might simply have sprouted through the floorboards, and they too, she and Donald and some people who were standing in a group behind them, also floating and transparent, in double exposure like ghosts.

Meanwhile, shoes off, stockinged feet extended, slumped sideways in the welcoming softness, she was getting her right hand down between the arm of the chair and the cushion, almost to the elbow now, right down in the crease there, feeling for coins, or a biro or lost earring. You could find all sorts of things in such places if you got deep enough, as she knew from cleaning at home. Not just dustballs.

Once, in a big hotel at Eaglehawk Neck in Tasmania, where she had gone to play in a bridge tournament, Tess Hyland had found a used condom. Really! They must have been doing it right there in the lounge, whoever it was, late at night, in the dark. She hoped her fingers, as they felt about now, didn't come across anything like that! But she was ready — you had to be. For *whatever*.

The tips of her fingers encountered metal. She slipped lower in the chair, settling in a lopsided position, very nearly horizontal, like a drunk, and closed her fist on one, two, three coins, more — and a pen, but only plastic.

'For heaven's sake,' Donald exploded.

Maybe she looked as if she was having an attack. She abandoned the pen. With some difficulty she wiggled her fist free and, pushing upright, smoothed her skirt and sat up, very straight now and defiant. Donald, with a puzzled look, went back to his novel but continued to throw her glances.

She snapped her handbag open, met his gaze and, very adroitly she thought, slipped the coins in. Two one-dollar pieces, a twenty cents and some fives. Not bad. She estimated there were about thirty such armchairs in the lounge, plus another half-dozen three-seaters. Up to a hundred dollars that would make, lurking about as buried treasure in the near vicinity. Quite a haul if you got in before the staff.

She wondered if she could risk moving to the third of the armchairs round their table, but decided she'd better not. Donald was already on the watch.

What pleased her, amid all these ghostly reflections, was that the coins down there in their hidden places, like the ones she had just slipped into her purse, maybe because they had slipped deep down and smuggled themselves out of sight, had retained their lovely solidity and weight. That was a good trick.

What she had to do was work out how *she* might manage it.

MID-MORNING. They were out under the sails beside the pool. Donald was writing again. She wondered sometimes what on earth he found to say. She had been with him all the time they were here. Nothing had *happened*.

On the wide lawn bodies were sunbaking, laid out on folding chairs, white plastic, that could also become beds, their oiled limbs sleek in the sun.

Three Japanese boys who looked like twelve-year-olds, and not at all the sort who would rape nuns, were larking about at the deep end, throwing one another over and over again into the pool. They were doctors, down here, Donald had discovered, to celebrate their graduation.

Four women in bikinis that showed their belly buttons and yellow-tanned bellies – women as old as herself she thought – were at a table together, sipping coloured drinks. They wore sunglasses and a lot of heavy gold, though all one of them had to show was a stack of red, white and green plastic bangles up her arm. She recognised her as a person she had spoken to once before, maybe yesterday. She was from a place called Spokane. Or was she the one from Tucson, Arizona? Either way, she had found their encounter disturbing.

Spokane! She'd never heard of it. Never even knew it existed. A big place too, over four hundred thousand. All learning to talk and walk and read and getting the papers delivered and feeling one another up in the backs of cars. This woman had lived her whole life there.

What you don't know can't hurt you, her mother used to say. Well, lately she'd begun to have her doubts. There was so much. This Rock, for instance, those people in the *camps*. All the time she had been spooning Farax into Douglas, then Donald, these people in Spokane or Tucson, Arizona, had been going to bed and the others into gas ovens. You couldn't keep up.

'Where is it?' she had asked the woman from Tucson, Arizona, who was perched on the edge of one plastic chair with her foot up on another, painting her toenails an iridescent pink.

The woman paused in her painting. 'Well, do you know Phoenix?'

'What?'

'Phoenix,' the woman repeated. 'Tucson is a two-hour drive from Phoenix. South.'

'Oh,' she'd said.

So now there was this other place as well. She'd never heard of either one. But then, she thought, these people have probably never heard of Hurstville!

Still, it disturbed her, all these unknown places. Like that second *bed*.

There were six old men in the spa, all in a circle as if they were playing ring-a ring-a-rosie, their arms extended along the tiled edge, the bluish water hopping about under their chins.

They were baldies most of them, but one had a peak of snow-white hair like a cockatoo and surprisingly black eyebrows, in a face that was long and tanned.

Occasionally one of them would sink, and as he went down his toes would surface. So there was more to them than just the head and shoulders.

These old fellers had not lost their vim. You could see it in their eyes and in the champagne that bubbled up between their legs. The spa was *buzzing*. Most of it was these old guys' voices. It was like a ceremony, that's what she thought.

She shifted her chair to hear them better.

'Tallahassee,' she heard. That was a new one! 'Jerusalem.'

She pretended to be looking for something under her chair, and trying not to let Donald see, jerked it closer to the spa. These old fellers were up to something.

Gnomes, is what she thought of. The gnomes of Zurich. Shoulders, some of them with tufts of white hair, long faces above the boiling surface. Hiding the real source of things, the plumbing. Which was lower down.

She had never fathomed what men were really up to, what they wanted. What it was they were asking for, but never openly, and when they didn't get it, brooded and fretted over and clenched their jaws and inwardly went dark, or clenched their fists and beat one another senseless, or their wives and kiddies, or rolled their eyes up and yearned for in a silence that filled their mouths like tongues.

The pool was whispering again.

'Odessa,' she heard. 'Schenectady.' Then, after a whole lot more she couldn't catch, very clearly, in a voice she recognised over the buzzing of the water, 'unceremonious', a word she wouldn't have picked up if she hadn't heard it on a previous occasion.

Unceremonious.

MRS Porter stood in the middle of her room and did not know which way to turn. Each time she came back to it, it was like a place she was stepping into for the first time. She recognised nothing.

When something like that happens over and over again it shakes you. As if you'd left no mark.

It wasn't simply that the moment she went out they slipped in and removed all trace of her. It was the room itself. It was so perfect it didn't need you. It certainly didn't need *her.*

She thought of breaking something. But what? A mirror would be bad luck.

She picked up a heavy glass ashtray, considered a moment, then flipped it out the window. Like that cockroach. It disappeared with a clunk into a flower bed.

Well, that was a start. She looked about for something else she could chuck out.

The one thing she couldn't get rid of was that Rock. It sat dead centre there in the window. Just dumped there throbbing in the late sunlight, and so red it hurt her eyes.

To save herself from having to look at it she shut herself in the bathroom. At least you could make an impression on that. You could use the lav or turn the shower on and make the place so steamy all the mirrors fogged up and the walls lost some of their terrible brightness.

The place had its dangers of course, but was safe enough if all you did was lower the toilet lid and sit. Only how long could a body just sit?

Unceremonious.

He had saved that up till the last moment, when he thought she was no longer listening, and had hissed it out, but so softly that if she hadn't had her head down trying to catch his last breath she mightn't have heard it at all.

What a thing to say. What a word to come up with!

She thought she might have got it wrong, but it wasn't a word *she* could have produced, she hardly knew what it meant. So what was it, an accusation? Even now, after so long, it made her furious.

To have *that* thrown at you! In a dingy little room in a place where the words were strange enough anyway, not to speak of the food, and the dim light bulbs, and the wobbly ironwork lift that shook the bones half out of you, and the smell of the bedding.

One of her bitterest memories of that dank little room was of Leonard kneeling on that last morning in front of the grate and putting what must have been the last of his strength into removing the dust of France from the cracks in his boots. His breath rasping with each pass of the cloth. His body leaning into the work as if his blessèd soul depended on the quality of the shine.

And then, just minutes later, that word between them. 'Unceremonious'.

For heaven's sake, what did they expect? How many meals did you have to dish up? How many sheets did you have to wash and peg out and fold and put away or smooth over and tuck under? How many times did you have to lick your thumb and test the iron? How many times did you have to go fishing with a safety pin in their pyjama bottoms to find a lost cord?

Angrily she ripped a page off the little notepad they provided on the table between the beds and scribbled the word. Let someone else deal with it, spelled out there in her round, state-school hand.

She opened a drawer and dropped it in. *Unceremonious*. Posted it to the dead.

Then quickly, one after another, scribbled more words, till she had a pile of ripped-out pages.

Dimension, she wrote.

Bon Ami.

Flat 2, 19 Hampstead Road, West End, she wrote.

Root, she wrote, and many more words, till she had emptied herself, like a woman who has done all her housework, swept the house, made the beds, got the washing on the line, and, with nothing to do now but wait for the kiddies to come home from school and her husband from work, can afford to have a bit of a lie-down. She posted each page in a different drawer until all the drawers were occupied, then stretched out on one of the beds, the one on the left, and slept. Badly.

Back home in her unit, dust would be gathering, settling grain by grain on all her things: on the top of the television, between the knots of her crocheted doilies, in the hearts of the blood-red artificial roses that filled the glass vase on her bedside table.

On one petal of each rose was a raindrop, as if a few spots of rain had fallen. But when you touched the drop it was hard, like one of those lumps of red-gold resin they used to chew when they were kids, that had bled out of the rough trunk of a gum.

If it was rain that had fallen, even a few spots, her things would be wet and the heart of the rose would have been washed clean. But what she found herself sitting in, in her dream, was a slow fall of dust. Everything, everything, was being covered and choked with it.

Well, it's what they'd always said: dust to dust – only she hadn't believed it. The last word. *Dust*.

It worried her now that when she'd made her list she had left it out, and now it had got into her head she'd never be rid of it. She'd just go on sitting there for ever watching it gather around her. Watching it fall grain by grain over her things, over *her*, like a grainy twilight that was the start of another sort of night, but one that would go on and on and never pass.

The Hoover, she shouted in her sleep. Get the Hoover.

She woke then. On this double bed in a room from which every bit of dust, so far as she could see, had been expunged.

And now, at last, the others arrived.

One of them lay down beside her. She refused to turn and look, and the bed was wide enough for her to ignore him, though at one point he began to whisper. More *words*.

The others, a couple, lay down on the second bed and began to make love, and so as not to see who it was who had come to her own bed, and most of all not to have to listen to his words, she turned towards them and watched. They were shadowy. Maybe black.

She didn't mind them using the bed, they didn't disturb her. Probably had nowhere to go, poor things. And they weren't noisy.

She must have gone back to sleep then, because when she woke again the room seemed lighter, less thick with breath. She was alone.

There was a humming in the room. Low. It made the veins in her forehead throb.

She got up and went, in her stockinged feet, to the window.

It was as if something out there at the end of the night was sending out gonglike vibrations that made the whole room hum and glow. The Rock, darkly veined and shimmering, was sitting like a cloud a hundred feet above the earth. Had simply risen up, ignoring the millions of tons it must weigh, and was stalled there on the horizon like an immense spacecraft, and the light it gave off was a sound with a voice at the centre of it, saying, *Look at this. So, what do you reckon now?*

Mrs Porter looked at it askance, but she did look. And what she felt was an immediate and unaccountable happiness, as if the Rock's new-found lightness was catching. And she remembered something: a time when Donald had just begun to stand unsteadily on his own plump little legs and had discovered the joy of running away from her towards a flower he had glimpsed in a garden bed, or a puppy dog or his brother's red tricycle. When she called he would give a quick glance over his shoulder and run further. Suddenly unburdened, she had had to hang on to things – the sink, Leonard's Stelzner upright – so as not to go floating clean off the linoleum, as if, after so many months of carrying them, inside her body or on her hip, first the one, then the other, she had forgotten the trick of letting gravity alone hold her down.

Now, looking at the Rock, she felt as if she had let go of something and was free to join it. To go floating. Like a balloon some small child – Donald perhaps – had let go of and which was free to go now wherever the world might take it. She glanced down. She was hovering a foot above the carpet.

So it had happened. She was off.

Immediately she began to worry about Donald. She needed to get word to him.

That did it. She came down with a bump. And with her

heart beating fast in the fear that it might already be too late, she made for the door. She needed to reassure him, if he didn't already know, that she hadn't really minded all those times when he'd hung on to her skirt and dragged her off to look at this and that. So full of need and bullying insistence, she saw now, because if she didn't look, and confirm that yes it was amazing, it really was, he couldn't be sure that either he or it was there.

She had gone grudgingly, and looked and pretended. Because she had never given up the hard little knot of selfishness that her mother had warned would one day do her in. Well, her mother was wrong. It had saved her. Without it she would have been no more than a space for others to curl up in for a time then walk away from. All this, in her new-found lightness, she understood at last and wanted to explain to the one person who was left who might understand it and forgive. Still wearing the frock she had lain down in, she flung the door open and, barely hearing the click as it closed behind her, stepped out into the hotel corridor. Only then did she realise that she did not know the number of Donald's room.

'You fool, Dulcie,' she told herself. The voice was Leonard's. In these latter years, Leonard's had become the voice she used for speaking to herself. It made her see things more clearly. Though Leonard would never have said to her the sort of things she said to herself. 'Stupid *woman*. Bloody old fool.'

She walked up and down a little. All the doors looked the same.

She put her ear to one, then to another, to see if she could hear Donald's snoring, but behind their identical doors all the rooms preserved an identical breathless silence.

A little further along, beside the door to a linen closet where she had sometimes seen a trolley stacked with towels and the little coloured bottles and soap packs that went into the various bathrooms, there was a chair. In a state now of angry alarm, she seized occupation of it and sat, commanding the empty corridor. She'd been too quick off the mark. She needed to sit now and have a think.

But the corridor, with its rows of ceiling lights and doors all blindly closed on their separate dreams, gave her the creeps. She felt breathless.

She made for a small flight of stairs at the far end that went down to a door, and when she opened it, and it too clicked shut behind her, found herself outside the building altogether, standing in her stockinged feet on stone flags that were still warm. The warmth came right up through her, and all about were night-flowering shrubs, and bigger trees with boughs that drooped. She took a good breath. The air was heavy with scent – with different scents. Night insects were twittering. All was clear moonlight, as still as still.

She began to walk – how simple things could be! – enjoying her own lightness and wondering if she wasn't still asleep and dreaming. Only in dreams did your body dispose of itself so easily. She walked on springy lawn. But they must have been watering it, because almost immediately her stockings were soaked. She sat down on a low wall and peeled them off, and when she looked back gave a little laugh at the look of them there on the shadowy grass. Like two snakeskins, a couple. That'll make 'em guess!

Soon she was in a car park, empty but flooded with moonlight, then out again into soft sand. Red sand, still with the warmth of the sun in it, but cooler when you worked your naked toes in. Luxurious. She waded to the top of a dune and let herself go, half sliding, half rolling, till she came to a stop and was on level ground again. She righted herself and, seated in warm sand, checked for broken bones. All around her the bushes, which were spiky and had seemed dull by day, were giving off light like slow-burning fireworks. Big clouds rolled across the moon, thin as smoke, then darker. There was a twittering, though she could see no birds. Everywhere, things were happening – that's what she felt. Small things that for a long time now she had failed to notice. To see them you had to get down to where she was now, close to the ground. At kiddie level. Otherwise there were so many other things to demand your attention that you got distracted, you lost the habit of looking, of listening, unless some kiddie down there dragged at your skirt and demanded, 'Look, Mum, look.'

That twittering for instance. She knew what it was now. Not birds but the Station Master's office at Babinda. It was years, donkey's years, since that particular sound had come to her, yet here it was. Must have been going on all around her for ages, and she was too busy listening to other things to notice.

Babinda.

For a whole year after she was married, with Leonard away in New Guinea, she had been with the Railways, an emergency worker while the boys were at the war. Those were the days! She was off the shelf, so that was settled, and she had no domestic responsibilities. She had never in her life felt so free. She loved the noise and bustle of the Station Master's office when things were on the go; the buzzing and tinkling when the First Division was held up by floods below the Burdekin or when, outside the regular timetable, a Special came through, a troop-transport with all the boys hanging out the windows wolf-whistling and calling across the tracks to where she was walking up and down with a lantern, to ask her name. Then the long sleepy periods when nothing was happening at all and you could get your head into *Photoplay*.

The Station Master, Mr O'Leary, was a gardener, his platform a tame jungle of staghorns, elkhorns, hoyas, maidenhair ferns in hanging baskets, tree orchids cut straight from the trunk. He was out there in all weathers in his shirtsleeves whispering to his favourites. 'Hullo, ducky,' he'd be singing, 'here's a nice drop of water for you. That's a girl! You'll enjoy this.'

She'd pause at her knitting to listen to him. He used the same tone when he was talking to her. It made her feel quite tender towards him. But he was always respectful – she was, after all, a married woman.

Sometimes, in the late afternoon, when everything was at a low point and even the bush sounds had dropped to nothing, he would talk of his son Reggie, the footballer, who had been in her class at primary school and was now a POW in Malaya. Reggie had played the mouth organ, that's what she remembered. A chunk of honeycomb at his lips and his breath swarming in the golden cells, that's what she remembered. *The Flight of the Bumble Bee*.

'It's a blessing his mother's already gone,' Mr O'Leary would tell her softly while the light slanted and turned pink. 'At least she's spared the waiting. Once you've got kiddies, Dulce, you're never free, not ever. I spend half my time asking myself what he's getting to eat, he's such a big feller. If he's got a mate an' that. I'm only half here sometimes.'

She listened and was sympathetic but did not understand, not really. Douglas and Donald were still way off in the future, waiting there in the shadows beyond the track; they had not yet found her. But she liked listening to Mr O'Leary. No one had ever thought her worth confiding in, not till this. She felt quite grown up. An independent woman. She was all of twenty-three.

Under the influence of the many unscheduled trains that were running up and down the line, all those lives the war had forced out of their expected course, she was led to wonder what direction she herself might be headed in. Odd, she thought now, that she had never considered her marriage a direction, let alone a terminus. But that was the times, the war. Everything normal was suspended for the Duration. Afterwards, anything might be possible.

'You won't find me stickin' round once the war is over.'

This was Jim Haddy, the Station Master's Assistant. 'No fear! I'll be off like a shot. You watch my dust!'

At sixteen, Jim Haddy was the most amazing boy she'd ever come across. He was so full of things, so dedicated. He thought the Queensland Railways were God and got quite upset if you threw off at them or said things like, 'You know the theme song of the Queensland Railways, don't you? "I Walk Beside You".' He thought Mr O'Leary was 'slack' because when they went out with their flags and lamps and things to wave a train through, he left the tabs on his waistcoat unfastened. Jim was a stickler. He did not roll his sleeves up on even the muggiest days. Always wore his soft felt Railway hat. And his waistcoat, even if it was unbuttoned in front, was always properly buckled at the sides.

He was a soft-faced kid who got overexcited and had, as Mr O'Leary put it, to be watched. He knew all there was to know about the Royal Houses of Europe, and talked about the Teck Mecklenburgs and the Bourbon Parmas as if they owned cane farms down the road, and Queen Marie of Romania and King Zog as if they were his auntie and uncle. He spent a lot of the Railway's time settling them like starlings in their family trees on sheets of austerity butcher's paper.

'What a funny boy you are,' she would tell him dreamily as she leaned over his shoulder to watch.

The summer rain would be sheeting down, a wall of impenetrable light, and when it stopped, the view would be back, so green it hurt your eyes, and the earth in Mr O'Leary's flower beds would steam and give off smells. The little room where they sat at the end of the platform would be all misty with heat. She'd be thinking: When I get home I'll have to take Leonard's shoes out of the lowboy and brush the mould off. 'Where *is* Montenegro?' she'd ask, and Jim was only too happy to tell, though she was none the wiser.

That boy needs watching.

But she had lost sight of him. Like so much else from that time. And from other times. She was surprised now that he had come back, and so clearly that as she leaned over his shoulder she caught the vinegary smell of his neck under the raw haircut.

'What happened to you, Jim Haddy?' she found herself asking in her own voice, her feet in the powdery red soil. 'Where are you, I wonder? And where are Queen Marie and King Zog?' She hadn't heard much of them lately either.

'I'm here,' she announced, in case Jim was somewhere in the vicinity and listening.

She looked about and saw that she was in the midst of a lot of small grey-green bushes, with daylight coming and no landmarks she could recognise.

'My God,' she said to herself, 'where? *Where* am I? This isn't my life.'

Off in the distance a train was rumbling in over the tracks: a great whooshing sound that grew and grew, and before she knew it passed so close to where she was standing that she was blown clear off her feet in a blaze of dust. It cleared, and she realised that high up in a window of one of the carriages as it went thundering past she had seen her own face, dreaming behind the glass and smiling. Going south. She picked herself up and got going again.

The Rock was there. Looming. Dark against the skyline. She made for that.

The sun was coming up, hot out of the oven, and almost immediately now the earth grew too hot to walk on. The bushes around her went suddenly dry; her mouth parched, she sat down dump. There was no shade. She must have dozed off.

When she looked up again a small boy was squatting in front of her. Not Donald. And not Douglas either. He was about five years old and black. He squatted on his heels. When her eyes clicked open he stared at her for a moment, then took off shouting.

When she opened her eyes again there were others, six or seven of them. Shy but curious, with big eyes. They squatted and stared. When she raised a hand they drew back. Dared one another to come close. Poked. Then giggled and sprang away.

At last one little girl, older than the rest, trotted off and came back with some scraps of bread and a cup full of water. The others looked on while the little girl pushed dry crusts into the open mouth, as if feeding a sick bird, and tipped the cup. The cup was old and crumpled, the child's fingers rather dirty. Oh well, she thought, it's a bit late to be worrying over my peck of dirt.

She swallowed, and the children watched as her old throat dealt with the warmish water, got it down.

She saw that it was a test. To see what she was. Old woman or spirit.

No need to look so puzzled, she told them, though not in so many words. It's just me, Dulcie MacIntyre. It's no use expecting anything more. This is it.

But they continued to watch as if they were not convinced.

She lay like a package while they sat waiting. As if, when the package finally unwrapped itself, it might contain something interesting. Oh well, she thought, they'll find out. If they're disappointed, that's their lookout.

After a while she must have seemed as permanent and familiar to them as any other lump of earth because they got bored, some of them – the littlies – and went back to whatever game they'd been playing when that first one interrupted them, shouting, 'Hey, look what I found! Over here!'

But two or three of them stayed. Watching the old lizard turn its head on the wrinkled, outstretched neck. Slowly lifting its gaze. Shifting it north. Then east. The dry mouth open.

They fed her dribbles of water. Went off in relays and brought back armfuls of dry scrub and built a screen to keep the sun off, which was fierce, and moved it as the sun moved so that she was always in shade. She had never in all her life felt so closely attended to, cared for. They continued to sit close beside her and watch. They were waiting for something else now. But what?

'I told you,' she said weakly, 'it's no good expecting anything more.' They had been watching so long, poor things. It was a shame they had to be disappointed.

They must have waited all day, because at last she felt the sun's heat fall from her shoulders, though its light was still full in the face of her watchers. Then a shadow moved over them. The shadow of the Rock. She knew this because they kept lifting their eyes towards it, from her to it then back again. The Rock was changing colour now as the sun sank behind it.

The shadow continued to move, like a giant red scarf that was being drawn over them. The Rock, which had been hoarding the sun's heat all day, was giving it off now in a kindlier form as it turned from orange-red to purple. If she could swing her body around now to face it, to look at it, she might understand something. Might. But then again she might not. Better to take what she could, this gentle heat, and leave the show to these others.

I'm sorry, she chuckled, I can't compete.

She was beginning to rise up now, feeling even what was lightest in her, her thoughts, drop gently away. And the children, poor things, had their eyes fixed in the wrong place. No, she wanted to shout to them. Here I am. Up here.

One of the little ones, sitting there with a look of such intense puzzlement on his face, and baffled expectation, was Donald. I'm sorry, Donald, she said softly. But he too was looking in the wrong place.

THE big fish dolphin lay stranded. The smaller waves no longer reached it. There were sandgrits in its eyes, the mouth was open, a pulse throbbed under its gills. It was changing colour like a sunset: electric pink and mauve flashes, blushings of yellow-green.

'What is it?' Betty Olds asked. 'What's happening to it?'

'Shush,' Isobel told her.

So they sat, all three, and watched. The waves continued to whisper at the edge of the beach. The colours continued to play over the humped back and belly, flushing, changing, until slowly they became less vivid. The pulsing under the gills fluttered, then ceased, and the flesh, slowly as they watched, grew silvery-grey, then leaden.

'What happened?' Betty asked again. 'Is it dead now?'

'I think so,' Isobel told her. Then, seeing Betty's lip begin to quiver, put her arm around her sister's shoulder and drew her close. 'It's all right, Bets,' she whispered. 'It was old.'

Dulcie said nothing. She too was breathless. This was a moment, she knew, that she would never forget. Never. As long as she lived. She also knew, with certainty, that she would live for ever.

The Domestic Cantata

The Domestic Cantata

STARTING back before he stumbled, the man groaned, then raised his voice in protest.

'Maggie,' he shouted. 'Maaggieee!'

The ten-geared blue-and-gold Galaxy had been propped against the panelled wall of the staircase and was sprawled now on its side in the hallway outside his room, like a giant insect that had blundered in and expired there, or a stunned, irides-cent angel – one more example of the chaos they lived in, the clutter and carelessness. Nobody in this house, so far as Sam could see, ever rinsed a coffee mug or returned a book to its shelf, or threw out a newspaper, or picked a wet towel up off the sopping bathroom floor. He knew the savagery he was assailed with had nothing to do, specifically, with the bike, but he kicked it just the same, and saw even as he did so what a spectacle he was making of himself. A grown man in the hallway of his own home, putting his boot into a defenceless machine!

Maggie had appeared at the kitchen door.

'Maggie,' he moaned, '*look* at this!' His voice had the arch and droop of classic lament. 'That boy wants a good hiding. Look at it!' A good hiding was a phrase that Sam McCall was excessively fond of. It belonged to the world of his boyhood – maybe even of his father's boyhood, though the truth was that neither he nor any one of his children had ever had a hand laid on them.

Maggie looked, but not at the bike. Hot blood suffused his brow. There were veins in his neck.

'I'm sorry, love,' she said mildly, and came out into the hallway drying her hands on her skirt. 'I tell them and they don't listen.'

She reached down, hoisted the bike upright, and stood for a moment, bare-armed, poised on her solid legs as if, tempted by its promise of velocity, she might be about to leap into the saddle, sprint down the hallway, over the threshold and away. Instead, she turned the beast into its stall under the stairs.

'There,' she said. All was restored, made good again.

Sam watched. Quiet but unappeased.

'Would you like a cup of coffee, pet?'

He shook his head.

She waited. He might be amenable to some other distraction.

'Well,' he said in a tone of aggrievement, 'I'll get back to it. I came out to make a phone call.'

What he meant was that the moment of tender sociability that had drawn him away from his work had been spoiled now and was irretrievable. He turned, went back to his workplace, and a moment later she heard, tentative, in one chord, then another, the notes of the piano.

Redeeming a football boot he'd failed to notice, she set it on the bottom step — she'd carry it up later — and went back to the kitchen, a little song rising in her throat, set off perhaps by a suggestion in one of the chords. She sang three or four bars of it, then returned in silence to the sink, where, in a high, soft head voice, she launched into the rest while she topped and tailed celery sticks and scored a dozen radishes that, when they were plunged into cold water, would open and transform themselves into peppery, pink-and-white roses.

TWELVE years ago, when they first moved in, this house had seemed perfect.

It was a big Federation house on three levels, with pierced work above the solid doors and in the archway between the ground-floor rooms, leadlight windows that in the early morning threw dancing colours on the walls, and balconies that broke out in unexpected places on a view of palm crowns and glinting water. The children had been more manageable then, and fewer.

These days, everything above the ground floor, which Maggie tried to keep clear, had been abandoned to general mayhem and din. She tolerated this, and only intermittently dealt with it, so long as there was no clattering on the stairs, no shouting in the hallway and, above all, no argument with the law that 'down here', and the garden outside their father's window, was the sacred realm of Silence. Silence, in this house, was a positive not a negative commodity, a breathing space and pause that was essential not only to the production of their father's work but to the work itself, as they knew very well from counting out the fixed measures of it, either in their head or with the muted tapping of a foot, when they played or sang.

But silence, outside music, was hardly absolute.

'What about the birds?' Miranda had demanded once, meaning the bad-tempered Indian mynahs that carried on an incessant warfare around the bottlebrush and pomegranates below their father's window, screaming and driving off the natives.

She kept her voice civil, draining it of any suggestion – she was twelve then – of rebelliousness or irony. Her father already suspected her of the first. He did not consider her old enough, as yet, for the second.

'Nature', he told her, 'is different.'

Miranda held her tongue but made a face at the twins, who each raised an eyebrow and looked away.

It was Cassie, too young for the codes that were in operation here, who in all innocence had demanded, 'But what about us? Aren't *we* nature?'

'Of course you are, darling,' Maggie told her. 'What Daddy means is, he knows what distracts him. Little people stomping. Shouting in the hallway or on the stairs. You know that.'

They all did, and accepted it for the most part without question. However they might whisper among themselves, and complain against their father's moods, his grouchiness, his angry descents and tyrannies, they acknowledged that he was himself a force of nature, a lightning rod for energies, for phenomena that people were impressed by and wrote about in the newspaper in terms that Miranda tended to mock – but only the terms, not the fact. She would read these pieces aloud at the breakfast table, while Sam, his face screwed up with distaste and embarrassment, shook his head – disguising, he hoped, a certain measure of delight – and Maggie said flatly, 'Well, I didn't understand a word of that. But what would I know? I only sang the thing.'

'Impeccably,' Miranda quoted.

Now it was her mother's turn to make a face.

Their father's alternation of moods constituted the weather of their lives, which, like the weather itself, it was useless to quarrel with or resist.

In his phases of exuberant good humour he could be wilder and noisier than any of them. Then there were what their mother called his 'dumps', whole days it might be when he was like a ghost at the table and even Cassie could not get a good word out of him, and all you heard at mealtimes, since no one else dared speak either, was the clink of knives and spoons against crockery and the grinding of jaws.

He lived in two worlds, their father – with, so far as they could see, no traffic between them.

When it suited him he was like a boy who had never grown up, full of stories made up on the spot about stones that yodelled and perambulating washing machines that went on trips to Vienna or London and gave performances as Brünnhilde at the Met.

He would settle into a beanbag and watch cartoons with them, utterly absorbed, producing great hoots of laughter at things even they thought silly. Then in the middle of one of his rambling tales, full of grunts, whistles, clicks and hums, the mood of boisterous hilarity in him would lapse and go underground; he would ease off his lap whichever of the littlies had climbed there and, without a word of explanation, go off. They would wait a moment to see if it was just a call of nature, in which case he would be back. But mostly it wasn't. He had been *struck*. Just like that – *kazoom*, as Tom put it.

You got used to it, of course, but it was disconcerting. Annoying too. *They* couldn't have got away with it.

So however much they stood in awe of whatever force it was that he had given himself up to, they resented it, and took their own form of revenge.

Asked what it was that their father did, Miranda would say blandly, 'Oh, he works for the council. He's a sewage inspector.' Or as Tom once put it, 'He's a burglar.'

Intimidated by his father and puzzled by a side of him that did not keep to the rules, Tom had conceived a picture of Sam as an anarchic schoolboy, pretending to be hard at work behind closed doors but in reality reading a comic, or picking his nose, or no longer there at all but off robbing a bank.

It was a boyish vision, to be explained not only by Tom's easy tendency to attribute to others what he would most wish for himself but by the resentment he felt at being the odd man out. Not only because he was the only boy in the family but also because, through some quirk of nature, he alone among them had no ear. He suffered this affliction without complaint, and even allowed himself to be teased about it with clownish good humour, but in a household where singing was as natural as speech he felt disabled, and since his first inclination was to conform, it unnaturally set him apart. He also felt, painfully, that Sam, whom he longed to please, was disappointed in him.

Lately, out of defiance, not of his father but of fate, he had taken to sneering at every form of 'artiness' as 'female business'.

It would have surprised Tom to know that his father understood his perplexity and was undismayed. Composing, for Sam, was work – it was the only thing he had ever been good at – and music a condition that could manifest itself in other ways than as notes on a page or in flights of calibrated sound. He was waiting for Tom to stop feeling sorry for himself and discover his own form of the thing.

They must have had some inkling, Sam felt, of what nature was up to in Tom's case, when they named the girls Miranda, Rosalind, Cressida and — in a moment of recklessness — Cassandra, but for the boy had immediately settled on Tom. Not even Thomas, but Tom. Tom-tom. There was, from the beginning, something wonderfully bull-like in him that would not be rarefied — even, Sam suspected, by time. He had grown up around his own literalness, and to Sam was all the more precious for it.

As for Maggie, though she believed without question in the energy Sam poured into his work — always had, from the first note he struck in her presence — the deeper music of the household flowed, for her, from what each of her children, with all their different natures and needs (even the twins, Ros and Cressie, were of contrary colour and temperament), brought to the routine and daily muddle of their lives: hurt feelings, tantrums, head colds, the shooting pain of a new tooth pushing into the house, complaints of misunderstanding and unfairness, squeals of protest at a shampooing against head lice or as a strip of Elastoplast was ripped off. For all the time and fret this cost her she would not have had it otherwise. Not one little difficult nature, or demand, or crotchet. Not one. Though she was glad she did not have to find a system of notation for it, and even more that she did not have to sing it.

SAM, looking sleek and youthful, his locks wet-combed from the shower, wandered into the kitchen, on the prowl now that he was done with work for the day, for something he could pick at — a stick of celery, a sliver of carrot, something one of the children had been up to.

'Where is he, anyway?' he demanded, meaning Tom. He was still fretting over that business with the bike. 'They'll be here any minute now. Can't we eat as a family for once?'

'He's taken his surfboard to Manly,' Maggie told him, busying around behind him. 'He did ask. I said it was OK. He's to be back by five.'

'And the girls?'

'They're at the pool.'

There was an open-air saltwater pool just ten minutes away, on a walk along the Harbour.

'Miranda should have stayed,' he grumbled. 'You shouldn't have to do all this.' Including the guests, there would be more than a dozen of them. He picked a round of cucumber out of the tuna salad, ruining one of her attempts at symmetry, and leaned with his back to the refrigerator.

'What can *I* do?'

'Open the wine and get me something to drink.'

Instead, he came up from behind, put his arms around her and buried his face in her hair. Maggie laughed.

'That was lovely,' she told him, 'but what about my drink?'

He opened three bottles of red, set them on the bench with the corks laid across their mouths, then drew her a glass of flagon white with soda.

For a few minutes they moved easily together in the space between table and cupboards, her stacks of empty egg boxes, the spilled waste from the bin; not touching, but in an easy association of bodies that was a kind of dance before the open-mouthed wine bottles.

The upper part of the house, its rooms all disorder and stopped noise, hung above them like a summer cloud, dense but still, alive with events that were for the moment suspended. The door to his workroom was closed for the day, its flow of sound also suspended, but on a chord that continued to reverberate in his head and teasingly unfold. It was there, humming away, and could wait. He would find his way back to it later.

Maggie turned and looked at him. Seeing herself reflected in his gaze, she brought the back of her hand to her forehead where a strand of hair had come loose.

It was difficult to say at such moments, she thought, whether this was before or after; whether the children were about to come bursting back into their lives from the pool, from the surf, all wet towels and hair, complaints and appetites, riddles, the smell of suntan oil and Bacon Crispies – or whether they were still waiting in youthful expectancy in that one year when there had been just the two of them, in the long nights, the short days. Not so long ago really.

They stood for a moment outside time, outside their thickened bodies, in renewed youthfulness. He nibbled. She sipped. The chord moved out through the house, discovering new possibilities in what might have passed for silence.

The doorbell rang.

'Damn,' she said. 'That'll be Stell. They're always early.'

At the same moment, from the back porch, came the voices of the girls, little Cassie's breathless with grievance.

'Mummy, they tried to run away from me.'

'We did not.'

'They were chasing boys.'

'We were *not*.'

The bell sounded again.

'You get it,' Maggie told Sam, and turned to face the onslaught.

'Now, Cassie,' she told the child, who was clinging to her hip, 'stop whingeing. We've got visitors. Lars and Jens are here. Cressie – Ros – you should be ashamed of yourselves.'

Miranda, hair dyed pink and green in the punk style she now affected, stood in the frame of the doorway, frowning, unwilling to be drawn in.

'And so should you, miss,' Maggie told her. 'I let them go with you because you're sixteen and supposed to be responsible. Sometimes I wonder.'

But the rebuke, as Miranda knew, was ritual. There was no conviction in it.

'Now go and get yourselves decent, all of you. Before the real guests appear.'

THE real guests were an American visitor, Diane Novak, and her friend Scott McIvor, a much younger man than they had expected who turned out to be a local sailmaker. The others were family: Maggie's sister Stella and her two boys, Lars and Jens, and Stella and Maggie's old singing teacher, Miss Stinson. Then – invited unannounced by Miranda, it seemed, but more likely uninvited and hastily vouched for – Miranda's 'best friends' of the moment, an odd pair called Julie and Don, also known as 'The Act'.

Sam was appalled. 'How did *they* get here?' he demanded fiercely, the minute he got Maggie alone.

'I don't know,' Maggie told him. 'Any more than you do. I suppose Miranda asked them. They'll be all right. I've put all the kids out in the sunroom. You just look after the drinks. And, Sam, love,' she pleaded, 'try not to make a fuss.'

Julie was an intense, waiflike creature. Tossed out of home (or so she claimed) by her stepfather, she had taken herself out of school and was living now in a squat – a plywood cubicle in an empty warehouse at Marrickville. Like Miranda she was sixteen. She got herself up, Sam thought, like an anorexic teenaged widow, entirely in black, and painted her lips black and her fingernails as well – in mourning, Sam had once suggested, for her own life.

Her partner Don, the other half of The Act, was a slight, sweet-faced boy, girlish but not it seemed gay, whose pale hair had been trained to fall perpetually over one eye and who affected little pink silk ballet slippers that Julie had embroidered with vivid scarlet and emerald-green thread. Julie was a designer. She created fashion garments from scraps picked up at the Salvation Army and St Vincent de Paul op shops. Miranda today was wearing one of Julie's 'creations', a recent present. It was a flared skirt made entirely of men's ties, in heavy satins and silks, a little grimy some of them but all vivid in colour and glossily shimmering.

She was always giving Miranda presents. Trashy jewellery she bought with her outsized allowance, miniature artworks of her own devising and of a crazy intricacy: cages in search of an inmate, efficient tiny guillotines involving razor blades and springs – bad-luck charms all, which Sam did not want smuggled in among them. Offerings, he had once observed, to some god of ultimate unhappiness.

'Honestly,' Miranda told him. 'I can't believe you'd say a thing like that! You're so ungenerous! And you think Julie's the crazy one.'

Miranda liked to scare them with lurid accounts of what Julie, poor thing, had 'been through'. How at seven she was abused by a favourite uncle. How three months ago she'd been raped in her plywood cubicle by half a dozen ethnic youths but had declined to press charges.

Was any of this true? Or was it, as Maggie assured him, just another of Miranda's stories? Designed to shock them into admitting how out of touch they were, how little they knew of what was really going on.

'Young people these days see all sorts of things,' Maggie told him, trying for an unconcern she did not quite feel. 'Things we had no notion of. They survive, most of them – if they're sensible. Miranda is *very* sensible, you know that. All this is just showing off. She wants you to be impressed.'

'Impressed!' Sam exploded.

'In your case, love,' she told him with a twisted smile, 'that means scared.'

'Well, I am,' he admitted. 'I'm bloody petrified. I don't know how you can be so cool about things.'

But that was just the point, the point of difference between them. And it was the mystery of this, more than anything Maggie actually said or did, that had its effect on him, a belief that Maggie did know something he did not, and that he could rely on this to get him through all doubts and difficulties. It was what she offered him. He had no idea what it might be that he offered her in return. Now, ignoring the irruption of Julie and her pallid companion into what was meant to be a private celebration, he followed Maggie's instructions and set himself to dealing with the drinks, but was not happy. It was a mistake – that's what he now decided – to have made his first meeting with Diane Novak a family affair.

For one thing, it had become clear that she hadn't made this trip 'down here' only to see him. However eager she appeared to be, and full of interest in his workplace, the house, the bottlebrush with its sprays of pink-and-gold blossom that drooped over the front porch – 'Callistemon, I think,' she pronounced accurately – all the flow of energy in her, and it was considerable, was towards the young sailmaker, Scott, one of those easy-going, utterly likeable, ponytailed young fellows from good North Shore families and the best private schools who, instead of following their fathers into accountancy or the law, went back, led by nothing more radical than their own freewheeling interest, to trades their grandfathers or great-grandfathers had practised, and became carpenters and did up houses, or built boats, or made surfboards or sails.

Diane Novak was from Madison, Wisconsin. Three years ago Sam had come across one of her poems in an anthology and was led to set it to music. Later he sought out others and had ended up with a loose cycle. He wrote to her. Diane Novak wrote back. A correspondence developed.

Correspondence.

He had never given much consideration to the word till then, but 'correspondence' and all it implied seemed entirely rich and right for what had since then flowed so easily between them: the current of curiosity and interest, of shy revelations on his part, flights of extravagant fancy on hers; jokes, wordplay, essays in boldness that took them, he had sometimes felt, to the edge of flirtation; small hints at the erotic. A hint too of darker things. Disappointment. Pain. Which his music had found in the poems, and which corresponded, he felt − there! that word again − to something in himself that had remained to this point wordless, though not entirely unspoken.

There was nothing dangerous in it. No suggestion of an affair, even a long-distance one. He passed all Diane's letters on to Maggie, though he suspected she did not read them, and could, without fear, have shown her his own. The deeper connection was impersonal. It lay in the inwardness with which he had taken her words, felt out the emotion there that had given them just their own shape, weight, texture, and found music for it. Released, she might have said, the music that was already in them and in her. She recognised that. Had felt it strongly as something secret, though not quite hidden, that he had subtly but again secretly made plain, for which she was grateful to the point of an agreeable affection that constituted a correspondence of an even more intimate kind. Inexpressible, or rather not needing expression because he had already expressed it for them in the thing itself – the music.

So there was no need for them to meet, she told him. They had already done that, in their own chaste but public consummation, *there*.

In the meantime, they could joke about passing one another as intimate strangers on the moving walkway in some airport, Hawaii or Atlanta, or pressing fingertips on either side of a glass partition in Anchorage.

When she wrote out of the blue announcing a visit, he had assumed, foolishly, and with some trepidation, that she was coming because of him. But then, from her hotel, she had called and admitted to another interest 'down here', this Scott the sailmaker, whom she had met at a poetry reading in Seattle. And now they were seated, Diane Novak, this Scott, who at twenty-seven or so was a good twenty years younger than his companion, at the big pinewood table in their front room, together with Maggie's sister, Stella, and Miss Stinson. Maggie and Diane, Sam thought, seemed entirely relaxed and easy with one another, like old friends united in understanding.

Of what? he wondered. Him?

Only now did it strike him that Maggie might have her own correspondence with Diane Novak. Through the words he had found music for. To which Maggie, in performance, had brought an exploratory sense, which she was now testing, of the other's shifting emotions, but also her own presence and breath. Is that why he felt so uncomfortably displaced, the only one here who seemed out of tune with the occasion?

The truth was, he was confused.

Very blonde and tanned, very carefully presented, but in a stringy way that was a mite too 'American', Diane Novak was not what he had pictured. There were angularities to her that he had not foreseen. Something in the way she came at things – too directly, he thought – set him ill at ease. He wondered now if there had not been in her letters a suggestion of – what? Artfulness and high self-mockery that she had expected him to share but that he had mistaken or missed.

In her letters, not in the poems. She was rounder, softer there. Or was that because he had translated the poems so fully into Maggie's sphere?

Either way, while remaining excited, fascinated even, he had begun to doubt his clear sense of Diane Novak, and was disconcerted by the speed with which she and Maggie, for all the differences between them, had caught one another's tone.

DIANE Novak was also disconcerted. She had brought presents, of course: jewellery of various kinds for the girls, a Ferragamo scarf for Maggie. For Sam a pair of Indian moccasins. He had received them, she thought, as if they were an exchange, not quite adequate, for something she had deprived him of, rather than as a gift, and was suddenly aware of all those little signs of unease she had felt between the lines of his letters and put out of mind, but which in the man himself were too close to the surface to be ignored. Goodness, she thought, what have we got here? She was disturbed a little, amused a little, but also touched.

Because the music he had found for her was so inward, so

intuitive and acute, she had assumed a degree of knowingness in him that had led her into a kind of playful exaggeration that she saw now might have been a mistake. He wasn't at all knowing. He was, for all his sleekness, altogether boyish and at the mercy of his own wild starts and emotions.

Proprietorial too, she saw. Of herself, of Maggie. Of everything. She would have to be careful of wounding him. She would have to rely on Maggie to get them through.

Thank goodness, she thought, for Maggie.

She shot Sam a glance that was meant to be reassuring, collusive even, but all he did was look alarmed, and she was reminded yet again of how much of what life cannot deal with may be taken up, taken care of and reconciled, in the work.

She was well aware of what this meant for her own work, and had assumed that he too must know it – which is why she had responded so completely to him. She saw now that he might not. And saw too, almost too clearly, how much of 'life' his work might have to make up for.

Scott, meanwhile, had transferred his attention to Miss Stinson, who, seventy-five if she was a day, was glowing in the full light of his interest.

He was amazing, Scott. He had a fund of attention, of youthful excitement over this, that – everything in fact – that seemed inexhaustible and which he bestowed, in an unselfconscious way, on everything in his vicinity. Which was a bit of a problem really. She knew from her own case how easy it was to be misled. But not, in her own case, dangerously; she was pretty skilled, at this point, at protecting herself from ultimate disappointment.

Miss Stinson was telling them how she had discovered Maggie and Stella, while Stella, the subject of the story, sat placid and indulgent, but frowning. It bored her to have these ancient wonders trotted out again – as she would have said, for the forty-second time. Any glory they involved was more important, these days, to Miss Stinson than to Stella herself, who had long since put well behind her the tattered, if once glowing, clouds they trailed.

'Such funny little things, they were,' Miss Stinson told. 'With no shoes, and scars on their knees, real harum-scarums. Tomboys.' They were her next-door neighbours, their father a removal man. They were always hanging over the fence to hear the scales that rose and fell behind the blinds of the little house she shared with her sister, and the big practice pieces their students performed. Longing to join in. Well, she had taken them on at last, in exchange for a couple of hours of ironing each week, because their mother had wanted something more for them – but without much enthusiasm. And lo and behold, miracle of miracles, by one of those quirks of fate that make you wonder at things – life was such a lottery, so unexpected, so unpredictable – little Stella Glynn had turned out to be just what her name suggested – a star. The one undisputed triumph of Miss Stinson's career. She won the Sun Aria. Went to study in Paris, then London. Sang at Covent Garden and the Met and was for ten years an international 'singer of renown', and was still described that way when her records turned up on local radio. But the gift she had been endowed with had never meant as much to Stella as it did to others. As soon as she could manage it she gave up the irregular life of glitter and savage discipline, married her Swede, and came home. These days she co-managed a successful travel agency. It suited her to a T.

Scott, dazzled to find himself in the presence of a real star, even one who seemed little interested in her own faded glow, was leaning intensely towards Miss Stinson, who was telling her story now, in an oddly flirtatious way, entirely for him.

'Go on,' he said, when Miss Stinson paused and seemed for a moment to be following some vivid memory of her own. 'What happened then?'

'Isn't this amazing,' he said aside to Diane, with no hint of irony.

Diane was quietly amused. Clearly, whatever else she might be to Scott McIvor, she was not a star.

Sam too was listening, also moved in his way by the familiar tale.

Long ago when they were all young, it was Stella he had been drawn to. She had obsessed and tormented him.

He was studying piano then with Miss Stinson's sister, Miss Minnie. Without Stella, he thought, his real life – the one he had imagined and must at all costs have – would be forever closed to him.

He had been wrong; had almost made a fatal error, and not only of the heart. When he listened these days to the two pieces Stella had inspired in him, and which he had written for her extraordinary voice, he got a cold feeling at the base of his spine that was only partly for what came back to him, unbidden, of that old attraction, and the young man's bitter hurt with which it was still sometimes infused.

What scared him more was the echo he caught, the *pre*-echo, of the works he might have gone on to produce; the way his nature, his own gift might have gone if Stella, grand as she was, had continued to be his goal and inspiration. But she had been wiser than he was. Crueller. More honest. Less vain. She had understood, long before he saw it, that the true voice of what he might have in him was Maggie's. When he saw it too he was dismayed and humbled, then swept away by how obvious it was.

Miss Stinson was right. How unexpected, how simple life could be. Though not, perhaps, just at the moment.

He turned his attention to the sunroom where the children were gathered. Frowned. Got to his feet. Maggie, seeing his frown and reading the question in it, waited a beat then followed.

Sprawled on the floor out there the twins were engaged in a game of Monopoly with their cousin Jens. Cassie, who distrusted Jens and often complained about him, but succumbed immediately to the smallest attention he showed her, had been permitted to mind his cash. Jens, of course, was winning. Lars, Stella's older boy, was plugged into a Walkman. Miranda and the two interlopers, as Sam thought of them, were in a huddle of green, pink and ash-blond heads half hidden behind the door.

Sam surveyed the scene and settled on Jens and Lars as the source of what he felt in the air as a threat of imminent disorder. They had only to step across the threshold, these two, for the twins to be transformed from awkward, leggy little girls stuck on Michael Jackson to beings who gave off a seductive glow that terrified him, it was so naked – though innocent of course. They didn't know what it meant.

Lars was sixteen. He played in a pop group and was reputed to have got a schoolgirl pregnant – they had actually heard this from the twins! He was keeping his distance today, big feet in Nike joggers thrust out into the centre of the room, head bobbing, eyes closed under bluish lids. A great six-foot *lump* attached to a Walkman, exerting some sort of diversionary influence on the Monopoly board by disabling the twins, who could never quite ignore him.

But Jens was the one. It was Jens with his berserker's blue eyes and con man's smile who was the killer.

'I hope you'll tell that Jens he's not allowed upstairs. I don't want him going through my things.'

This, earlier in the day, from Cassie, who was possessive of her 'treasures'.

'The last time he was here he walked off with a scent bottle I was keeping. He's a thief!'

And here she was, three hours later, entirely under his spell.

Once, when he was five, they had surprised Jens with his thing out, attempting to put it into one of the twins.

Stella, who ought, Sam thought, to have been as appalled as he was, had laughed when he faced her with it.

'Oh for heaven's sake, Sam, he's five years old!' she told him. 'It'd be like marshmallow in a moneybox.'

She and Maggie had collapsed at that, and Sam, enraged, had felt once again what a gap there was between the way he saw things and the world these sisters came out of, and so easily reverted to the moment they were together. Two minutes in one another's company and they were barefooted kids again, back in that disastrous household that had once, he admitted, when he was young, seemed so liberating. The easy-going care-lessness and good humour. The very amenable terms these sturdy, down-to-earth sisters had appeared to be on with their own very different styles of beauty and with the world – with Life, as he would have put it then.

Well, he was less indulgent these days of that sort of care-lessness. He knew now what it led to. On a daily basis.

Eighteen years he and Maggie had been together, but there were times when he was astonished all over again by how differ-ently they took the world and what it threw at them.

As for Jens, five years old or not, he could have killed the little shit. And he could have killed him all over again right now.

Maggie, who had come up quietly behind him, laid her hand very lightly on his back.

'What is it, love? What's the matter?' she enquired. But almost immediately one of the twins, Rosalind, complained: 'Mummy, Jens is cheating.'

'He *is* not,' Cassie told her.

'He is too.'

'Play quietly, girls,' Maggie said, barely paying attention. She was concerned now with getting Sam back to the table. She barely noticed the buzzing behind the half-open door where Miranda was closeted with her friends.

'What about Tom?' Sam now demanded, as if this all along was what had really been troubling him. 'You said five. It's gone half past.'

As if she knew any more than he did. The boy was fifteen.

'Oh, you know what he's like,' Maggie told him. 'He gets carried away. He'll be back.'

Stella's eye was on them from the table next door. Maggie caught it and winked.

'What are you two doing out there?' Stella called. 'Come here, Sam, and explain to Diane about fire-farming. You know what a dud I am, and Scott's no help.' She was sacrificing the sailmaker, who was too pleased to have been named by her in such a familiar way to take offence.

Maggie relaxed a little. If there was anyone who could break Sam's mood it was good old Stell.

IT was nearly six now and beginning to be dusk. The conversation at table was muted. The bottles of wine Sam had opened earlier, and one Stella had brought, stood empty before them among half-filled glasses and plates piled with peelings and scraps.

Diane Novak consulted her watch.

She was uncertain of the conventions here. People seemed settled in and gave no sign of moving, but she thought they should get going, that it was time to whip her sailmaker away. Suddenly there was a commotion from the sunroom – actual screams.

Miss Stinson, who was in full flight again, looked alarmed as the heads turned – she was deaf – and first Maggie, then Sam, then Stella, leapt to their feet.

'What is it?' she cried. 'What's happened?'

It was at moments like this that her 'condition', which for the most part she contrived very successfully to hide, came home to her – the prospect of not hearing the car that was bearing down to lift you bodily off your feet.

The scene in the sunroom when Maggie arrived was confused. It was Sam, immediately behind her, who took it all in and saw at once how things stood: Jens rushing past them to his mother in the hallway, Lars, still plugged in to his Walkman, upright now in the middle of the room, around him and under his feet small houses scattered as by a tornado among the dice and cards of the Monopoly game, the twins and Cassie, big-eyed all three, clinging together in the bay window. Still half out of sight behind the door, Miranda, Don and the girl Julie were scrabbling in a heap on the floor. It was Julie who was screaming. But she was also flailing her arms and kicking her legs while Don and Miranda tried to hold her still and shouted her name. It was only a moment before Sam, uncomfortably sprawled with the writhing body half under him, had her controlled, but in that moment, he thought, the room was like an animal pit, as the others must have seen, coming up behind Stella – the sounds that were coming out of the child's body so little resembled anything that belonged to human speech. Sam looked back over his shoulder to where Maggie had pulled Cassie and the twins, who were staring white-faced but silent, close against her. Jens had his head hidden in his mother's shirt.

A moment. Then it was past. They were back in their ordered lives again.

'It's OK, pet,' Maggie was telling Cassie, 'everything's fine now.'

She moved to relieve Sam, who was stricken, now that the girl was quiet, to find her sobbing against his chest. He let go and Maggie took over.

Picking Cassie up in his arms, Sam carried her past the others, the twins following, to the dining room, but turned back when Miss Stinson said, to no one in particular, 'I expect she's taken something, poor girl. They should find out what it is.'

That 'taken something' reminded him. Years back – twenty, twenty-five – Miss Stinson's sister, Miss Minnie, had 'taken something'.

In her late forties, Miss Minnie had fallen passionately in love with a bus driver and when, after a series of approaches and ambiguous responses, he had, deeply embarrassed, made it plain that she had mistaken his interest, the poor woman had swallowed a whole bottle of aspirin. She survived, but it was a shaming business and Miss Stinson had been devastated to find herself brought so close to a passion whose destructive consequences she too had to bear.

What surprised Sam was how entirely he had submerged and forgotten what to Miss Stinson must, for so long, have been a source of immediate and almost daily sorrow. He kissed Cassie briefly on the ear and told her: 'Here, sausage, why don't you go to Miss Stinson for a moment.' They were old friends, Cassie and Miss Stinson. 'I'll just go and see how Mummy is doing. And you girls,' this to the twins, 'why don't you make us all a good cup of coffee. A big pot. Real grains.'

But when Sam got to the sunroom, Maggie and the others were gone. Only the boy Don, with his floppy hair and lolly-pink slippers, was there, hovering on the threshold. Like everyone else, Sam had forgotten him.

It was Diane Novak's young man Scott who stepped in. 'Are you OK, mate?' he asked, at Sam's side. The boy looked tearful. 'Come on here.' He came obediently, and Scott, without self-consciousness, put his arm around the boy and held him close; and at just that moment, the women reappeared at the top of the stairs − Stella, Miranda, Diane. Maggie had shushed them off and remained with Julie.

'She'll be fine,' Stella told them, 'she's a bit overwrought, that's all.' She made a face at Sam, indicating that for Miranda's sake he should ask no questions.

Overwrought, they both knew, was an understatement, but for the moment must suffice.

Sam nodded. With a revulsion he could not hide, at least from himself, he turned away, but felt again in his back muscles and in the tendons of his hands the unnatural strength with which her body, slight as it was, had thrashed and jerked against his hold. Her hot breath in his ear. And the sounds that issued from her, wildered howlings at such a pitch of animal fury and uncomprehending anguish that he had almost been overcome.

By her terrible closeness. By the birdlike fragility against his ribcage of her bones and the alien power they were endowed with as he used all his weight to keep her still.

Her presence had always unnerved him. The funereal black of the miniskirts and shawls she got herself up in, her black eye make-up and the black fingernails and lips. The toxic disaster stuff she carried. Which he was afraid might brush off on Miranda, or on Cassie or the twins.

Now Maggie too reappeared at the top of the stairs. 'She's sleeping,' she told them.

She came on down, touching Sam's hand briefly as she passed. The twins were at the kitchen door, with a pot of coffee and a tray of mugs. 'Good girls,' she said. They all made their way to the dining room and went back to being a party, but a single one now, sipping, passing things. Even Lars appeared, tempted by chocolate biscuits.

'Miss Stinson,' Maggie suggested, 'why don't you play us something.' In the early days of their marriage they had often had musical evenings. Miss Stinson had always played.

Too old and too much the professional to be coy, Miss Stinson got her ancient bones together and moved to the piano.

The Schubert she chose was safe, its fountain of notes under her fingers brightly lit and secure. The regretful middle section when it appeared, with its shifts, on the same note sequence, from trancelike sureness to throbbing hesitation, its wistfulness and quiet stoicism, spoke of a world of recoveries that could still rouse itself and sing. Even the repeats, which might have been too many, as she reached for them were new-found and welcome.

Sam, under the influence of the music, and the hour and the light, which seemed one, met Diane Novak's eye across the table. She smiled and nodded.

Nothing had been said. They had barely spoken. But he felt easy again. Their meeting had not, after all, been the central event of the occasion, but had not been a mistake.

The last notes died away. Miss Stinson sat a moment, as if she were alone out there, somewhere in the dark, and they, like shy animals, had been drawn in out of the distance to listen; drawn in, each one, out of their own distance and surprised, when they looked about, that music had made a company of them, sharers of a stilled enchantment. It was only when Miss Stinson, still absent and absorbed, lifted her hands at last from the keys that Tom, who had been waiting, respectful but impatient in the doorway behind them, bursting with his news, spoke up at last, red-faced and over-wrought.

'I had an accident,' he hooted.

He was triumphant, despite the bump on his forehead and his discoloured eye. 'I got hit by a board. I had to have stitches!'

Still pumped, still caught up in the world of mishap and risk he had come from, but torn now between the wish to astonish them and at the same time not to alarm, he came forward to show his mother the wound.

'It's not serious,' he told her. 'I had to go in an ambulance. Is that OK? Do we belong?'

It was true, it was nothing, nothing much. A gash that would heal, leaving a scar over his left eye that would be interesting. But it must have been close just the same, and because it was so physical, and came so soon after their earlier commotion, Maggie shocked the boy by suddenly clasping him to her and bursting into tears. He faced the others – his father, Miranda – over her shoulder and did not know what he had done.

'Honestly,' he told them, 'it's nothing. I hardly felt it.'

Sam, recalling how angry he had been with the boy, was suddenly heartsick. Tom saw it.

'Hey, Dad,' he said, 'I'm sorry. I didn't mean to upset you.'

'That's all right, son,' Sam told him, playing calm. 'We've had a bit of an afternoon, that's all. Come and get something to eat.' It surprised him that his tone was so much one that Maggie might have used. She too caught it, gave him a swift look, and laughed.

'Well,' she said, releasing Tom, then drawing him back to give him a light kiss on the corner of his mouth, 'welcome back from the wars.'

THE guests were gone, the children settled. Upstairs was quiet, all the lights out except in Tom's room; the rooms left and right down the hallway filled with quiet breathing, their windows half open to the summer night of clicking insects and the barely audible slow flapping past of flying foxes, the stirring of possums among leaves. Downstairs the washing-up was stacked in racks above the sink.

Sam and Maggie, having shut the kitchen door behind them, were in Sam's sleepout workroom, Maggie, with closed eyes, in an upright chair by the door, Sam at the piano. Idly his fingers struck a chord, the same one that earlier in the day, out in the kitchen, had led her to an old song that was there somewhere in the four ordinary notes. But what moved out into the silence now was full of other, stranger possibilities that brought the room into a different focus: the air, rather thick and heated; the bright ellipse of the lamp under its hood, where it lit the keys and the reddish wood of the piano; Sam's profile, lips slightly apart in anticipation; the glare of the louvres, parted to let in a scent of leaves and distant water.

'Do you want me to try it?' Maggie asked.

'You're not too tired?'

She made the ·effort, sprang upright. Sam briefly laughed. She took the sheet from the piano, and Sam handed her two more that she ran her eye over in preparation as his fingers found one chord, then, in a way that made her draw herself together and attend, another. And now the focus was in *her*. In her shoulders, her legs where she settled the column of her· body on the worn carpet, and reaching in the spaces of her head for the first note let out her breath.

Ah! Sam turned his head. He felt the whole surface of his skin thrill at the wonder of it, the purity of this voice she harboured so mysteriously in a body he had lived with now for nearly twenty years and which never failed to astonish him. Fleetingly their eyes met and Maggie smiled, as sounds he had with so much difficulty drawn out of himself now poured forth, without effort it seemed, on her breath, and on the same breath climbed and spread. So much part of her, of her actual being, yet entirely independent. As they had been of him too, even before she took them over, took them into herself, gave them life.

With the turn of his head Sam showed a different profile, and Maggie recorded it while all her attention remained fixed on the page and on what, with all her body's susceptibilities and claims in perfect collusion, she was miraculously trans-lating into this other self he had discovered for her, and which her breath, pushed almost to its limit, was once again amply reaching for.

UPSTAIRS, with the blanket drawn up high under his chin, Tom contemplated his sister Miranda, who sat on the edge of the low bed and regarded him with a look he preferred not to meet. She was preparing, he thought, to rebuke him. He felt warm and comfortably indulged. He did not want to be told, yet again, how hopeless he was. There had been a moment down there in the sitting room when he had been the centre of all their attention and concern – not just his mother's, his father's and Miss Stinson's, but everyone's, and had felt, beyond his usual awkward self-consciousness, a kind of glow, an assurance of how loved he might be. He did not want that spoiled.

But Miranda did not mean to spoil it. She wanted to tell him how fond she was of him, how often she thought of a time, before the twins appeared, when there had been just the two of them and he had been her dumb, soft, wet-mouthed little brother who needed her to watch out for him and trailed after her and did everything she did.

There were moments when she still saw him that way.

Recently, when she began to colour her hair and explore the decorative resources of the safety pin, her mother had told her angrily: 'This is very silly, Miranda, your father is disappointed. Is that why you're doing it? To get at him? And it's such a bad example!'

'Who to, for heaven's sake?'

Her mother had had to stop and think.

'To Tom,' she decided. 'You know how he copies everything you do.'

Miranda had laughed outright. 'Honestly,' she said. 'Tom!'

But it was true. He did follow, in his odd, half-hearted way. Careful always not to stray too far from his own stolid centre. He had acquired a pair of black parachute pants, put colour in his hair that would wash out for school, wore a stud in his ear.

'What *is* that?' their father had taunted. 'That *thing* in your ear. A hearing aid?'

She too wished he would stop trying so hard and just be his own lovable self.

What he really wanted, she thought, was that they should be twins; whereas what she wanted, in her contradictory way, was to be an only child. What she said now was: 'I could sleep here, if you like. On the floor.'

Tom was surprised. Wary.

'Julie's in my bed anyway. It'd be better if she just stayed there.'

'Well, if you want to,' he said. 'But I don't need it.'

'I know you don't,' she said. 'I do.'

He snuggled down into the blankets.

'I'm pretty tired now,' he told her. 'I might just go to sleep.'

'That's all right. I'll be tired myself in a bit.'

She took his hand.

His eyes were closed but he was smiling. Already sinking downwards into sleep.

Far off in the depths of the house their mother's voice rose in a long sweet arc of sound, pure and unwavering.

Tom heard it, a shining thread he was following in the dark that step by step was leading him down into his own private underworld.

Julie too heard it. Still stiffly awake in the next room, she was puzzled for a moment. She lay breathless, listening, salt tears in her throat — not for the music, though the throbbing of it seemed one with her own silent weeping. As if it had appeared just at this moment to reassure her that what she felt, her unassuageable misery, was part of something larger that was known, shared, and could take this lighter form, a high pure sound out of elsewhere. Something more than this hot welling in her throat, this salty wetness in her nostrils and on her lips.

Maggie was on the last page now, and aware, as she moved with ease along the line of notes, of the silence she was approaching, which began just a little way up ahead, where he had laid down his pen.

As she came closer to it Sam's head turned further in her direction and his eye caught hers. She was coming to what had stopped him.

He was looking right at her now, as she reached the small difficulty he had set himself there. Had set *her*. She closed her eyes, to free herself from his look of anxious expectancy, so that without anxiety she could allow what was purely physical in her to take over and get her through. She heard his breath go out. Then silence.

But not quite silence. A slight hissing of night through the parted slats of the louvres. Nature. Then again their breathing.

'That's it for the moment,' he said – unnecessarily, but to return them, she understood, to the ordinariness of speech.

She nodded. Laid the last sheet beside the others on the stand.

Her body was still attuned to what she had just been so caught up in. She felt the vibrations still. No longer emanating from her, they went on where the music continued to flow and spread. Beyond the page. In his head. In the silence which was not quite silence. On the lines of score-paper as yet still empty.

Which would sit where she had just set down the last uncompleted page, in the dark of this room, after he had put the lamp out and closed the door behind them, and they had gone upstairs, undressed, lain down side by side in the dark; for a few moments simply going over the day's events, Diane Novak, whatever it was that had afflicted the child – not one of their own – who now lay sleeping across the hall, Tom's accident, Miss Stinson. Till once again he turned to her and whispered her name.

And this, waiting below.

To be resumed. To be continued.

www.vintage-books.co.uk